D1245418

THE FOREIGN AFFAIR

DAVID C. DAWSON

ABOUT THE BOOK

Book Three in the award-winning series The Delingpole Mysteries.
By David C. Dawson

There's a murderer stalking the gay bars of Berlin.

It's September, the time of Folsom Europe, the city's annual festival for gay men in leather.

And Berlin's become a dangerous place for them.

British lawyer, and part-time sleuth, Dominic Delingpole is in town. He's come to Berlin to visit Matty, the teenage son he first met only a year ago.

When Matty is arrested for the attacks, Dominic teams up with German lawyer Johann Hartmann, a good-looking man with a seductive charm.

As they battle to prove Matty's innocence, Dominic and Johann discover the attacks are linked to a sinister, Russian-backed experiment.

But whose side is Hartmann really on?

This is a work of fiction. Names, characters, organizations, places, events, and incidents are either products of the author's imagination or are used fictitiously. Any resemblance to actual persons, living or dead, or actual events is purely coincidental.

Text copyright © 2020 by David C. Dawson

ISBN: 978-1-9162573-3-7

Cover design by: Garrett Leigh @ Black Jazz Design

For Mum, who read all my other books, but won't be able to read this one.
Thank you Mum. You gave me so much support.

1

Berlin, September 2019

IF DOMINIC had known that death in all its untidiness was about to strike only a mile away from where he sat, he would have thought twice about revisiting this European city, with all the happy memories it had once brought him.

He shifted his position on the wooden seat at the entrance to the cemetery and stared absently at the line of headstones in front of him. The late afternoon sun shone through the trees, backlighting their leaves in a vivid display of green turning to gold. The dappled light gave the cemetery an aura of peace and calm. Here, death was ordered into tidy lines, given sepia tints with vases of flowers and faded photographs.

Dominic stood and followed the gravelled path as it swept around in a broad curve on the eastern side of the cemetery towards a newly created garden. Halfway along, he stopped by a small, stone basin set into the boundary wall. Dominic put his canvas bag down on the ground, and from it he removed a glass vase and a bundle of roses. He filled the vase from a metal watering can and placed it on the flat edge of the stone basin. He took the roses from their wrapping and arranged them as best he could in the vase.

Flower arranging was not Dominic's strength, and he struggled to make the display look passable. After several minutes he abandoned his attempt. Anyway, the wind blowing up from the east would quickly rearrange his handiwork. He stuffed the flowers' wrapping into the canvas bag, picked up the vase and resumed his brisk walk along the path.

A hundred yards farther on, Dominic stepped off the path and onto the grass. He followed a rough track that was worn by regular visitors that diligently cared for the graves of their loved ones. He kicked through the growing pile of leaves scattered across the ground. A short distance from the track, he came to a small, black headstone. Its inscription was simple:

Bernhardt Freude my lover and friend

Dominic stopped and faced the headstone. He breathed deeply and the scent of wild blueberry shrubs flooded his nostrils.

"Here we are again," said Dominic softly. "I promised I'd return."

He dropped the canvas bag onto the wet grass in front of the gravestone and kneeled on the makeshift mat. Carefully, he placed the vase of roses behind the low gravestone and adjusted some of the blooms, not wanting a single one to be obscured. Satisfied with his arrangement, he sat back on his haunches, the palms of his hands resting on his thighs.

"Who'd have thought it?" he said with a smile. "Here I am, once again on my knees in front of you."

He sighed.

"But it's too late for that now, my friend. More than a year too late."

Dominic stared at the name on the gravestone for a moment before bowing his head in thought.

"Hey, Dad."

Dominic looked up when he heard the voice and turned his head towards the path. A young man stood with his hands in his pockets. He wore a collarless, white shirt with its sleeves rolled up, and narrow-leg black jeans tucked into a pair of heavy black boots, the laces half tied. Despite the heat of the afternoon, he wore a Russian *ushanka* hat with the earflaps tied together on top. His long brown hair hung down over his shoulders.

"Matthias!" Dominic waved at his son. "I'm not late for our supper date, am I?"

"No, Dad." The young man stepped off the path and walked towards Dominic. "We've got plenty of time. But I thought I'd come and pay my respects as well." Matthias looked around him. "All the years I've visited Berlin. But it wasn't until last year I came to this graveyard for the first time. It's the last resting place of Marlene Dietrich you know."

"I'm surprised someone your age knows anything about her. Bernhardt was a big fan." Dominic opened his arms wide and embraced his son. Matthias towered over him. Dominic was six foot, but Matthias was another three inches taller. They held each other until Dominic patted his son's back and gently released his arms.

"I only met Bernhardt once." Matthias turned towards the gravestone. "He was very kind to me. I can't imagine what you must feel, Dad."

Dominic shrugged.

"Apart from Jonathan, he was my closest friend," said Dominic. "Bernhardt was very good to me over the years.

Which shows the kind of man he was. After all, he didn't have to be. Not after I ran out on him."

"Oh, come on, Dad," said Matthias. "You were eighteen years old, and he was your..." He looked down.

Dominic smiled.

"After your mother? Yes, Matthias. He was my second significant love."

Matthias smiled awkwardly and fiddled with the sleeve of his shirt.

"Are you okay if you call me Matty? Only Mama still calls me Matthias, and I don't really like it anymore."

"Sure, Matty." Dominic tried out the name. "Is that what your friends at university call you?"

Matty nodded. "One of the guys did when I first arrived and it's sort of stuck."

"Matty." Dominic tried the name again. "It sounds good."

"I wish I'd known you when I was growing up." Matty said. "Eric would have been an okay stepdad. If I'd been straight. He took me to football, judo lessons, taught me to sail and stuff."

"I'm not sure I could have fulfilled those kinds of duties," Dominic replied. "I'd have probably taken you to museums and musicals. Perhaps things worked out for the best."

He bent down and picked up the canvas bag. Straightening, he smiled at Matty.

"Come on. Bernhardt won't mind if we go for a walk. But not far. My feet are killing me. It feels like I've walked all over Berlin today. I love sightseeing here. But I always end up doing too much."

"Why don't we go straight to the restaurant?" Matty suggested. "What time did you book it for?"

"Five thirty." Dominic checked his watch. "They won't

mind us being a bit early. They know me well enough in there after all these years."

Dominic and Matty headed back towards the cemetery gates. At a crossing in the path Dominic stopped. "Another time, we must go and pay our respects to her." He pointed to his left.

"You mean Marlene?" asked Matty. "It's the kitschiest grave I've ever seen. Alex took me there one day last spring."

"Ah. Your mysterious boyfriend, Alex. When do I get to meet him?"

"Oh, come on, Dad." Matty seemed embarrassed. "It's only been seven months. I don't think we've got to the 'meet the parents' stage yet."

"You saying that makes him even more intriguing." Dominic laughed. "Now I definitely want to meet him." He squeezed his son's shoulder, and the two men headed back to the outside world.

The aroma of hot cheese and cooked pork hit Dominic's nostrils as soon as he pushed open the door of the Alt Schwäbisch Restaurant. It was in Albestrasse, a ten-minutes' brisk walk from the cemetery. Despite being early evening, the large dining room was already half full, and the sound of animated chatter ricocheted off the bare floorboards of the restaurant. Hanging on the whitewashed walls were the stuffed heads of wild boar and deer, their glassy-eyed stares fixed and lifeless.

"Do we really have to eat here, Dad?" Matty pushed up against Dominic in the narrow entrance of the restaurant and closed the door behind them against the wind. "Can't we go somewhere less...German?" He whispered the final word into his father's ear.

"I like to eat German food when I'm in Germany," Dominic replied. "And I wanted to bring you here. I've eaten in this place a lot over the years. And it was where Bernhardt liked us to eat."

The restaurant offered a limited menu based on variations of traditional southern German cooking. It was principally pork in a heavy sauce, served with dumplings. Dominic noticed Matty surveying the hunting trophies on the wall with disapproval.

"Are you against it because it's Schwäbisch?" asked Dominic with a smile. "You're not becoming a snob towards your southern German compatriots are you, young Matthias?"

Before Matty could protest, a tall, buxom woman of mature years came up to them.

"*Grüss Gott*, Herr Delingpole!" she shouted above the noise of the restaurant. "It's good to see you again, after so long."

She embraced Dominic and kissed him enthusiastically on both cheeks.

"And this must be your younger brother, also from England."

Dominic saw the horror on Matty's face. He hurried to correct the error.

"No, no, Frau Consten," he said. "Please let me introduce you to Matthias. He's my son."

Frau Consten looked at Dominic with a confused expression.

"But I thought you were—"

Matty saved the situation by holding out his hand in greeting.

"I'm delighted to meet you, Frau Consten," he said in German. "My father tells me this is the best restaurant in Berlin."

"Oh, *schätze!*" said Frau Consten. She reached forward

and clutched Matty in a warm embrace, kissing him three times on either cheek. Dominic chuckled as his son's face went bright red with embarrassment.

Frau Consten finally released Matty from her grip. She turned to Dominic with a beaming smile.

"But where is the lovely Jonathan? You were married last year already, *nein*? I haven't seen either of you since then."

It was the moment Dominic still dreaded. He cleared his throat and readied himself.

"I'm afraid he's no longer with us, Frau Consten."

"He's gone away? Is he travelling with his work? He is opera singer, *nein*?"

"No, no." Dominic cursed himself for using a confusing euphemism instead of saying it straight. "He died. Jonathan's dead. It was last September. A year ago."

"*Mein Gott!*" Frau Consten said the phrase so loudly the other diners stopped speaking and turned to look at them. Dominic felt his face flush with embarrassment.

Frau Consten leaned heavily against the wall behind her. Her mouth opened and closed several times, but she struggled to say anything.

"How...? When did it...? You must be..." With an effort Frau Consten pushed her bulky frame away from the wall and embraced Dominic once more. Her shoulders heaved and she sobbed noisily into his shoulder. Dominic glanced sideways into the restaurant. The diners continued to stare at them. Those who caught his eye quickly looked away and resumed conversation with their fellow diners.

The sobbing subsided into loud sniffles. She relaxed her grasp of Dominic and looked up at him.

"It must have been very sudden?"

"In a way." Dominic wanted to spare this friendly, motherly woman the details of his husband's slow, lingering death. How Jonathan had taken a bullet in the chest as the two men attempted to protect a friend of theirs. How Dominic cradled Jonathan in his arms as they waited for the air ambulance. The months he waited by Jonathan's bedside, hoping he would wake from his coma. And that final afternoon, when the medical team told Dominic there was nothing more they could do for his husband.

But, instead of explaining the details, Dominic pulled out a handkerchief from his pocket and gave it to Frau Consten. She blew her nose heavily, wiped it clean, and offered the handkerchief back to Dominic. He held up his hand to decline it politely. "We were on our honeymoon. In California."

"On your honeymoon? *Mein Gott!*"

"He didn't suffer any pain."

"I am very sad for you, Herr Delingpole." Frau Consten sighed. "Jonathan was a beautiful man. Very naughty. Always with me he made jokes. But I know he was not meaning it." She tipped her head to one side and stared at Dominic. "How are you feeling, Herr Delingpole? You say it was a year ago? How are you now?"

It was a question Dominic always found difficult to answer. How he was changed from day to day. Mostly he felt he could cope with life, especially if he was busy at work. But some days were dark. That was when he needed all his effort simply to get out of bed and function at a very basic level.

"I'm fine," he said. "It gets easier as time passes."

Frau Consten turned to Matty.

"You must take good care of your father, young man." She wiped her eyes with Dominic's handkerchief. "Unbelievable. Jonathan murdered. Such a beautiful young life snuffed out."

She reached for two leather-bound menus and cleared her throat loudly.

"Follow me," she said. "I will get you seated and then bring you two beers. On the house. To toast your dear husband, Herr Delingpole. I have the best table in our restaurant for you."

Frau Consten strode off through the restaurant. Dominic and Matty did their best to follow her as she cut a path through the sea of tables. Some of the diners stared at them as they walked past.

"Here." Frau Consten gestured extravagantly at a table by the window. "From here you can watch all the men in their leather, if you like that sort of thing. You know it's the Folsom festival this weekend? Men come from all over the world to Berlin to flaunt themselves in the street." She handed Dominic and Matty menus as they took their seats. "I bring you your beers," she announced and left.

"Are you okay?" Matty asked.

"I haven't done that for a while." Dominic opened his menu. "I've told pretty well everybody now. I'd forgotten she didn't know. It's a bit like coming out. It gets easier the more you do it."

"Dad?"

Dominic looked up to see the concern on Matty's face.

"Are you really okay?"

"I am today." He nodded in the direction of the bar. "Especially when Frau Consten called you my younger brother."

Matty laughed. "How old does she think I am?"

"You should be flattered." Dominic flicked through the pages of his menu. "We should both be flattered. You, because she thinks you're a handsome young man, older than your nineteen years. And me, because—"

"Because you don't look like you're in your forties." There was a mischievous smile on Matty's face.

"You know very well I'm only thirty-nine," retorted Dominic.

"You'll be forty in a few months' time."

"What is your obsession with age all of a sudden?" Dominic sat back in his chair and looked quizzically at his son. "Tell me, how old is your man Alex?"

Matty opened his menu and studied it closely. "Is it important? After all, it's only a number."

"I see."

Dominic closed his menu and put it on the side plate. "Is there something you've got to tell me, Matty? You've not fallen for one of your lecturers, have you? Because if you have, I need to warn you that—"

Before Dominic could continue, Frau Consten arrived with their drinks.

"Your beers, gentlemen." She placed two tall steins on the table. "A gift from me in memory of Jonathan. *Pröst!*"

She took a notepad and pencil from her apron pocket.

"Tell me your order," she said. "Today is Thursday, and we become very busy because all the men in their leather arrive for the festival. I recommend you have the *Maultaschen* before we run out of it. It is the chef's specialty."

"That's pasta stuffed with loads of pork, Dad." Matty turned to Frau Consten. "I'm vegetarian."

"*Kein problem*. We have vegetarian *Maultaschen*. And for you, Herr Delingpole?"

"I'll have that as well," Dominic replied.

"*Gut.*" Frau Consten scribbled on her notepad. She paused to watch two men dressed in leather walk past the window. "If only your husband was here now, Herr Deling-pole. He would be dressed just like that. But he would look far more handsome." She collected their menus and headed for the kitchen.

Dominic picked up his beer stein. "*Pröst*, Matty."

"To absent friends, Dad." They clinked glasses and drank.

"So tell me about your young man," Dominic said. "You've hardly told me anything."

2

BERLIN CITY SERVICE Engineer number 459 pulled up outside the Prinzknecht Bar in Fuggerstraße and switched off his moped's engine. BCSE 459 dismounted the City Transport Department electric moped he had stolen earlier and pulled it back onto its stand. He took off his leather gloves, removed his mirror sunglasses and helmet, placed the helmet carefully on the seat, and put the sunglasses back on.

BCSE 459 pulled out a packet of cigarettes and a lighter from the top pocket of his jacket. He inhaled and allowed the smoke to escape through his nose. His hand trembled as he felt the initial hard kick of the nicotine.

It was five thirty on Thursday afternoon, and there was already a crowd of men standing outside the bar. The majority of them were dressed in leather. Some in full motorcycle suits, others wore heavy leather jackets with chaps or jeans. A few wore harnesses, to show off the hours they'd spent working on their bodies in the gym. The Prinzknecht Bar was the main rendezvous point for men that had come to Berlin to take part in the annual Folsom

Street Fair. It was a pilgrimage for gay men from around the world whose fetish was to wear leather or rubber. Berlin Folsom was named after the original fair, first held in Folsom Street in San Francisco in 1984. As well as German, BCSE 459 could hear men speaking languages from as far away as Russia, Brazil and Japan.

He watched the crowds for several minutes while he enjoyed the momentary high the cigarette gave him. It was Russian. Unfiltered and raw. The hot smoke risked scorching his throat as the thin paper tube burned towards its end.

In addition to the crowd of men standing outside the Prinzknecht Bar, BCSE 459 could see there were a few more inside. But he knew by eight o'clock that evening the bar would be packed.

Perfect. While it remained quiet he could do what he had to do with minimal risk of being disturbed by one of the leather-clad drinkers.

BCSE 459 took one last drag on the stub of his cigarette and tossed it into the street. He pulled on his leather gloves, removed the small, black rucksack from his back and opened it. Everything was in its place. The red light of the clock on the timing mechanism glowed in the darkness of the rucksack. It displayed two times: the time now and 20.00.

The activation time.

Nothing had been disturbed. BCSE 459 fumbled to refasten the rucksack's two straps. It was difficult to grasp them through the stiff leather of his gloves. Finally, the straps latched into place and he carefully lifted the rucksack back onto his shoulder. He picked up his helmet from the seat of the moped and walked over to the main entrance of the Prinzknecht Bar.

BCSE 459 was conscious that the men standing outside were checking him out. He had been instructed to wear a leather jacket, tight leather jeans and tall motorcycle boots. He was told it would help him to blend in. His hair was also close-cropped like many of the men around him. As he walked inside, he enjoyed the thrill of being noticed. Possibly of being admired. He was a good-looking guy after all.

A group of men wearing one-piece leather biker suits stood at the bar talking to the barman. BCSE 459 nodded to them as he approached. He pulled out his Berlin City identity card and held it out in readiness. Meanwhile, his mind reviewed the briefing he had been given earlier. The barman broke off his conversation with the bikers.

"What'll you have?" he shouted above the sound of a pounding club anthem playing through the speaker system. The barman wore leather jeans and was stripped to the waist. A large eagle was tattooed across the top of his chest.

"I'm from the City Health Department." BCSE 459 showed the identity card. "You should've received a call earlier. To tell you I was coming." His German was almost flawless. The slight hint of Russian was lost in the noise of the bar.

"Wait a minute," replied Eagle Tattoo. "I'll get Ulrich."

He took the identity card and walked to the other end of the bar counter. The place was dimly lit, and BCSE 459 pulled his sunglasses down his nose to see over the top of them. Eagle Tattoo was talking into the ear of another man who wore a leather waistcoat. The man, presumably Ulrich, inspected the card and stared across at BCSE 459 for a few moments. BCSE hastily pushed his sunglasses back up his nose.

Ulrich nodded to the man with the eagle tattoo and they

walked to the front of the bar. Eagle Tattoo handed the identity card to Ulrich and resumed his conversation with the bikers.

"Hello, I'm Ulrich." He held out his hand in greeting. "You know we're about to get really busy in here. What do you need to do?"

BCSE 459 smiled.

"Don't worry. It should take me twenty minutes at most. I have to check the quality of the air being pumped out by your air-conditioning system." He patted his rucksack. "I have gas analysers in my bag. If you can show me the units, I'll get it done as quickly as possible."

Ulrich grunted. "And if we're not up to spec? What happens then?"

"Oh, you get my report. And my report goes to the city council. And you have twenty days to sort everything out."

"We're not going to get shut down tonight?" Ulrich looked annoyed. "This is about to be our busiest time of the year. We'll lose a fortune if you close us now."

BCSE 459 held up his hand to placate the barman. "Please don't worry. I'm sure it'll be all right. And if not, as I say, you have twenty days."

Ulrich grunted again and ducked under the countertop to join BCSE 459 on the other side. "Follow me," he said and led the way to a large metal unit fixed to the sidewall of the bar.

Twenty minutes later, BCSE 459 told Ulrich that all the measurements were satisfactory. He would send his full report to the city council and tell them the air quality of the Prinzknecht Bar was approved for another twelve months. The two men shook hands. BCSE 459 picked up his rucksack and headed back to his moped parked outside.

The bag was much lighter than when he'd first entered the bar.

"Forty?" Dominic's fork was frozen in mid-air, its cargo of vegetarian dumpling inches from his mouth. "He's older than me."

Matty stared at his father, a look of annoyance on his face.

"Is that a problem?"

Dominic rested the fork on his plate, the dumpling uneaten. He took a drink from his beer while he let his son's new revelation sink in. Matty's boyfriend was twice his age. It was a surprise. But then there were lots of age-gap relationships that worked. The composer Stephen Sondheim's to start with. No, for Dominic, it was not the age gap that was his main concern.

"I'd have thought relationships with lecturers would be strictly forbidden at the Technische Universität."

"He's not a lecturer." Matty shook his head. "He's a visiting professor."

"But presumably he does some teaching?"

Matty ran his finger around the rim of his beer glass. He said nothing.

"How did you meet?" asked Dominic.

Matty took a long drink from his glass and set it back down on the table. "He was doing some classes in abstract algebra."

"So he does teach."

"No." Matty stabbed at a dumpling with his fork and shoved it in his mouth. As he chewed, he continued to speak. "He was a student in the class. So was I. He sat next to me and we got talking. He's an amazing guy."

"If he's a professor, why is he attending an undergraduate course in abstract algebra? What's he a professor of, anyway?"

Matty pointed his fork at Dominic.

"You know, you're beginning to sound a lot like Eric. I didn't think you'd be so disapproving."

Dominic was stung by the comment. Matty rarely had a kind word to say about his stepfather. He painted the picture of a very traditional, provincial man with a narrow outlook on the world.

"I'm not disapproving," Dominic protested. "I'm... surprised. Please. Tell me more about him. Any pictures?"

Matty sniffed. He pulled out his phone and flicked through the photographs. Dominic tried to catch a glimpse of what was on his son's phone. Matty sat back in his chair. Finally, he turned the phone around to show Dominic.

"His name's Professor Alexeyev Krovopuskov, and he's professor of biomechatronics at ITMO University in St Petersburg. He's on an exchange trip organised between Germany and Russia."

Dominic took the phone and studied the image on the screen. He had to admit that Professor Krovopuskov was a handsome man. And very youthful. The picture showed him with his arm around Matty's shoulder at Berlin Pride earlier that year. With broad grins creasing up both their faces, they could have been of similar age.

"Biomechatronics? What on earth's that?"

Matty took the phone from Dominic. He seemed excited to be able to enlighten his father.

"It's the big leap forward in man–machine interfaces. It's how we'll be able to control everything in the future." Matty shoved the phone back in his pocket. "Well, not the future. They can do it now actually. People with prosthetic limbs have been able to move electromechanical fingers simply by thinking. They've been doing loads of work on it in Russia, and Alex is sharing his knowledge with the Universität. He's a leading expert on the subject."

"Really?" Dominic was puzzled. "I didn't think there was much love lost right now between Russia and Germany."

Matty waved his hand dismissively. "Oh, that's maybe true at the government level, but we academics carry on regardless. There's so much knowledge to share. Political barriers shouldn't get in the way."

Dominic smiled to himself at Matty's idealism. If only the world was that simple. But he was happy Matty was already referring to himself as an academic. Perhaps he would stay on at the Technische Universität once he completed his undergraduate degree in mathematics. For Dominic, mathematics was a foreign language and always had been. He admired the ease with which his son had sailed through his first year.

"So, outside your joint passion for academia, what else do you and Alex have in common?"

Matty looked sideways at Dominic. "Dad. When you say that, it sounds like you actually mean, 'Alex is so much older than you, so you can't possibly have the same amount of life experience for a meaningful relationship.'"

Dominic sighed. "No, I didn't say that at all. And as I said before, I'd like to meet him."

"Well, I'm meeting him at eight over at the Prinzknecht Bar in Fuggerstraße. I suppose you could come with me. But, as I said before, I don't think it's got to the 'meet the parents' stage yet."

Dominic was crestfallen and Matty laughed. "Don't be

like that. I'm sure you'll meet him eventually. You'll like him. He's very outgoing. Very lively. Great fun to be with. He loves opera. He's a lot like..."

"Go on," encouraged Dominic. He knew what Matty had intended to say.

Matty sat back in his seat and smiled at his father.

"I'm sorry," he began. "I was going to say, he's a lot like how you described Jonathan. But that's a bit clumsy of me." He reached for his glass and took a sip of beer. "I'm sorry," he said again.

Dominic laid a hand on Matty's arm. "Don't be afraid of talking about Jonathan. I'm very pleased you've met someone who makes you happy. If he's anything like Jonathan was, I imagine he's a bit of a handful."

Matty laughed. "Oh, God yes. We were in this bar the other night, and they started playing some traditional Russian dance. God knows why. Next moment, Alex is up on the table dancing like some demented Cossack. I didn't know where to look."

"That sounds like Jonathan all right." Dominic smiled fondly. "You know it was three years ago when he persuaded me to come here to Folsom for the first time. He danced "You're the One That I Want" from *Grease*, dressed in full leather, in the middle of Fuggerstraße. I was so embarrassed."

"I didn't know you'd come to Folsom before." Matty poked at a dumpling on his plate. "I mean, when you said you were coming for Folsom I was a bit surprised. Are you actually, you know, into leather?"

Dominic had taken a drink from his glass. He choked on a mouthful of beer at Matty's question and hurriedly set the glass back down on the table. It was well over a minute before he could stop coughing and answer Matty's question.

"I'm really not," he said. "But Jonathan is. I mean, he was." Dominic paused and took another mouthful of beer to clear his throat. He still found it difficult to talk about his former husband in the past tense. He set the glass back on the table and smiled at Matty. "Jonathan loved anything which involved dressing up. And he was certainly very sexy when he wore leather biker gear and a harness."

"And you?" asked Matty. "Dad? Am I going to see you in full leather tomorrow?"

Dominic laughed and struggled to stifle another coughing fit. "Don't worry, Matty. I'm not going to embarrass you. But I wanted to come to Berlin at this time of year. It was the anniversary of Bernhardt's birthday yesterday. And I had a lot of fun when Jonathan and I came for Folsom. I even wore a harness and jeans to go around the bars with him. I had to, to stop him nagging me."

Matty laid a hand on his father's arm.

"You miss him, don't you, Dad?"

Dominic looked down at Matty's hand. He was unused to this level of affection from his son. They had only established contact a year ago. He was grateful Matty had welcomed him into his life after years of separation.

"Terribly," he replied. "It's a little over a year since he was shot. I was so convinced he was going to survive. He was so full of life. I couldn't imagine him ever... You know... He lived life at a hundred miles an hour... And he dragged everyone else along with him... Those three months while he was in a coma. I really thought..." Dominic ran out of words. Matty held his arm tighter.

"At least he won't have felt any pain," said Matty. "They did everything they could for him. If he'd survived, if he'd ever woken up from the coma, he might have been in a terrible state—"

Dominic rested his hand on top of Matty's. "Don't. Please," he said. "Every day I'm reminded that I'll never get to speak to him again. Even to say goodbye..." His voice faltered.

"Right, Dad," said Matty. "Let's finish up here and go over to Fuggerßtrasse. We can have a drink in Prinzknecht Bar, and perhaps you'll meet Alex. Anyway, we'll raise a glass to Jonathan."

Dominic smiled. He ran his fingers through his son's long hair.

"I'm so glad we're back in touch," he said. "You're the best thing that's ever happened to me."

3

THE BRIGHTLY painted yellow-and-red train on S-Bahn line 2 rattled into Humboldthain station and wheezed to a halt. The pneumatic doors clattered open and discharged maybe a dozen passengers onto the empty platform. The sun was setting, but a warm breeze still rustled the leaves of the trees surrounding the entrance to the station.

Professor Alexeyev Krovopuskov strode along the platform, a large black bag slung over his shoulder. He jogged up the stairs of the over-bridge, walked out of the austere 1930s station exit and onto Hussitenstraße. In this sleepy neighbourhood of north Berlin, there were few cars around. He crossed the street and headed for the park. It was a longer walk to his office at the Berlin Technische Universität than if he had continued via the street. But it was a prettier walk through the park, especially at this time of year when the leaves were turning gold.

Through the trees he could see the remains of two concrete towers. They were the Humboldthain Flak Towers. Huge concrete structures built by the Nazis to defend Berlin in the Second World War. These days their only useful purpose was to provide a good vantage point from which to view the city. The unusually warm weather had tempted students away from the university and into the park that afternoon. Some dawdled along in small groups along the path that Alexeyev followed. Others, dressed in fashionable running gear, jogged past him with intense, earnest expressions.

He reached the far side of Humboldthain Park, crossed Gustav-Meyer-Allee and entered the plain, red-brick building that housed the Biochemistry faculty of the Technische Universität. Alexeyev shared an office with three other faculty members on the fourth floor, overlooking the park.

When he pushed open the door, he found the office empty. His colleagues must have already gone down to the main lecture hall for a staff meeting. It was irritating that the dean of the faculty always called the meeting late on a Thursday afternoon. Alex had hoped to stay at home all day and work from the apartment in Schöneberg the university had lent him. That morning he had arranged with Matty to meet around eight in the evening at Prinzknecht Bar for a drink. The bar was a few minutes' walk from his apartment. It was very inconvenient to have to make the half-hour journey out to the university in the far north of the city for an annoying piece of academic administration.

Alex walked over to his desk by the window and unloaded the bag from his shoulder. He took out his laptop, opened it up and unlocked it with his fingerprint. The project report he had been writing appeared on the screen. He sat down and flicked through its pages. It was only twenty minutes before the meeting was due to start. Enough time to review what he had written that morning.

Before Alex had got very far through the document, an

alert for an incoming video call flashed up in the top right of the laptop. It was from Professor Michael Zimmermann.

"Hey, Mickey! *Wie geht's?*" the Russian asked in his limited German. The face on the screen was that of a balding, middle-aged man. A bushy beard could not completely disguise his sagging, heavy jowls.

"*Privet,* Alex," replied Professor Zimmermann from the screen. His deep voice rumbled on the laptop's loudspeaker. "*Khorosho, spasibo.* You know, we're on an open connection, so we must be careful. It's Thursday evening here and I'm bored. So I decided to see how things are with you. You know it's eight months this weekend since we swapped places. Here I am, a German in Russia. And there you are, a Russian in Germany." He raised a small glass to the camera, filled with what was more than likely vodka. "*Prosit!*"

"*Na Zdorovie!*" replied Alex. He raised an empty hand to the laptop camera. "Is it really eight months already, Mickey? I can't begin to thank you for making this happen. My life is transformed. It's so wonderful here. I can finally be myself without fear of being beaten up."

Professor Zimmermann nodded. "I'm sure it's true. I have to say, even I'm surprised by how much attitudes here have changed since I last visited five years ago. Your mother country Russia has developed some very tough laws regarding people like us. Of course, for me, it's not a problem. All I do is sit in the apartment and watch terrible television. Or go to the café and sit on my own. But for you, when you were living here, it must have been very difficult."

"More than difficult. It became very frightening." Alex checked the clock on his computer. "I'm sorry, Mickey. I can't stay talking for long, I'm afraid. I've got to go to a staff meeting in ten minutes."

"Oh, yes. The famous Thursday afternoon bore-fests,"

replied Professor Zimmermann. "I thought you'd be exempt, given that you're only supposed to be there for a year."

"No one's exempt, Mickey. And I'm sure they'll notice if I don't turn up. Someone will report me."

Professor Zimmermann's smile seemed to fill the screen. "And I'm sure you want to keep your nose clean, especially if you want to get an extension to your twelve-month stay."

"I don't know if I do, Mickey." Alex shrugged. "It's wonderful here. But you know. I have responsibilities back there in Russia. I have to face facts. I can't stay here forever."

"Maybe," replied Professor Zimmermann. "But I'm sure your brother is being cared for extremely well. Perhaps he's getting better care than you can give. You should think about yourself for a change. By the way, how is that young man you mentioned? Have you seen him again?"

"Yes, I have." Alex smiled. "A lot. Matty's very bright. Very..." He searched for the right word. "Emotionally mature. We have so much in common. I'm going back to Schöneberg after the staff meeting to meet up with him. It's Folsom this weekend."

Professor Zimmermann laughed. His laugh made a deep rumbling noise, even over the little speaker in the laptop. "I remember it well. Such a sight. Max and I would sit on our balcony and watch all those men in leather in the street below. It was always interesting to watch."

The professor sighed and shook his head.

"Of course, Max is gone three years now. But you, Alex. You have someone. Go and enjoy yourself." He chuckled. "Why don't you go to the leather party this weekend?"

"No, no," Alex said hastily. "It's not really our thing. But we'll probably go and watch."

Professor Zimmermann's laugh rattled the laptop speaker again. "Each to his own, I suppose." He shrugged.

"Now. To business. I called to ask you about the American conference in November."

"The biomechatronics conference at MIT?" asked Alex. "Are you going?"

"I've been asked to give a paper about advanced neurological control interfaces. And I have a proposition. Would you present the paper with me jointly?"

Alex was flattered by Professor Zimmermann's invitation. Like Alex, the professor was a specialist in biomechatronics. The two men had met at a conference two years previously, found that they got on well together, and had quickly agreed to collaborate. Professor Zimmermann was over fifteen years older than Alex and was very paternalistic towards the younger Russian. It was Professor Zimmermann who had suggested the academic exchange.

"It's very kind of you to ask, Mickey," Alex began. "As you know, I've long been an admirer of the work you're doing on animal brain implants. There's great potential to replicate the work in humans. I'm glad MIT's invited you. You deserve it. What did you have in mind?"

"I'm so pleased you're interested," replied Professor Zimmermann. "Let me explain my idea a little more."

Professor Michael Zimmermann stared out of his living room window at the Neva River. It was a pleasant view across to the Hermitage on the opposite bank. The apartment was a valuable perk of the academic exchange he had entered into with Alex. It was in a perfect location in St Petersburg. A ten-minute walk to the university, and very close to museums and libraries that were related to his second passion after his academic work, Catherine the Great.

Admittedly, the apartment had been very draughty during the remains of the freezing, damp winter. The ancient windows were no longer a good fit for their frames. But the heating system was efficient enough. And in the last few months he had enjoyed the white nights, when the sun virtually never set. Even at this time of the evening in early September, there was still a faintly discernible orange glow in the sky. He sighed. With his husband dead three years, he had no one to share it with.

As he turned from the window, the intercom buzzed. Professor Zimmermann paused for a moment. It was rare for anyone to visit. He had made few friends since he had arrived in St Petersburg. These days, Michael preferred to keep his own company.

He crossed the floor of the living room and into the hall-way. On the small video screen of the door intercom he could see a woman standing outside the main front door to the apartment building. She had long, blonde hair and wore a black coat with fur trimmed around its collar. It was an unusual choice. The temperature was beginning to drop in the evenings, but it was still very mild for September. As Michael watched the video screen, the woman raised a cigarette to her mouth and inhaled. He pressed the button on the intercom.

"Yes? Who is it?" he asked.

The woman stared at the camera mounted above the front door and smiled.

"Is that Professor Zimmermann?"

"I am he. Who are you?"

"My name is Patrikova. Professor Patrikova. We arranged to meet tonight. I apologise. I am a little early."

He had forgotten. The woman had emailed him a few days before. She had said she was returning to St Petersburg on the Thursday and asked to see him urgently about a research project she was involved in. Reluctantly, he had agreed to the meeting.

"Ah, yes. I remember now. You'd better come up. Third floor."

He pressed the door-release button and watched the woman enter the building. He walked through the open doorway behind him into his study and crossed to the desk. He unlocked the laptop screen and began to type the name Patrikova. The search engine retrieved the page he had read three days before.

Professor Katerina Vniz Patrikova. Professor of Psychiatry at Moscow State University. Currently working in St Petersburg Correctional Hospital, specialising in the re-education of the criminally insane.

Before he could read any more, there was a knock at the door. He closed the lid of his laptop, went back into the hallway, and opened the front door. The woman he had seen a moment before on the video screen stood on the landing outside. She was taller than he had imagined, with high cheekbones and a small, thin-lipped mouth. She extended a gloved hand towards him.

"Professor Zimmermann? I am Professor Katerina Patrikova."

He took her hand and shook it.

"Professor Patrikova." He stood aside and gestured into the apartment. "Please. Come in."

She stepped into the hallway and looked around. "It's such a pleasure to meet you, Professor Zimmermann. I've read so much about your work. I was surprised – and delighted – to learn that you were here in the city."

She walked into the small living room and crossed to the window. Professor Zimmermann closed the front door and followed her. "Please," he said. "Call me Michael. Would you like some tea? Or something stronger?"

Professor Patrikova was staring out of the window. "What a wonderful view you have. Is that the Marble Palace over there?"

She turned away from the window and raised a hand to her cheek in a display of ostentatious contrition.

"I'm sorry for being so forward, Professor Zimmermann. I mean, Michael. But you're very lucky to live here." She began to remove her gloves. "Please. Call me Katerina. And, yes. I would love some tea."

"May I take your coat?"

"Thank you, but no," Katerina replied. "I won't detain you long."

Michael crossed to a tall, polished wood cabinet on the far side of the room and retrieved a small teacup and saucer from its shelves. He returned to the table next to the window, filled the cup with tea from a chrome-plated samovar and offered it to Katerina.

"Do you take sugar?"

"No, thank you." Katerina placed her gloves and coat on the table and took the cup and saucer from him. I have no need."

Michael picked up his own cup and refilled it. He sat on a chair at one end of the table and indicated the chair opposite him.

"Please. Sit. How can I help you?"

Katerina sat at the table and took a sip from her teacup.

"I'm working with a team on a research project to reduce the population of our jails in Russia," she began. "A small group of us are working with patients at the Correctional

Hospital. It's about forty minutes from here. Across the river." She gestured towards the window. "You'll probably not know about it. It's very...discreet." She took another sip of her tea. "The patients have committed criminal acts, but they weren't of sound mind at the time of the offence. Our project aims to restore their mental condition to a point where they can become useful members of society again."

"As a matter of fact," Michael said. "I am aware of the hospital. But how can I help? I'm not a psychiatrist. My work is with brain–computer interfaces." He drained his cup and placed it back on its saucer.

"That's exactly how you can help us." Katerina smiled. "The problem with conventional drug treatments for mental health conditions is that we can't see into the brain. We have very poor feedback on the effectiveness of the drug. Now." She held her teacup with both hands, took another sip from it, and regarded him over the rim of the cup. "Our team has succeeded in managing a patient's brain activity using a series of neural implants."

Michael stared at her. "You're surely not suggesting...?"

Katerina smiled again. "Let me tell you about this particular patient and what we've been able to achieve. Then you'll understand why I've contacted you."

4

DOMINIC HANDED his credit card to Frau Consten.

"*Alles gut*, Herr Delingpole?" Frau Consten slid the card into the slot of the portable card reader and waved the machine in the air. "I have trouble with Wi-Fi," she said apologetically.

Before Dominic could answer Frau Consten's question his phone chirruped.

"Well, you don't have trouble with Wi-Fi," Matty said. He grabbed Dominic's phone from the table before Dominic could reach for it. "I recognise that sound anywhere." He looked accusingly at his father. "When did you start using dating apps?"

Frau Consten handed back Dominic his credit card. "Ignore your son, Herr Delingpole. He's only jealous that other men in Berlin find a good-looking widower like yourself attractive."

"Oh, Dad." Matty turned Dominic's phone around to show him the screen. "You're using Papi? Dating for daddies? What are you looking for? Twinks?"

"Not at all," Dominic protested. He was acutely embarrassed. He had forgotten about the Papi app that a friend had mischievously installed on his phone shortly before the trip to Berlin. He took the phone from Matty. "I've been meaning to delete it."

"Oh, yeah?"

Dominic checked the time on his phone. "What time are you meeting Alex? It's well after eight."

"Oh, shit." Matty picked up his own phone and checked through his messages. "That's strange. He hasn't messaged me. He said he had to go to some staff meeting at the university this afternoon. But that should have finished ages ago. He was going to text when he was leaving."

"Where are you meeting?"

"At the Prinzknecht in Fuggerstraße." Matty made a call and held the phone to his ear. "He must be there by now." He looked across to Dominic. "Look. Why don't you come along for a drink as well? Then you can meet him."

Dominic smiled.

"I thought you weren't at the 'meet the parents stage' yet?"

Matty took the phone away from his ear. "It's not connecting. That's strange." He turned to Dominic and shrugged. "Maybe we are."

Frau Consten handed Dominic's card back to him.

"*Alles klaar. Vielen dank.*" She smiled at Matty. "It was a pleasure to meet you, young man. Take care of yourself. You know there are some wild parties happening this weekend. Crazy people everywhere."

The restaurant door opened and four men dressed from head-to-toe in leather walked in.

"See what I mean?" she said and smiled to greet the new arrivals.

Dominic and Matty walked up the stairs from the U-Bahn platform at Viktoria-Luise-Platz. It would be a brisk five minutes' walk through the leafy Schöneberg district of Berlin to the bar.

But not tonight.

They walked around the park and onto a tree-lined street called Welerstraße. Stark white light from old-fashioned, cast-iron streetlamps illuminated the darkness. Dominic and Matty crossed Geisbergstraße and continued on towards Fuggerstraße, the heart of the weekend's Folsom leather party and home to the Prinzknecht Bar.

They had only advanced maybe a hundred yards when they found themselves surrounded on all sides by crowds of people. In the distance, Dominic could see blue flashing lights reflecting off the windows of the buildings. Groups of people were standing around talking excitedly. The vast majority were men, many of them dressed in leather. But mixed in with the weekend partygoers were residents from the houses and apartments that lined the street. Occasionally they would gesture in the direction of Fuggerstraße farther down the street. Dominic glanced up to the apartments above and saw more people at the railings of their balconies, peering into the street below.

Matty had stopped walking and was talking in German to two men in front of them. He broke off to translate for Dominic. There was a look of shock on his face.

"They say Fuggerstraße's closed," he began. "The police have sealed off the street."

"Why? Has there been an accident?"

Matty spoke to the two men again. Dominic's German was limited, but he heard the name "Prinzknecht" mentioned.

After several minutes of rapid talking, Matty turned to Dominic. This time, his voice was shaking when he spoke.

"They've evacuated the Prinzknecht Bar. Something's happened. They're saying people have been killed. We can't get into the street."

Dominic put his arm around his son's shoulder.

"Killed? What happened? Was it a fire? It's not a bomb, is it?" Dominic thought back to the terrible attack on a gay pub in London's Soho back in the 1990s. A homophobic terrorist planted a nail bomb that killed three people and injured seventy.

Matty shook his head.

"Nobody seems to know. These guys were about fifty metres from the bar when the police told them to get as far away as possible. The officers didn't seem to know what it was, but they said something about gas."

"Gas?"

Matty had his phone to his ear and made no reply. After a short pause, he held it away from his head and glowered at it.

"It's not connecting." His eyes were wide and furious. "I can't get through to Alex. He's not answering."

Matty stared past Dominic at the street full of people ahead of them.

"Come on," he said. He ducked away from his father's arm and pushed through an opening in the crowd. As he did, he called over his shoulder. "We can get more information up there."

"Matty." Dominic called out to the retreating figure of his son. "It's not safe."

But Matty was fast disappearing into the sea of bodies. Dominic hurried after him. It was fortunate Matty was tall.

Although he was all but swallowed up by the crowd, his distinctive *ushanka* fur hat bobbed up and down above the heads of everyone. Dominic managed to get behind him and grabbed Matty by the shoulder.

"Matty. Wait. It's not safe."

Matty stopped and looked at Dominic impatiently.

"Dad. There'll be a police line somewhere up there. They won't let us get much farther. But at least there might be someone who'll know a bit more."

Before Dominic had a chance to reply, his son turned back and pushed into the crowd once more. Dominic decided he had no choice but to follow.

As they got closer to the blue flashing lights, the street became more congested with throngs of people. Dominic reached again for his son's shoulder. Matty took his father's hand. And so they continued up the street. Hand in hand. Father and son.

Ahead of them the crowd was thinning out. There were several police cars parked in the street, as well as three ambulances and a fire engine.

Around fifty yards before the junction with Fuggerstraße, their progress was blocked by blue-and-white police tape. Four police officers stood in front of the tape. Matty released his father's hand, walked up to one of the policemen, and began talking in German. Beyond the police line Fuggerstraße was almost empty. He could see four or five firemen standing in the street. They were wearing gas masks. A paramedic, who was also wearing a gas mask, pushed a wheelchair past the firemen towards Welerstraße. In the wheelchair was a man in jeans and a T-shirt. He had an oxygen mask strapped to his face. More paramedics carried bodies on stretchers. Dominic was shocked by what he saw. It was as though they had been plunged into a war zone.

"Dad."

There were tears in Matty's eyes.

"What is it?" asked Dominic. "What did he say?"

"It is the Prinzknecht. People were collapsing and throwing up. Everyone else thought they were drunk to start with. Then it happened to more and more. Then there was panic." Matty ran his hand through his hair. "Alex. He must have been... That's why I can't..."

Dominic placed his hands on Matty's shoulders to reassure him.

"They'll have a list of the injured. Alex might not have been in there. We don't know for certain yet." He squeezed his son's shoulders. "Can you ask how we find out who was in there?"

Matty turned back to the police officer. Before Matty could speak, the officer shrugged and answered Dominic's question in English.

"It's too early. There were many people. They're taking the injured to hospitals all over the city. You'll have to wait for the news reports."

"How many people?" Dominic asked.

The police officer shook his head. "Many people."

"If he wasn't in the bar," Dominic said to Matty. "Where would Alex go?"

"I guess he'd go back to his apartment. But why isn't he picking up?"

Dominic pulled out his own phone from his pocket. "Maybe they're jammed. All these people around here making calls. Or maybe they've blocked them. They do that sometimes when there's been an incident like this." He put his phone to his ear. "I'm calling you now. Check your phone."

Matty took his phone from his pocket, but Dominic shook his head. "It's not connecting. The network must be overloaded. I'm sure Alex is trying to call you as well. Where does Alex live?"

"It's not far from here." Matty was trying to make a call again. "Nollendorfstraße. We can walk it. But we'll have to go the long way around. It's on the other side of Fuggerstraße." He took his phone away from his ear and glowered at it with frustration. "If only I could get through." He looked at Dominic. "Thanks, Dad."

"Come on." Dominic smiled. "Lead the way."

They headed back through the groups of people standing around in Welestraße. After five minutes walking, the crowd thinned, and the two men turned onto another pleasant, tree-lined street with smart apartment houses on either side.

"I love this part of Berlin." Dominic knew Matty was worried and tried to keep a conversation going to distract him. "It's still got a Bohemian edge, despite all the money coming in to Berlin." Matty made no response, but Dominic kept on with his monologue.

"Christopher Isherwood lived near here. In the 1930s."

"I know, Dad." Matty sounded irritated. "The apartment's opposite Alex's."

They turned left onto a wider street. On the corner was a large burger and beer restaurant with tables outside. The tables were crowded with diners. Matty stopped and stared in through the windows. Inside the restaurant was an enormous television screen showing news pictures from Fuggerstraße.

"Come on, Dad." Matty walked up to the entrance. "I want to hear what they're saying."

He pushed open the door and entered the restaurant. In the middle was a long, American-style bar. The television screen was fixed to the wall behind it. Matty led the way between the tables. There was a noisy crowd of people three or four deep at the bar. Matty cupped his hand around his ear to listen to the commentary from the television news. After several minutes of listening, he spoke loudly in Dominic's ear.

"Whatever it was, it happened around eight. That's about an hour ago. They say people thought a few guys were drunk to start with. But then it became too many. There was panic and an...*ansturm*. How do you say...?" He clicked his fingers. "A stampede. People rushed for the exit. They think something like forty people are affected by the gas. And they were all inside the bar."

Dominic spoke directly into Matty's ear. The noise from the bar crowd was loud and the German television reporter's voice boomed above it.

"How are they affected?"

"They say two people are dead. But there may be more. Hang on." He turned back to the television. On the screen appeared a shaky video from somebody's phone, recorded at the entrance of the Prinzknecht Bar. The images showed men shouting, pushing and jostling past the person holding the phone. There were looks of either terror or anger on their faces. After a little over five seconds, the image shook violently, and the news report cut back to a reporter in the studio.

"He says there's speculation that it's some kind of nerve gas," said Matty. "The doctors don't know how to treat the casualties arriving at the hospitals. They're either unconscious or vomiting and hysterical." He remained almost hypnotised by the revelations from the news report.

Dominic found it difficult to believe what Matty had told him. He had read about the fears of either nuclear materials or nerve gas falling into the hands of terrorists. But he had always believed there would be strong enough safeguards in place to stop it happening. A chemical weapon had been used in a small town in the UK a couple of years ago. But that had been targeted at a former Russian agent.

More video from someone's phone appeared on the screen. This time it showed the inside of the Prinzknecht Bar. There was no evidence of an explosion. No smoke or flames. But a crowd of very scared people holding their hands over their faces, stumbling past the camera. Dominic was puzzled by the speed at which the television station had received the videos.

"If the internet's locked down," he asked Matty. "How come these pictures have been uploaded from people's phones?" he asked.

Matty turned to his father. There was a broad smile on his face.

"You're brilliant," he said. "They must have found Wi-Fi." He gestured around him. "And I bet they have it here. Maybe I can get hold of Alex on one of the hundreds of apps he's got on his phone."

"Why don't we just go over to his apartment?" asked Dominic. "You said it's not far from here."

But Matty had already pulled out his phone and started flicking through the messaging apps. Dominic marvelled at the speed with which his thumbs worked. He had never mastered the technique of two-thumbed typing on a phone. His messages were usually an embarrassment of mistyping or awkwardly wrong words helpfully supplied by the phone's auto-complete. His musing was cut short when a man pushed hard against him.

"Matty! Hey, Matty!" the man shouted. He pushed Dominic to the side and reached past to grab Matty's shoulder. Matty turned his head and let out a yell.

"Alex! Oh, my God. I've been trying to call you since forever."

5

ALEX'S APARTMENT was on the top floor of an old building in Nollendorfstraße. The entrance hall was a statement of opulence. Its high ceiling, together with large mirrors attached to the walls on either side, gave an impression of space and grandeur. A tiled floor led to an ancient elevator at the far end. The elevator was a cramped, wood-panelled box with a sliding concertina gate. The three men squeezed in. Alex heaved the metal gate shut and pushed the button for the top floor. The elevator jerked into action. It creaked and groaned as it lumbered up the building.

"Here we are," said Alex when the iron cage shuddered to an abrupt halt. He grasped the handle of the concertina gate and pulled it sideways sharply to release them from their confinement. "Matty, you lead the way. I'll send the elevator back down to the ground."

Dominic followed his son along the corridor. At the end on the left was a dark wood front door. Matty reached into his pocket and pulled out a key attached to a large metal tag. He opened the door, stepped into the hallway and switched on the light.

"You have a key?" asked Dominic.

Matty shrugged. "Of course. Why not?"

Dominic wanted to say there were a thousand reasons why a student should not have a key to a visiting professor's apartment. His lawyer's instinct jumped to the confidentiality issues related to personal student information. If Matty wanted, he could look at any other student's files Alex might keep in the apartment. But Dominic decided that to speak out at this point would be inappropriate.

"Please, Mr Delingpole." Alex had arrived behind him. "Come inside. I think we could all do with a drink." He turned to Matty. "There's that bottle of Grauburgunder in the fridge, Matty. Let's drink that."

Matty stepped into the large, old-fashioned kitchen opposite. Alex led Dominic down the hallway to a living room. The apartment was spacious, but it was filled with heavy, clumsy-looking furniture that made it appear cramped and untidy. The living room was furnished with enormous, brocaded, high-backed armchairs. In the middle of the room was a large, brown leather couch. The couch faced a set of tall glass doors that opened onto a small balcony.

"Please." Alex gestured to the couch. "Make yourself at home."

Alex crossed to the glass doors, opened them, and stepped out onto the balcony. There was the distant sound of sirens and the hubbub of crowds in the streets close to Fuggerstraße. There was a clutter of textbooks and academic papers scattered across the couch. Dominic decided it would be better to follow Alex onto the balcony.

"Cigarette?" Alex offered a packet embellished with Russian logos on its side.

Dominic shook his head. "I don't, thanks very much."

"Do you mind if I do?"

"It's your place. Please do whatever you want."

Alex tapped out a cigarette from the packet. He put it between his lips and lit the tip with a Zippo lighter. In the light from the flame, Dominic could see a thin scar on the side of Alex's face below his hairline. Alex inhaled deeply on the cigarette and shoved the lighter back in his pocket.

"So. Mr Dominic Delingpole." He blew a smoke ring into the evening air. "Matty's real father. I never thought I'd be allowed to meet you. Although Matty tells me so much about you."

Alex's Russian accent sounded even stronger when he pronounced Dominic's name. It was like the voice of a villain from a seventies spy movie.

"All good, I hope?"

"Oh, yes." Alex exhaled another smoke ring. "He's in awe of you. And also very protective. What brings you to Berlin? The Folsom leather party?"

"No," replied Dominic. "Well, yes, in a way. It holds happy memories for me. But I also came to see Matty."

"What do you mean, 'in a way?'"

Dominic sighed. "I don't know if Matty told you, but my husband died almost exactly a year ago. I didn't want to be on my own as it's the first anniversary of his death. Matty was here ready to start his next year of university, so I thought I'd come and visit him."

Alex tapped the ash from his cigarette over the rail of the balcony into the street below. "Yes, Matty did tell me. I'm very sorry for your loss. It must have been a great shock."

Dominic had still to find an adequate response when people offered sympathy for Jonathan's death. There were few people he wanted to talk to about it. One was his personal assistant, Gillian. Her husband had died five years before, and she gave Dominic the kind of informal and informed counselling only someone who themselves had experienced the death of a partner could provide. Since he had got to know Matty, he had gained confidence to confide in him. His son showed remarkable empathy and maturity, despite being only nineteen years old. But when anyone else offered condolences for Jonathan's death, Dominic's response was usually guarded and neutral.

"Thank you."

"He was murdered, yes?"

Dominic was not enthusiastic for the first conversation with his son's boyfriend to go down this route.

"Yes," he replied reticently.

Alex said nothing. A gap in the conversation Dominic felt obliged to fill. "He was shot. Murdered. Although he didn't die until over three months later. The man who shot him was pointing a gun at someone else at the time. Jonathan sort of got in the way."

"And what happened to the man who shot him?"

"He's in jail. In America. That's where it all happened. In California."

Alex stubbed out his cigarette on the rail of the balcony and tossed the stub into the street below. He sighed and stared across at the building opposite.

"Had you been together very long?"

"Three years. We'd only just got married. We were on our honeymoon."

"Oh, my God, Mr Delingpole. That's terrible." Alex was visibly shaken.

"Please. Call me Dominic."

Alex smiled. "Thank you, Dominic. In St Petersburg I grew up in a family where it was considered impolite to call someone by their first name until invited to do so. It may seem quaintly old-fashioned to you, but I rather like the custom. Especially with someone who is..."

"Someone who's your boyfriend's father?" suggested Dominic. "I'm not sure which of us is the more awkward here."

"Neither of you, I hope." Matty had arrived with their drinks. He handed a glass of white wine to Dominic. "Are you feeling awkward, Dad?" He handed a glass to Alex, kissed him on the cheek and looked at his father. "Because if you are, don't. Be happy for me." He raised his glass. "And let's all be happy we weren't in the Prinzknecht Bar tonight."

Dominic raised his glass. "You're right. We're all very fortunate." He turned to Alex. "Matty and I were deep in conversation at the restaurant and forgot the time. If Matty had been there when he was due to meet you then it would be very different. For both of you."

Matty took a drink from his glass. "It's not like you to be late, Alex," he said. "Did your meeting overrun?"

"No," replied Alex. "It was mercifully short. But it was only after I got on the U-Bahn that I realised I didn't have my phone with me. So I had to go back to look for it."

Matty clicked his fingers. "Is that why you didn't answer when I was trying to call you? Do you know where it is?"

"No idea. It wasn't in my office. And I checked the meeting room we'd been in. And the corridors."

"Perhaps one of your colleagues picked it up and handed it in?" suggested Dominic.

"I checked with security," Alex replied. "And they've not received anything. I must have dropped it somewhere between the university and the station." He turned to Matty. "It's really annoying. I've got to catch my flight to Helsinki early tomorrow morning. I'm going to the symposium, remember? Maybe I can buy a cheap phone at the airport. Otherwise I'll be out of touch."

"I know. You're going to be stuck without a phone," said Matty. "But it's only a couple of days, isn't it? And you've got your laptop. We can talk on that."

"Five days." Alex turned to Dominic. "It's so stupid isn't it? I've only been without my phone for a few hours, and already I feel naked. Completely lost."

Dominic was about to reply, but the deafening siren of an emergency vehicle racing along the street below them made any sort of response redundant. The three men leaned over the balcony to see what was happening. Two ambulances followed behind an escort of police motorcycles.

"I've never seen so many blue lights in one evening since I've been in Berlin." Alex moved away from the balcony and stepped back into the living room. "Come on. Let's put on the news and see if they're saying anything more than we already know."

Alex walked across to a small television set on a book-shelf and switched it on. Dominic and Matty hung back on the balcony.

"He seems very nice," Dominic whispered.

Matty laughed.

"Nice?" he repeated without bothering to whisper. "Nice? Is that the best you can offer?"

Perhaps it had been a lame word to use. Dominic wracked his brain for a better choice of adjective. Alex was tall and broad shouldered with close-cropped hair. The thin scar Dominic had seen on the side of his face gave him a sexy allure. But it seemed a wholly inappropriate word to use about his son's boyfriend.

"Don't you think he's sexy?" asked Matty. "He's brilliantly

clever, fit and good-looking. And he can bench press nearly a hundred and ten kilos."

Dominic rapidly tried to calculate if this was good or not. It sounded a lot. It was his own weight plus about half again. He concluded it was impressive.

"Matty! Come in here."

"I bet you think he's sexy," Matty said to Dominic. "And you're too embarrassed to say."

He walked back into the living room before Dominic could respond. Dominic followed him. Alex was sitting on the couch pointing at a bald man in glasses being interviewed on the news.

"Listen to this man."

"Who is he?" asked Matty.

"Listen." Alex was annoyed. His knee bounced up and down violently with nervous energy. He clenched and unclenched his fist as he stared transfixed at the television screen. Matty sat on the couch beside Alex with his hands rested on fists as he listened to the television interview. Dominic could not understand what the man on the screen was saying, as he spoke in rapid German. Dominic perched on the arm of the couch and watched his son's apparent mounting anger.

Matty's face got redder by the second. He kept muttering "*Scheiße.*" Finally he threw his arms in the air. "How could they even allow him to be on television?"

"Who is he?" asked Dominic.

Matty's eyes were wild with fury. "He's some ultra-right-wing conservative. I wouldn't be surprised if he's AfD."

Dominic was puzzled. "I didn't think Alternative for Germany had any presence in Berlin? What's he saying?"

"The extreme right never go away. We have to be vigilant." Matty pointed at the screen. "That *Arschloch* says that men who parade their pathetic fantasies on the streets are an obscenity. He says they're an affront to public decency, and the men in the Prinzknecht Bar deserved to die." Matty spat out the words. His German accent was suddenly much stronger. More guttural.

"And you don't like them giving him a platform for his views," Dominic said.

"Exactly."

Matty stood and shouted at the man on the TV.

"Do you know how much Berlin Folsom raises for charity each year? And do you know how much tourism it brings to the city?" He turned to Dominic. "Folsom is all about celebrating how tolerant this city is. It brings in people from all over the world. These people are pathetic."

The interview ended, and the picture changed to a reporter standing by a barrier on the edge of Fuggerstraße. He talked to the presenter in the studio in rapid German. Again, Dominic was frustrated by his lack of language skills.

"What's he saying?" he asked.

"This is terrible." Matty returned to his seat on the couch. He put his arm around Alex and rested his head on his shoulder. Tears formed in his eyes. "Ten people are confirmed dead, and there are more than seventy in a serious condition in hospital." He lifted his head from Alex's shoulder. "You could have been in there."

Alex kissed him on the forehead. "So could you." He looked across at Dominic. "Or your father. We were all incredibly lucky."

Dominic smiled back at Alex. It was clear how fond he was of Matty. He felt more reassured about Alex than when he had first met the Russian professor in the bar. "Do they know who did it?" he asked.

Matty shook his head. "They're speculating. The authorities aren't revealing anything. The reporter's confirmed it's some kind of nerve gas. But no one seems to know."

"Are we safe?" Dominic asked. "Do they think they might attack somewhere else?"

Matty shrugged. "They've not locked down the city. There's no curfew."

"I guess they might close off the odd street." Dominic stood. "I ought to go back."

"Where's your hotel?" Alex asked.

"Oh, Dad's not staying in a hotel," Matty answered before Dominic could speak. "He's booked a place through *StayGay*. You know? The website where you stay with a gay guy in his house and hope to get off with him."

"Good luck with that." Alex laughed.

"That's not the idea at all," Dominic protested. "It's simply a B & B for gay men where the owners live on the premises. This one's run by a very nice young gay couple. I think they're far too into each other to bother with an old man like me. And anyway, they're hardly ever there."

"You can always use Papi if you get lonely." Matty winked at his father.

"You're on Papi?" Alex asked. "I think I'm on it too. I must look you up."

"A friend put it on my phone for a joke," Dominic said. "I keep meaning to delete it."

"Don't do that." Alex unhooked himself from Matty's arm and stood. "You might get some fun while you're here in Berlin." He walked over to the bookcase. "I don't mean to be rude, but I must gather a few things for my trip tomorrow. How far is this gay B & B? Are you sure you won't stay?"

"It's only ten minutes' walk from here," Dominic replied. "Thanks for the offer but I'll be fine. Besides, you need to get up early tomorrow."

"Well, if you change your mind." Alex winked at him. "But I understand if you've got a better offer from your hosts at *StayGay*."

"Honestly, it's not like that—"

Matty laughed. He stood and embraced his father. "Now don't tell me you're all embarrassed." He whispered into Dominic's ear. "Perhaps I was wrong. Maybe we are at the 'meet the parents' stage."

6

ALEX STOOD on a chair and grappled with a small, brown leather holdall in the bedroom cupboard. It was wedged behind a box of textbooks. He swore as he realised he had no option but to remove the heavy box to retrieve the bag.

"Why don't you store your luggage under the bed?" Matty said from the doorway as Alex manhandled the box of books from the cupboard.

"Because I didn't expect to be travelling quite so soon." Alex climbed down from the chair and dropped the box onto the floor. "Now I've got two trips. The symposium in Helsinki tomorrow. And Zimmermann's asked me to present a paper with him in America later this year."

"What time's your flight tomorrow?" asked Matty.

Alex climbed back on the chair and pulled down the holdall. "Six."

"You've not got long before you have to get up again." Matty entered the bedroom and launched himself onto the bed. He checked the digital alarm clock on the side table. "Seven hours. Hardly worth going to bed." He pulled two pillows towards him and cuddled them like a giant teddy

bear. "Your bed is so much more comfortable than mine."
He stretched out luxuriously. "And so much bigger."

Alex laughed. "You can stay here for the next few days if
you like." He dropped the holdall on the bed. "But I was
hoping you'd come to Helsinki."

Matty wrinkled his nose. "I really want to. Honestly. But
it depends what my tutor says tomorrow."

"Rasmussen? He rates you very highly. You've got
nothing to worry about there."

"Really?" Matty sat up. "He doesn't tell me anything."

"Ah." Alex picked up the box of books and climbed onto
the chair to put it back in the cupboard. "Perhaps I shouldn't
have said anything." He looked down at Matty. "So. Are you
coming to Finland?"

Matty smiled. "For sure. I'd love to see Helsinki. But you
end up paying for everything..."

Alex closed the cupboard and jumped down to the floor.
He stood at the end of the bed with his hands on his hips.

"Why? Are you worried you might look like a toy boy?"

"Fuck off."

Alex walked around to the side of the bed and sat on the
edge. "I've left an open ticket with your passport on the side
in case you do." If you decide..."

"I'm sorry," Matty said. "It's only. I don't know. It feels a
bit weird sometimes. Like, the age thing shouldn't be a
problem—"

"Then why make it one?" Alex stretched out a hand and
ran his fingers through Matty's hair. "It's not an issue for me.
And after tonight I think it's less of an issue for your father."

"You think so?" Matty kissed Alex's hand. "I don't think
he had much of a chance to think about it this evening. With
everything that's happened."

Alex kissed Matty on the lips. He stood up, walked back

to the foot of the bed and opened the holdall. "I like Dominic. He seems to be a straightforward man. Very shy and cautious." Alex smiled. "Unlike you."

"What do you mean by that?"

"It's not a criticism. But I can't imagine Dominic ever got involved in student politics like you do."

"They're not student politics." Matty sounded offended. "They're politics." He moved down the bed and squatted on his knees in front of Alex. "Mama's always been very active in the party. She says it's too easy for our rights to be stolen away. She and Dad – I mean Stepdad – have often argued about it. But she's right. Look at what happened in Russia. Once, it was a shining light for socialism. For communism. Now it's caved in to capitalism, with a government run by a bunch of mafia crooks."

Alex opened a drawer behind him. He pulled out a selection of clothes and shoved them into the holdall. "What do you know about life in Russia under communism?"

"I know that it was fairer then." Matty folded his arms and sat back on his haunches. "That there was less of a divide between rich and poor. Did you know that before the fall of communism, the top ten percent in Russia had about a fifth of the country's wealth? Now they own half the country's wealth. It's no different to America."

Alex removed a shirt from its hanger and carefully folded it. "Did I ever tell you my father was held in jail until Gorbachev came to power? He was professor of linguistics at Moscow State University. A thinker. Hardly a dangerous man. His mistake was to refuse to write what the Party ordered. So, when I was four years old, they decided to make an example of him. I was ten when they finally released him."

"I didn't know that."

"I have something for you to read. I'll go and find it."

Alex went back into the living room and walked over to the bookcase. He looked along the shelves until he found the books he wanted. On his way back to the bedroom, he picked up his passport from the table by the door.

"Here." Alex placed one of the books on the bed in front of Matty. "You can start on this while I'm away. It's a long read. It's very valuable. So treat it well." He tapped the front cover of the remaining book he held in his hand. "I've got another one. We can read it in parallel, and you can tell me what you think."

Matty carefully picked up the faded copy of *Doctor Zhivago* by Boris Pasternak and thumbed through the pages.

"You've got to be kidding me," said Matty. "It's in Russian."

Alex laughed. "Too challenging? Imagine how hard it was for my parents to read this book. It was banned in Russia." He opened his copy and turned the pages. "Think. A love story was considered a threat to the Communist Party." He pointed at the book in Matty's hand. "These copies are very important. They were part of a batch printed by the CIA and distributed illegally in the Soviet Union. Ten million of them. Some say it's thanks to the CIA that Pasternak won the Nobel Prize for Literature."

"Why did the CIA print them?"

"Propaganda." Alex immersed himself in the text of *Doctor Zhivago* and read a section to himself. "It's still beautiful. The Americans wanted the Soviet ban on this wonderful book to backfire on them. They wanted the Party to look foolish. Instead, the Kremlin banned it right the way up to 1988. The year before the fall of the Berlin Wall."

Matty closed his copy of the book and held it out to Alex.

"I'll never manage to read this. I can barely read Cyrillic. I promise I'll get myself a German language edition and start reading it."

Alex held up his hand to refuse the book. Instead, he picked up his phone and searched for a page on the internet. "You don't need to buy a copy. I found a free German translation online the other day." He smiled at Matty. "Now we can read it together while I'm away. Isn't that romantic? Of course, *Doctor Zhivago* is more than a love story."

"What's it about?"

"So much." Alex sat on the bed and put his arm across Matty's shoulders. "It's about love. And war. And how our moral values can change in war. It's about class and hierarchy, and how it always exists, even in a communist system."

"No wonder it was banned."

Alex smiled. "Oh, Pasternak was even more contentious than that." He leaned across and kissed Matty on the lips. "I think if he'd been alive today, he'd have written about people like us."

"Really?"

Alex sighed. "Of course. In Russia, a relationship like ours is considered scandalous. As a gay couple, we have no legal rights. In effect, the present regime has made us illegal."

Matty leaned forward and rested his forehead against Alex's.

"Come on. There's not much point going to sleep tonight. You'll be leaving in a few hours. Let's be illegal."

Hodan rattled the large, metal door of the lock-up garage in frustration. The door was never locked. She had been coming to sleep here for the last three months. Every night, shortly after nine thirty, she arrived in this quiet dead-end street. The line of concrete garages was unlit. Hidden away.

A friend she had met at a feeding station in the city had told her about it. The first time she had come to explore she had struck lucky with the second garage door she had tried. It had been unlocked. Inside, the garage had been empty. That night, she had laid out her bedding roll, arranged her meagre possessions, and closed the door. For the first time in weeks she had slept safely, away from the night-time danger of the parks. Away from the smells and the noise of the U-Bahn stations, where homeless people like her slept. She had returned to the garage each night. Every time, she had found the door unlocked, exactly as she had left it.

But tonight was different.

The long walk out here had been for nothing. She kicked the door, squatted down on the ground and thought about where she could go. At least the evening was warm. If necessary she would have to sleep in the open. In one of the parks. But she hated the parks. Homeless women she had met in the shelters warned her of men who roamed the makeshift camps occupied by homeless refugees in Berlin's parks. They preyed on vulnerable women like her. The staff at the shelter she had gone to in Kreuzberg that afternoon had told her they might have a place for her next month. But she would have to report back to the shelter every day to safeguard her place on the waiting list.

Hodan stood and stretched her aching muscles. She decided to investigate the other lock-up garages. Perhaps one of those had become vacant and was now unlocked. She walked along the line of ten garages, trying the handle of each of them with a growing sense of futility. They were all locked. She thought about searching for another street of garages, but darkness had fallen, and the lack of street lighting made her feel vulnerable.

She walked back to the top of the street. If she turned left she would head back along the main street to central Berlin. To the right was the River Spree, and the construction site for the new office blocks.

Hodan hesitated.

Perhaps one of the cabins used by the construction workers might be unlocked. It was worth checking, if she could find a way into the site. Otherwise it was a long way back to the heart of Berlin.

As she walked towards the construction site she could see a ten-foot-high fence surrounding its perimeter. The fence was topped off with barbed wire. The site was impenetrable. Hodan stopped at the double gates set into the fence. They were locked and chained. On top of the gates was more barbed wire. Hodan sighed. It was futile.

She looked to her left and saw the River Spree. Now she had got this far, she might as well go and see it. In all the time she had slept in the lock-up garage, she had never ventured down here to explore it before.

For a desolate, riverside construction site, the view was pleasant. Tranquil. The moon was almost full, and its light glinted on the surface of the water. About fifty yards downstream was a large boat moored on the opposite bank of the river. Strings of lights festooned its mast like nautical Christmas trees. A sign described it as a 'luxury hostel for backpackers'. Upstream was a riverside bar. Beyond it there was darkness, punctuated by the red warning lights attached to tower cranes. They were like large, motionless UFOs suspended in the sky and marked yet another construction site.

Hodan watched the river. It was peaceful here. But the

water made her anxious. It was a reminder of her terrifying journey across the Mediterranean six months before. It had been the worst part of the flight from her native Somalia. She walked back towards the main street.

Which was when she saw the hole in the fence.

It was neatly cut. A three-foot square hole at ground level. Perhaps another homeless person had had the same idea as her. Or maybe they were simply hoping to steal from the construction site. The latter was the more likely explanation. Whatever the reason, Hodan might still find a place to sleep for the night without the long walk back into central Berlin.

Once again, she hesitated.

What if the person who had cut the hole was still inside the perimeter fence? It was probable they had cut the hole that evening. The owners of the construction site would not allow such a breach in their security to continue for longer than a day. If the person who had cut the hole was still inside, he was likely to be a man. And if he were a thief, he would be hostile to a potential witness like Hodan seeing him.

It was a risk.

Hodan's aching limbs quickly made up her mind for her. She climbed through the hole in the fence, taking care to avoid snagging her bags of bedding and possessions on the jagged edges of the cut wire. Straight ahead was a small office block of temporary cabins stacked on top of each other. A steel staircase on one side gave access to each of the three floors of the structure.

An optimistic thought entered Hodan's head. Perhaps the workers left the doors of the offices unlocked, putting their trust in the tall fence around the site. Her hopes briefly raised, she hurried towards the door of the first of the offices at ground level.

It was locked. She went along the block, trying each door in turn. Every one of the doors was locked. Undeterred, she headed up the staircase to the offices on the next level. At the door of the third office along she struck lucky. It was unlocked. The small temporary office was empty, save for a few boxes of protective clothing shoved in a corner.

Perfect. Hodan closed the door behind her, unrolled her sleeping mat and settled down for the night.

7

THE ALARM rang at three thirty the next morning. Matty stirred from a deep sleep. His eyes remained closed and he felt Alex kiss him on the cheek.

"Don't move, my love." Alex kissed him again. "Go back to sleep. I'll get dressed in the living room and creep out. See you after the weekend?"

Matty rolled over and squinted open his eyes. The bedroom was lit only by the bluish glow of the alarm clock. Alex stood with his back to him at the end of the bed. He was naked. Sorting out underwear and socks from a drawer.

"Safe journey." Matty decided not to answer Alex's question. "Did you have to get such an early flight?"

"I've got a lot to do before it starts," Alex replied. He stared across at Matty. The soft light in the room highlighted the muscular curves of Alex's body, although there were the hints of love handles developing around his waist. Matty felt his cock stiffen, knowing he had been entwined with this body only a few minutes ago.

"I'll message you," Alex continued. He picked up a

handful of clothes, walked over to the bed and reached across to kiss Matty on the lips.

"Go back to sleep, sexy man."

There was a faint glow of dawn in the sky when Hodan woke up. She could hear a noise. She remained curled up in her makeshift bed and listened intently. After a few seconds a door slammed. It must have been the construction workers coming on shift. If they caught her she was sure they would report her to the police.

Cautiously she sat up, crawled over to the window and looked outside. On the ground about ten feet below her was the storage area for the site's machinery. There was a line of forklift trucks parked on one side, and a line of pneumatically powered equipment on the other.

There was the flicker of a shadow to the left. She ducked down below the level of the window and held her breath. There was no sound. Slowly, she lifted her head to peer into the storage yard below her.

A man stood in the middle of the yard, staring out at the construction site. He was tall and broad, with close-cropped hair, and carried a large, brown holdall. He had no bright orange jacket or protective helmet, like the construction workers Hodan had seen. Perhaps he had arrived early at the site, she thought. Or perhaps he was a thief. Perhaps he was the one that had cut the hole in the fence she had crawled through earlier.

The man picked up a large hammer from the ground and shoved it into his holdall. He swung the bag onto his shoulder and walked forward a couple of steps. He stopped and suddenly looked directly at Hodan.

Hodan ducked below the level of the window. She scrambled across the floor of the cabin to her few possessions, rapidly packed them into her backpack, and headed out of the door. She crept down the metal staircase outside, trying to make as little noise as possible.

At the halfway point she turned on the stairway and saw the man from the storage yard. He was striding away into the heart of the construction site. Perhaps he had not seen her at the window. Hodan waited on the staircase and watched as the man approached a tall metal tower. It was a white-painted steel cylinder, over thirty feet high. On the top of it was a platform with a small guardrail around its edge. Halfway down the cylinder, giant, flexible pipes emerged from its side. One of the pipes hung close to a cement mixer truck.

Hodan had seen one of these towers before, on a construction site in central Berlin. She had watched fascinated as two men had manipulated a large pipe from the tower and sprayed cement into preformed moulds. It had seemed to produce an endless supply of thick sludge.

The man reached the base of the tower and started to climb the vertical ladder on its side. He rapidly reached the top, dumped his holdall on the platform, and stood facing a metal hatch. He took the hammer he had removed from the storage yard and began to attack the hatch. After only a couple of blows the hatch fell open.

The man bent down, picked up the brown holdall, and threw it through the open hatchway. After a few moments' hesitation, he grabbed a rail above him, swung himself into the air, and dropped out of view. Down into the depths of the cement maker.

Hodan struggled to understand what she had seen. Why would a thief climb into a cement maker? How would he get out again? She waited for the man to re-emerge. But there was no sign of him. She hurried down the staircase, contemplating what she had witnessed.

―――

After Alex left for the airport, Matty slept until eight. Friday dawned bright and sunny, and light streamed in through the gap between the bedroom curtains. He stretched his limbs and relished the extra space the large bed afforded him. He rolled over, yawned extravagantly, and thought about the day ahead.

He had a day free from lectures, and it was his father's last few days in Berlin. Matty had arranged to meet him at the Schwüles Museum at eleven. This museum of gay history was near the Tiergarten. They planned to have lunch at the café by the lake, and afterwards they would go for a walk. Matty looked forward to finding out more about his real father's past. They had yet to discuss how Dominic had met his mother, Amélie, in a small south German town near Munich. He wanted to know if there had been any spark of love in the relationship at the time Matty was conceived. He wanted to know why Dominic had left her and travelled on to Berlin, where he had met Bernhardt, his first male lover.

But then, twenty years later, did it still matter? Matty sat up, shielded his eyes against the daylight penetrating the bedroom, and considered the question.

His mother had surrounded him with love as far back as he could remember. His stepfather was very different. Matty's mother always deferred to Eric as the head of the household. Eric in turn expected Matty to play the role of the dutiful stepson, who would one day succeed him as head of the small construction firm in southern Germany he owned. He was not an unkind stepfather, but he was distant and cold. Would things have been different if Matty had grown up with Dominic as his father?

Matty climbed out of bed and walked across the room to draw the curtains. He pulled the windows wide open and inhaled deeply to breathe in the cool air of the morning.

Of course things would have been different. It was an illogical question to ask, and a useless point on which to speculate. History had happened and could not be changed. What mattered was the present. Since Dominic had made contact with his mother three years ago, Matty had taken a long time to reconcile himself with the inevitability of history. His real father had departed Germany and returned to England even before Matty was born. But it was not a malicious act on Dominic's part. He had been unaware that a night of passion had resulted in the prospect of a baby boy.

Matty's mother was from a Catholic family. She had told Matty on more than one occasion that an abortion had never been an option for her. Her family had made that clear. But nor was it an option she would have chosen herself. What she had looked for was a husband to provide stability for her imminent family. Eric had been her sweetheart at school. Their parents had been on a regular, dinner-party level of friendship. He had been the obvious candidate to secure respectability for her condition in the provincial, Bavarian community.

Matty went into the kitchen to brew some coffee. There was a note from Alex propped up against the coffee maker. It read:

No more than two cups per day! See you Monday, caffeine freak xxx

He smiled and recalled that it was Alex that had persuaded him to keep in touch with Dominic after their first few meetings.

"Why on earth not?" Alex had asked. "This man's an important part of your history. Don't lose him now he's found you."

Looking back to that time, Matty found it difficult to comprehend why he had been so reluctant to maintain the contact. Probably because he had feared how it might change his relationships, not only with his stepfather but with his mother as well.

He put fresh beans into the coffee maker and switched it on.

His fears about Dominic had proved groundless. Instead, he had found the perfect father to confide in about his sexuality. Eric was yet to learn of Matty's seven-month relationship with Alex. He had reacted badly enough when Matty came out at the age of sixteen. He knew his stepfather would struggle to comprehend his relationship with Alex, a man twice his age. When Matty had told his mother, she had said she would tell his stepfather, "When the time is right."

That time had yet to come.

His phone buzzed with the arrival of a new message. It was from his tutor:

This afternoon's meeting is important. We must discuss Professor Krovopuskov. I will see you at 14.30.

Matty leaned back against the kitchen countertop. So his tutor finally wanted to talk about Alex. That sounded ominous.

"I thought you said it wasn't a problem?"

Dominic spoke to his son in a whisper. They had been looking at a display of 1980s homoerotic photography when Matty had told him about the message from his tutor. Dominic wanted to keep his conversation with Matty confidential. But a small group of leather-clad men stood nearby, clearly enjoying the images on the wall in front of them. His son had picked a bad moment to announce he was about to be cross-questioned by the university about his relationship with a professor twenty years his senior.

"It's not," Matty whispered back. "Alex isn't my tutor. He doesn't take me for any lectures. He's not even a permanent member of the faculty staff. Why should it be a problem?"

"If it's not a problem, why does your tutor want to talk to you about it?" countered Dominic.

"I don't know. I'll find out later."

Matty turned away from the display of photographs. He walked towards a leather sling in the middle of the room. Dominic followed reluctantly. He had found Berlin's gay museum a fascinating place up until this point. It related the city's long history of being a safe haven for people rejected by conventional society. The section on persecution during the rise of Nazism and throughout the Second World War had been very moving.

Now they were in a gallery celebrating the liberating times of the 1980s and 90s, when sex clubs had flourished, and Berlin became the go-to destination for the fetish community. He hoped Matty would not ask any awkward questions about dungeons or sex toys. Dominic was a shy man, and he felt their relationship would need to develop a lot more before their conversation could enter such intimate terrain. Matty rested his hand on the steel support of the sling and looked over at him.

"Have you ever been in a sling?" Matty's question cut through the quiet of the gallery. Dominic was convinced every visitor turned to stare him. His face flushed.

"Are we done in here?" Dominic asked in a loud whisper. "Let's go for a coffee downstairs. We can talk more about your tutor there."

Matty gave the sling a gentle push, and it swung back and forth on its chains. He grinned at Dominic.

"I'll take that as a maybe."

Matty walked over to his father and put his arm around his shoulder. "There's not much more to say about my tutor. For the moment. But I want to ask you about Mama. So coffee's a good idea. Why don't we go over to the Tiergarten now?" He gestured around to the other visitors. "We might be able to talk a bit more freely there."

<hr>

The leaves on the forest of trees in the Tiergarten glowed a rich, verdant green in the afternoon sunshine. Many of the trees were relatively new, no more than sixty or seventy years old. They had been donated to the park from all over Germany in the winter following the end of the Second World War. A fuel shortage had forced desperate Berliners to cut down hundreds of trees in the Tiergarten. It had taken many years to reforest the four-hundred-year-old park.

Matty led the way along a well-maintained footpath towards the café by the side of the lake.

"You know," Dominic began. "I can't tell you very much about your mother. We only knew each other for a month. She was staying in the same hostel in Munich where I was. She'd run away from her parents for the summer."

Matty laughed. "I can imagine why. Oma is very scary.

Opa was lovely. It was so sad when Opa died two years ago. Mama dressed in black for him for nearly a year."

They arrived at a small platform overlooking the lake. Matty stopped and rested on a rail at the edge of the platform. Dominic joined him and together they gazed at the lake. There were several small boats on the water. Amateur oarsmen navigated them clumsily and erratically, to the amusement of spectators on the shore.

"Did you love her?"

Dominic turned to Matty. He felt his face flush. It was not for the first time that afternoon. Matty was asking a lot of very direct questions.

"I was eighteen, Matty," he said. "I don't think I knew what love meant. She was – she is – a lovely person. We had some very good times together."

"Clearly." Matty smirked. "I imagine that's how I happened." He looked back at the boats on the lake. "Sorry. That was a cheap comment. But why did you leave her behind in Munich?"

Dominic was puzzled. "Didn't Amélie ever tell you? It was she who went back home. Her father, your Opa, had his first heart attack. It was the start of his ill health."

Matty sighed. "Mama never told me. I'd always thought you'd gone off to Berlin and left her behind."

"Is that what she said?"

Matty shook his head.

"Not in so many words. That was the impression she gave me. But now I think about it, it all makes sense. Mama's never really talked about you much. But she did say that the year she met you, it was the same year Opa had to stop work. And Oma became the breadwinner in the family. When Mama got married to Eric, Opa was ashamed he couldn't give his daughter the dowry he felt she deserved." He sighed again. "I'm sorry."

"Why?"

"Because I got the wrong idea about you."

Dominic smiled. "You thought I was some lothario, sowing his seed across Germany? You couldn't be more wrong."

"But then you got to Berlin and you met Bernhardt." Matty turned to rest his back against the railing. "So, Dad. Will you answer me a question?"

"It depends what it is."

"Do you like women, or men?"

"Oh. That question." Dominic lowered his head and rested his chin on the railing. He watched a small group of ducks paddle past him towards the bank where a young girl was scattering bread on the water.

"Well?"

Matty was staring at him expectantly.

"I thought I was in the first throes of love with Amélie. I didn't think of anyone else at the time. Then she left Munich when your grandfather had his heart attack. I wanted to follow her, but she said it wasn't a good idea." Dominic sighed. "She was probably right. I stayed in the hostel another couple of days. But it wasn't the same without her. So I got on the train and came to Berlin."

"But were you really attracted to men?" asked Matty.

"Not then." Dominic saw the dubious expression on his son's face. "No, really, Matty. If your mother had stayed in Munich, and I'd known she was pregnant with you, I'm sure I would have married her."

"But, what about Bernhardt? And Jonathan? And all the other men?"

Dominic laughed. "All the other men? I can assure you

there were only two other men between Bernhardt and Jonathan. I'm really not the slut you think I am."

"I didn't say that—" Matty's protests were cut short by his phone ringing. He pulled it from his pocket and checked the screen. "Sorry. It's my tutor."

The conversation was brief. By the end of it, Matty was upset.

"What's the matter?" asked Dominic.

"He says I've got to go into uni right now."

"Why?"

"He says it's about Alex." Matty was distracted by his phone. "He says the police are there."

"The police? Why?"

"Why can't you get decent internet in the middle of Berlin?" Matty waved his phone above his head. "It's useless."

"Why are the police there?"

"He wouldn't say. All he said was, 'Haven't you seen the news?' That's what I'm trying to do now. But I can't get a fucking signal on this phone."

"I'll try on mine." Dominic shoved his hand into his pocket and pulled out his phone.

He opened the internet and chose a news service. "What are we supposed to be looking for?"

Matty took the phone from his father and flicked through the web pages.

"Shit."

Dominic tried to see the screen over Matty's shoulder.

"What is it?"

"This is madness. They've released a photograph of the chief suspect in the Prinzknecht Bar attack last night." Matty turned the phone around for Dominic to see.

It was a photograph of Alex.

8

DOMINIC FOLLOWED his son through the doors of the Mathematics Institute building. The cavernous entrance hall was practically deserted. In the far corner, a small group of students were sitting around a table talking loudly. Apart from them, there was no one else around.

"Where is everyone?" asked Dominic.

"It's early September, Dad." Matty led the way to a staircase sweeping up to the mezzanine floor above. "Not everyone's back yet." He stopped at the foot of the stairs and turned to Dominic. "Do you want to wait here while I go up? I'm not sure how long this will take."

"Don't you want me to come with you?"

"I'm not sure." Matty thought for a moment. "I think it would be really weird. I wouldn't normally have my dad come with me to see my tutor."

"This is different," Dominic replied. "Remember the police will be there. It might be a good idea to have a lawyer with you."

Matty shrugged. "But I haven't done anything wrong."

Dominic shook his head. "I'm afraid everything's going to get a lot more complicated. With Alex now a suspect—"

"But that's crazy," protested Matty. His raised voice echoed in the vast space of the entrance hall. A couple of the students in the corner looked up. Matty lowered his voice. "That's crazy," he repeated quietly. "Alex can't possibly be the one who set off that gas attack at the Prinzknecht Bar. They've got it wrong."

"Possibly," Dominic replied carefully. "But according to those news reports they've got him on CCTV. It doesn't look good. They're going to want to know where he is right now. Have you heard from him since he left for Finland?"

"He lost his phone yesterday, remember? He was going to buy a cheap one at the airport and call me from it so I'd have the number. Perhaps he didn't have time. Maybe he'll get one in Finland and call me from there."

"It's not a great time for him to go off-grid." Dominic put his hand on Matty's shoulder. "Come on. I'll come with you. Just in case."

Matty led the way up the stairs to the mezzanine floor. At the top they entered a long corridor. Matty stopped outside the second door along. The name card on the door read Professor Ralf Rasmussen.

"Rasmussen?" whispered Dominic. "That doesn't sound like a German name."

"No," Matty replied. "He's Danish. He's a good tutor but his German's lousy." He knocked on the door. After only a few seconds the door opened. A German police officer stood in the doorway.

"Herr Lange?" asked the officer. Matty nodded. The police officer looked across to Dominic. "*Und wer sind sie?*" he asked.

"*Dieser Mann ist mein Vater,*" Matty replied. "*Er ist englisch. Er spricht kein Deutsch.*"

The officer looked back into the room.

"*Ja, ja. Komm,*" said the voice of a man behind him.

The officer turned to Matty and Dominic. He motioned them to enter the room. A man with short blond hair and a moustache sat behind a desk facing them, his back to the window. An older man stood to his left. He was balding and wore heavy-rimmed glasses. Although tall, his hunched shoulders made him seem several inches shorter. It was as though he carried the troubles of the world upon his back.

"*Guten Tag,* Herr Lange," said the older man to Matty. He turned to Dominic and spoke in English. "Good day, Mr Lange senior."

"Actually, my name's Delingpole," said Dominic. "I'm a lawyer." He extended his hand in greeting. The older man ignored it.

"Why is your name different to your son's?"

"Matthias took his mother's name," Dominic replied. "We've been estranged for many years."

"I see," said the older man. He seemed unconvinced by Dominic's explanation. "You are from England?"

Dominic nodded.

"I see," said the man again. "I am Kriminalkommissar Schutz and this is Polizeimeister Weiß." He waved in the direction of the uniformed officer that had opened the door. "I am from the BKA, and Polizeimeister Weiß is from the Bundespolizei. You're familiar with our police system here in Germany, Herr Delingpole?"

"Only from a distance, Herr Kommissar," Dominic replied.

"Kriminalkommissar."

"My apologies Kriminalkommissar," Dominic said

hastily. "The BKA is the Bundeskriminalamt, responsible for terrorist investigations—"

"Very good, Herr Delingpole," interrupted Kriminalkommissar Schutz. "And are you an English lawyer who can practise here in Germany? Or merely a concerned parent?"

Dominic was disconcerted by the way the conversation was going. He felt he was about to be ejected from the room.

"I'm here to advise my son," he replied simply. He hoped it would be a sufficient answer to allow him to stay and help Matty.

Kriminalkommissar Schutz took off his glasses. He pulled an off-white handkerchief from his pocket and polished the lenses. It was only after he had completed the cleaning process that he replied.

"Very well. You may stay." He stuffed the handkerchief back in his pocket, put on the glasses and added, "For the moment. We only have a few questions to ask your son." He indicated two chairs in front of the desk. "Please. Sit both of you."

The blond-haired man seated at the desk extended his hand in greeting to Dominic. "Mr Delingpole," he said. "I'm Professor Rasmussen, Matty's tutor. I'm pleased to meet you. Although I'd have preferred it to be under happier circumstances."

Dominic shook hands with Professor Rasmussen and sat down. "Thank you, Professor. Me too. I'm pleased to meet you." He turned to Kriminalkommissar Schutz. "How may we help you, Kriminalkommissar?"

"I'm not sure you can help me at all," replied the chief inspector. "It's your son who holds the answers." He turned to Matty. "Where is Professor Krovopuskov?"

"He's at a conference in Helsinki," Matty replied. "He flew there early this morning."

"Did he call you or message you when he landed?" asked the Kriminalkommissar.

"No. He lost his phone last night. He was going to buy a temporary one at the airport and call me on it. But I've not heard from him yet."

"I see." Kriminalkommissar Schutz pulled out a small notepad from his jacket pocket and transferred it to his other hand. He reached into the pocket again and fumbled around as if searching for something. He snapped his fingers at the uniformed police officer.

"*Stift.*"

Polizeimeister Weiß hastily reached into his pocket and pulled out a pen. He handed it to the chief inspector, who took it without acknowledgement and turned back to Matty.

"What is the name of the conference? And where is Professor Krovopuskov staying?"

"It's called the Seventh Symposium on Biomechatronics Applications in Prosthetics," replied Matty. "It's at the Scandic Congress Center in Helsinki. That's where he's staying, also."

"I see." Kriminalkommissar Schutz flipped open his notebook. "That's what your tutor told us earlier." He stared down at Matty. His eyes were unblinking.

"What is your relationship with Professor Krovopuskov?"

Matty looked nervously at Dominic, who turned to the chief inspector.

"Kommissar, is that relevant—"

"Kriminalkommissar, Herr Delingpole," interrupted the chief inspector testily. "And yes, it is. Professor Krovopuskov is a key suspect in a murder investigation. A terrorist attack.

You have seen the news, no? We have him clearly on video at the scene of the outrage. It is logical that your son's relationship to this suspect is of great interest to us." He scratched the bridge of his nose. "You understand?"

Dominic sighed. He nodded at Matty.

"We're...good friends," Matty began.

"When did you last see Professor Krovopuskov?" asked the chief inspector.

"This morning. Around four. He left for the airport."

"You were in his apartment?"

"Yes."

"In his bed?"

"Kriminalkommissar," protested Dominic. "I really don't think that—"

The chief inspector glared at Dominic. "Be quiet, Herr Delingpole. Or I will have you removed." He switched his gaze to Matty. "Herr Lange. Are you lovers?"

"Yes."

"And yet, even though you are the professor's lover, you care not where he is, even when he is wanted for murder?"

"*Nein!*" Matty placed his hands on the table and rose to his feet. The chief inspector held up his hand and motioned him to sit down. Matty shook his head and resumed his seat. "I told you. He's in Helsinki. At the conference."

The chief inspector closed his notebook and put it back into his jacket pocket, together with the police officer's pen. He removed his glasses once more, reached into his pocket for the off-white handkerchief and resumed cleaning. The affected mannerism was beginning to irritate Dominic.

"The problem is, Herr Lange," said the Kriminalkommissar. "We have already checked with the Congress Center. And with the symposium. Professor Krovopuskov has not arrived. They've not seen him."

He leaned across the desk to Matty.

"So tell me, Herr Lange. Where is he?"

———

Kriminalkommissar Schutz arrested Matty ten minutes later.

Dominic was shocked. He demanded to accompany his son as the police officers led him out of the Mathematics Institute building to a waiting police car. The Kriminalkommissar was scathing.

"Herr Delingpole, I suggest you use your time constructively and find a proper German lawyer to help your son. Herr Lange is withholding vital information in a terrorist investigation. That is very serious. We have the power to detain him for twenty-four hours. Then we'll take him before the judge, and we can hold him for longer. When you find a proper lawyer, they will confirm that for you."

Dominic watched the police car containing his son leave the university entrance and drive away. He walked back towards the entrance of the institute. As he reached the top of the steps, he was forced to stand aside as a large group of students flooded through the glass doors. When he finally got back into the entrance hall it was crowded. It looked like an orientation meeting for new students. The hall was buzzing with a hundred or more conversations. Dominic felt claustrophobic. His chest tightened. A growing sense of panic welled up inside him.

He desperately missed his husband at moments like this. Despite Jonathan's compulsive jollity and occasionally irritating frivolity, he had been a good person to be with in a crisis. He badly needed him now.

The steady drone of excited conversation in the entrance

hall was loud. Dominic walked back outside. He took out his phone and made a call.

"Goodness, Dominic. You're not still in Berlin are you? We've been watching the news about the gas attack on that bar. Are you all right? How's your son?"

"I'm fine, Miles," Dominic replied. "And so was Matty. Until about five minutes ago."

"Good God. He's not injured is he?" The rounded, upper-class vowels of Miles Torrington QC were unmistakeable. The voice of England's most highly paid lawyer was the product of an expensive education at Westminster School and Oxford University.

"No." Dominic sighed. "Only arrested. I need a good recommendation for a German lawyer. And quickly."

"In trouble with the police?" Miles sounded amused by the information. "What's the young tearaway been up to? Dear Dominic. You've only been in touch with your son for less than a year and he's already following in your footsteps."

"Hardly." Dominic was indignant. "He's been arrested by the counter-terrorism branch of the Bundespolizei on suspicion of withholding information."

"Exactly," Miles replied. "I seem to remember you doing precisely the same thing with our boys in blue in Brighton a few years back."

Before Dominic had a chance to protest further, Miles continued.

"I'm afraid that sort of criminal law's not really my expertise, old boy. And certainly not German criminal law. Corporate computer fraud is more my bag. Hang on a minute while I give Penny a call. She might know someone. Or someone who knows someone."

Penny Torrington was Miles's wife. A human rights

lawyer with an international practice. Miles and Penny Torrington were known as the Park Lane Power Couple and regularly featured in society gossip columns. Dominic first met Miles when they were undergraduates together studying law at Oxford. Since Jonathan's death, Miles and Penny had frequently provided a sympathetic ear when grief had threatened to overwhelm Dominic.

"Bingo!" Miles's voice bellowed into the telephone after a rapid-fire conversation with his wife. "Penny's a wonderful woman. So glad I married her. She's got just the man for you. He's called Johann. Johann Hartmann. Splendid fellow apparently. Penny says he'll spring your boy from the cooler in no time. Who'd have thought it, eh, Dominic? Your boy up against the police. Like father, like son. A chip off the old block."

On the one hand Dominic was grateful to his friend for help. But he wished Miles would stop raking up Dominic's past run-ins with the British police every time they spoke. He sighed. Perhaps that's what friends were for.

———

Johann Hartmann had clearly been briefed to expect Dominic's call. Their conversation was short, but to the point. The lawyer was in the middle of a complex human rights case and very busy. He was prepared to meet Dominic at six o'clock at his offices on the north bank of the River Spree, close to Berlin's criminal court building. Dominic expressed his gratitude for seeing him at such short notice, and the call ended.

Dominic's next call was to his hosts at the B & B where he was staying. He was due to leave Berlin the following day. But with Matty arrested, he had no choice but to stay for longer. Fortunately, despite the crowds of partygoers that had descended on Berlin for the weekend, his hosts could accommodate him for at least another five days. He wondered how much more time he would need in Berlin.

His next call was to his personal assistant. Gillian would need to rearrange all his appointments for next week. Not easy to achieve on a Friday afternoon. He told her what had happened to Matty. Gillian chuckled.

"All I can say, Dominic, is, like father, like son."

"Not you as well." Dominic sighed. "Miles made the same comment. I do think it's unfair of you both."

"Don't be so over-sensitive." Gillian's reply was brusque. "Miles is quite right. Remember when that young man was in hospital in Brighton with a drugs overdose? You took it upon yourself to withhold quite a lot of information from Sussex Police I seem to remember. At the same time, you maintained you were only doing it to protect your client. Perhaps Matty's simply protecting his boyfriend."

"But they say they've got Alex on CCTV." Dominic rested his head on the wall of the Mathematics Institute. "The police seemed pretty confident he's their man. And to think I was having a glass of wine with him only last night."

"Oh come now, Dominic." There were occasions when Gillian sounded worryingly like Dominic's primary school teacher, a strict disciplinarian. "You know as well as I do how quickly the police jump to conclusions. It sounds to me like you're jumping with them. Let's hope that the lawyer Miles found is a bit more qustioning than you are."

Dominic had to admit Gillian was right. He had been too quick to presume Alex's guilt. Maybe it was because he was apprehensive about the older man's relationship with his son. Despite his conversation with Matty, he realised he still had misgivings. Perhaps now was the time to set them aside. Before he ended the call with Gillian, he promised her that he would be more supportive for both his son and Alex.

Dominic had nearly three hours to kill before his appointment with the German lawyer. He walked around the perimeter of the Tiergarten in the direction of the River Spree until he found a pavement café. He took a seat in the sunshine and ordered a pot of tea and a slice of *baumkuchen* with cream. To prepare himself for the meeting, he took out his phone and searched on the internet for Johann Hartmann.

The online biography proved that the man was exceptionally well-qualified to help Matty. He had graduated from Munich University and was the youngest graduate lawyer, or *Prädikatsjurists*, in Germany. In the last year he had successfully overturned the wrongful prosecution of two Syrian men accused of plotting an attack on the Berlin parliament building.

But Dominic was shaken by the black-and-white photograph of Herr Hartmann that accompanied his glowing credentials. He was very handsome. And bore a striking resemblance to his late husband.

9

A STRONG GUST of wind caught Dominic off-guard as he walked along TurmStraße on the north bank of the River Spree that evening. He staggered and came to a halt to catch his breath. Across the street was the imposing sight of Berlin's criminal court, the largest court building in Europe. It was built in the neo-baroque style of the early twentieth century and was one of the few buildings to be spared the ravages of Allied bombing on Berlin at the end of the Second World War.

Johann Hartmann's offices were a short distance farther on from the courthouse. They were in a bizarrely shaped modern block of glass and steel that seemed like it was on the verge of collapse. Floors jutted out at odd angles, and several appeared to be suspended without any visible means of support. Jagged beams of steel protruded from the sides and roof, as if to suggest the building had recently been the victim of an earthquake. Dominic recognised the style of architecture as deconstructivism. A style that deliberately avoided harmony and symmetry. It seemed a suitable metaphor for the way Dominic's life had suddenly turned upside down.

"Herr Delingpole. I'm delighted to meet you. Penny's told me a great deal about you."

Johann Hartmann's resemblance to Jonathan was even more striking in the flesh. He was a little shorter than Jonathan's six feet four inches and much leaner. Jonathan had always been an enthusiastic eater, particularly of bread and cakes. He had relied solely on the physical activity involved in his landscape gardening work for exercise. But it was Hartmann's extravagant and ebullient manner that most reminded Dominic of his late husband. The similarity was both attractive and disturbing at the same time.

They shook hands.

"I hope Penny hasn't told you too much about me," Dominic replied.

The German lawyer laughed. "Don't worry. She was very complimentary." He gestured towards a large sixties-style couch. It was set close to the window of the seventh-floor office. "Please. Have a seat and enjoy my glorious view of the Spree. Many people with offices in this strange building sit with their backs to the windows. I can't understand it. They miss so much. I prefer to keep in touch with the outside world. It's good for my soul." Johann Hartmann picked up a tablet computer from a bookshelf and joined Dominic on the couch.

"May I begin by expressing my condolences for your sad loss."

"Thank you." Once again, Dominic was uncertain how

to respond when presented with sympathy for Jonathan's death.

"Penny told me your husband was killed while you were on your honeymoon last year," Johann continued. "That's tragic. But how did you both become involved in the Charter 99 conspiracy in the first place?"

Dominic was taken aback by the question. Clearly Penny had given Johann a detailed briefing about him. He wondered what else she had said. He stared at Johann, who smiled and waved his tablet in the air.

"I did a little research before you arrived. You and your late husband seem to have got caught up in some pretty big adventures in the past few years. If it wasn't for you two, Charter 99 might have made the world a very frightening place."

Dominic shook his head. "No, really. It wasn't us who stopped them. We sort of stumbled across them and got in their way a bit."

"Don't be so bashful," Johann said dismissively. "You were key players in their defeat. And before that you managed to foil the plans of the Natural Family Association, who wanted to eliminate gay people from the world. Did you simply stumble into them as well?"

Again, Dominic was shocked by the question. Johann Hartmann had been very thorough in his research. Johann laughed.

"Don't worry, Dominic," he said. "I'm not stalking you. In fact, I'm a little in awe of you. The Natural Family Association was a very nasty group of people. You both did well to bring them to justice."

Dominic smiled. "I'm afraid you give us far more credit than is due. We really didn't set out to bring them down. It was more of a happy accident that they were caught."

Johann sprang to his feet and began to pace up and down in front of Dominic. The sudden movement startled Dominic. Partly because it was unexpected, and partly because it was exactly the sort of thing Jonathan would have done.

"No, no, Dominic. I disagree." Johann stopped pacing. He crossed to his desk. "You're a clever man. That's clear. And you're a good man. Another person would have simply walked away when faced with the challenges you encounter. But you don't." He picked up a tray from his desk. "Tea?"

Dominic laughed. "You're really too kind. And yes, I'd love a cup of tea. It's not been an easy day."

Johann carried the tray back to the window and set it down on a small table. "Penny introduced me to Earl Grey when she and I first worked together on a case five years ago. I love it. It's the only tea I drink now. I always take it with honey. So refreshing."

"Now that's a coincidence."

"Oh, good." Johann picked up a large china teapot and began to pour the tea. "You like it with honey as well?"

"No. But Jonathan did. I'd prefer it with lemon if you have some?"

"Of course." Johann set down the teapot, added a slice of lemon to one of the cups and handed it to Dominic.

"You're going to tell me you sing opera next." Dominic took a sip of his tea.

Johann snorted. "I hate it." He paused and frowned, as if reconsidering his statement. "Well, 'hate' is a strong word. Let's say, I've never understood it."

"Oh, but it's the most complete form of storytelling," Dominic protested. "Drama, music, dance and great spectacle."

Johann laughed. "No, no. You're describing musicals.

They're the complete form of storytelling. And they're my passion." He set the tablet on his lap. "Now. We must be serious. Your son's being questioned by the police on suspicion of terrorist activities. They can hold him for twenty-four hours. Then they have to go before a judge. That's when it will get really nasty."

"Yes. Kriminalkommissar Schutz told me as much. Is there anything we can do?"

"Maybe. But first, you must tell me everything you know."

Dominic went through the events of the past twenty-four hours. Johann typed rapidly as Dominic spoke. He occasionally interrupted Dominic's flow to ask a question for clarification. When Dominic had finished, Johann set down the tablet at his side and reached for his tea. He drained the cup, placed it on the tray and leaned back on the couch in silence. Dominic waited expectantly for him to say something. Finally, Johann spoke.

"It's unfortunate that it's a Friday evening. We have very little time to act. But I do have some people I can call. They might be able to help. Give me half an hour." He gestured to the teapot. "Please, help yourself to more tea."

"Thank you so much," Dominic replied. "Am I keeping you from something this evening?"

Johann smiled. "Well, it's the start of Folsom tonight. I was hoping to go to one of the parties. I'll make that my incentive to work hard and get a solution for you."

Like all gay men, Dominic was curious about the sexuality of each man he met. At least Johann had made plain his preference early on. Dominic could imagine the lawyer would be very popular at a Folsom party. The fitted white shirt Johann wore highlighted his athletic body. His eyes sparkled and his face radiated self-assuredness. Dominic's mind began to form a picture of Johann wearing leather chaps and a harness, topped off with a leather Muir cap.

"Is something wrong?" Johann asked.

Dominic awoke from his daydream to see Johann smile and wink at him. He felt his face flush as he realised he must have been staring at the lawyer a little too obviously.

"No, no."

"Aren't you here for Folsom?"

"No, no." Dominic shook his head. "I came to see Matty. And it's a few months since the first anniversary of my friend's death. I wanted to visit his grave."

"I'm so sorry." Johann touched Dominic's arm. "That means you lost two people in a very short space of time. Was he a close friend?"

"Yes. Well, we had been." Dominic smiled at Johann. "Many years ago, he was my first lover. I met Bernhardt here in Berlin. We kept in touch over the years. He was an international copyright lawyer."

Johann looked shocked. "Do you mean Bernhardt Freude?"

"Yes. Did you know him?"

"Oh, yes." Johann stretched back on the couch. He sighed, as if recalling a happy memory. "He and I were also lovers. Many years ago. Bernhardt wanted us to set up a law firm together. But I thought it would be unwise." He chuckled. "I think I made the right decision. But he was a wonderful man. So intelligent."

"How did you cope with Bernhardt's love of opera? After all, you hate it so much."

"I suppose I used to love it." Johann sighed again. "Perhaps that's why I hate it now. If I hear an excerpt from a Mozart opera, all I can think of is Bernhardt."

"You must have been close." Dominic instinctively laid a hand on Johann's arm. "How long were you together?"

"It was five years."

Johann stared out of the window for several minutes.

"Come." Johann sprang to his feet. "We have work to do. I have some calls to make. And you can use the spare laptop on my desk. I rarely use it these days. I prefer this wonderful device." He held up the tablet. "I use it for everything. I'm afraid it's even got Grindr on it. That's for when I get bored in court."

Dominic stared up at Johann with mounting alarm. Was the man coming on to him? It was hardly the right moment, what with Matty locked up in a police cell somewhere. Johann clearly noticed the concern on Dominic's face. He shook his head and walked across to his desk.

"I'm sorry, Dominic. It was a joke. But not appropriate. You have too much to worry about at the moment. Here." He indicated the desk phone next to the laptop. "Why don't you call the Congress Center in Helsinki? You can check whether the Kriminalkommissar told you the truth or not. And maybe you'll find out that Alex has in fact arrived there by now."

It was an excellent suggestion and gave Dominic the opportunity to do something practical for Matty rather than simply sitting around and waiting.

Over the next thirty minutes Johann paced up and down the office and held a series of conversations in rapid German on his phone. Meanwhile, Dominic settled himself at the glass-topped desk and called the Scandi Congress Center. The receptionist confirmed that Professor Alexeyev Krovopuskov had not checked into the hotel.

Dominic asked to be put through to the main desk of the biomechatronics symposium. It took some time for the receptionist to find anybody involved with the symposium. Helsinki was an hour ahead of Berlin and most people were at dinner. Finally, a woman's voice came on the line.

"Herr Delingpole? This is Anna Hokkanen from Scandi Conferences. You are seeking Professor Krovopuskov?"

"Yes, that's right," Dominic said. "Has he registered at the symposium? The hotel receptionist said he hadn't checked in."

"You are correct," replied Anna Hokkanen. "He left a message this morning to say he would be late—"

"He left a message?" interrupted Dominic. "How? Did he speak to someone?"

"I'm afraid I don't know. I was given the message by my colleague, and she's gone off-duty. Would you like me to read the message to you?"

"Yes, please."

"It says, 'I'm delayed in Berlin, but I'll catch the next flight. Apologies. I'll be there for the evening reception.'"

"Nothing else?" Dominic asked.

There was no reply from Anna Hokkanen. Instead, Dominic could hear her talking to someone else in Finnish. After several seconds she came back to the phone.

"Mr Delingpole. My colleague here tells me she saw Professor Krovopuskov on the television a moment ago. She says he's wanted by the police for the gas attack in Berlin. Is that true?"

Dominic ended the call and put the handset back on its rest. Johann was standing in front of him.

"He left them a message?" Johann asked.

"It seems he missed his flight this morning. I wonder if the police know that?"

"I'm sure they do," replied Johann. "If it's true, that is. We need to find out for ourselves. Give me a couple of minutes."

Johann made a call. After a lengthy conversation, he gave Dominic a thumbs up.

"That was interesting," Johann said a few minutes later. "My friend has access to the flight records out of Berlin. He was able to check if Alex got on the flight he was booked on this morning."

"And did he?" asked Dominic.

"He did. Which makes his message to the symposium very puzzling. Why did he tell them he was getting a later flight when he actually got on the one he was scheduled to catch?"

"It's not very helpful for Matty, is it?" Dominic said. His stomach felt like it was churning over and over. "I'm sure the police think Matty knew Alex was going to disappear. That's why they're holding him."

Johann smiled broadly. "Don't worry, my friend." He picked up his jacket from the back of a chair. "I've managed to track down the one person who can help us get Matty released. It took a combination of my old Munich University network and the pink network here in Berlin to find him."

He walked to the door of his office and opened it.

"Come, my friend. We'll have to call on him in person. I happen to know that, where he is right now, he'll be far too busy to take a call on his phone."

10

"WE'RE GOING TO CHURCH?"

Dominic stared at Johann as they stood on the platform of Turmstraße U-Bahn ten minutes later.

"In a manner of speaking."

The doors of the train clattered open. Dominic and Johann stood aside to let several passengers get out of the crowded carriage. As the last one stepped onto the platform, the two men pushed inside before the doors slammed shut behind them.

"There's a concert at the Zwölf-Apostel-Kirche in Schöneberg this evening," Johann continued. He grabbed the handrail above him as the train started with a lurch. "Manfred is a cellist. He's performing there tonight."

"I thought you said he was a judge?" The train braked and then accelerated again. Dominic lost his footing and fell against Johann. The tall German grabbed Dominic around his waist. For a few seconds Dominic was transported back to the September of three years before, when he and Jonathan had been in Berlin together for Folsom. He recovered his balance, pulled back from Johann and held on tightly to the handrail. The train rapidly gathered speed and plunged into the tunnel on its way to the Zoological Gardens interchange.

Johann smiled and dropped his arm away from Dominic's waist.

"He is a judge," Johann said. "But he's also an exceptionally gifted cellist. He could have performed professionally, but he chose to remain an amateur. Tonight's concert is..." Johann's forehead crumpled into a frown. "Well. Wait and see. Let's say, it's a very special concert tonight."

Despite Dominic's further questions, Johann refused to elaborate on the details. Instead, he pointed out the significant sites to see at each station along their route. As he spoke, Johann revealed his passion for the city. He had been born in East Berlin thirty-eight years ago, when it had still been part of the communist German Democratic Republic. When he was eight, the Berlin Wall had fallen, and West and East Germany had been reunited.

Johann described that night in December with great detail. His parents had been loyal members of the Communist Party in the former German Democratic Republic. Now that communism was dead, he recalled the fear they had had for their future. It had taken nearly a week for them to pluck up courage to cross the former boundary of the wall and venture into the West. Johann described the excitement he had felt when he had seen the bright neon lights of West Berlin. The department store windows full of tempting things to buy. The wide streets full of cars. The garish advertising hoardings. It had been as if the gates of heaven had been opened.

When they changed trains at the Zoological Gardens interchange they were able to get two seats next to each other.

"The nineties were a wonderful time to be in Berlin," Johann said loudly to Dominic, above the rattle of the train. "It was full of artists and Bohemians. It still is, despite the rise of the corporate monsters."

"But artists and performers have always been drawn to Berlin," Dominic replied. "Remember the KitKatClub in the twenties and thirties? Marlene Dietrich, Kurt Weill, Lotte Lenya?"

"It's true," agreed Johann. "But there's another reason why so many artists came to West Berlin after the war. Do you know it?"

Dominic shook his head.

"The government introduced conscription for the whole of West Germany in the 1950s," Johann continued. "Every young man had to do nine months military service."

The noise of the train got louder, and Johann moved closer to Dominic to speak directly into his ear. "But, if you lived in West Berlin, you were exempt. So lots of young men, who didn't like the idea of square bashing and learning how to kill people, moved to West Berlin when they got to age eighteen."

The train rattled into Nollendorfstraße Station and screeched to a halt. The two men got out and headed for the exit.

"And in my view," Johann said as he walked up the staircase alongside Dominic. "Those artistic young men are far more interesting. Which is why I love living here. Now. Prepare yourself for a surprise."

He led the way a few hundred yards down the street to a church on their left. A poster outside read:

Classic Meets Fetish

"You've got to be kidding me." Dominic laughed. "Your

judge friend is not only a gifted cellist but he's also into fetish?"

"And why not?" Johann asked. He winked at Dominic. "Manfred is stunning dressed in his Tom of Finland leathers. Come on. We'll creep in the back and see if he's sitting on the side. That is, unless he's performing."

Johann gently pulled open the door to the church. A tall, well-built man dressed in leather boots, chaps and leather shirt was standing inside. He raised a finger to his lips. Johann whispered in his ear. The man smiled, opened the inner door of the church and pointed to the audience sat on the left of the nave.

"Wait here," Johann whispered to Dominic. "I can see Manfred. He's over there. I'll go and get him and bring him out. There's an interval very soon anyway, so he won't be playing for a while. That's if he hasn't done so already."

Johann stepped into the church and crossed to the aisle on the far left. Several heads turned at the sound of his footsteps. Dominic could see the church was packed with men. Every one of them was dressed in fetish clothing, either leather or rubber. At the far end of the church was a leather-clad man playing a Beethoven sonata on a grand piano. It was a strange sight. By comparison, Johann was the odd one out, dressed in his formal suit, white shirt and tie.

Within a few minutes, Johann re-joined Dominic at the entrance to the church. This time he was accompanied by a tall man with short, jet-black hair. The man wore leather jeans and a shirt, tailored to accentuate his lean, muscular contours. His tall leather boots were highly polished, and he wore a black leather Muir cap and tight-fitting leather gloves. In all his years as a lawyer, Dominic had never met a judge under such bizarre circumstances. He wished it could happen more often. The man extended a leather-gloved hand in greeting.

"Herr Delingpole," he said. "Manfred Richter. Your reputation precedes you. I already know about your defeat of the Natural Family Association. The gay community is in your debt. I hope I can be of service to you."

The two men shook hands.

"Forgive me, Judge," replied Dominic. "But isn't the German word for 'judge'...?"

Manfred Richter laughed. "You're right. The German word for judge is 'Richter.' So my name is Judge Judge. When you're born with a name like Richter, your career is predestined." He glanced down at his leather jeans and then at Dominic. He smiled wryly. "You must understand, Herr Delingpole. I'm not normally dressed like this. Are you here to attend Folsom as well?"

"No," Dominic replied. "I came to visit my son. He's at the Technische Universität—"

"But now you're here in Berlin," the judge interrupted. "You should go to Folsom. Despite the gas attack, it will be very safe. The street party will be heavily policed after that terrible attack on the Prinzknecht Bar. It will be the safest place in the city, with lots of sexy police officers standing around. And there are always the parties to go to afterwards."

Dominic was surprised at Manfred's openness. He was a judge and held a very senior office. And yet here he was, dressed in leather, talking about Berlin's notorious sex parties. Manfred smiled back at him.

"You seem shocked, Herr Delingpole. Do you think it wrong that a judge should take part in these activities? Think. Who is it that grants licences to the sex parties? If our legal system goes to all that trouble to allow these events to take place safely, the least they can do is to let us take part as well. Perhaps we are more liberal here in Berlin than in England."

He turned to Johann.

"Let's go outside. There's less chance we'll be overheard."

He led the way outside to a stone bench beside the church. He sat at one end and motioned to Johann and Dominic to sit beside him.

"Now," said Judge Richter. "Tell me why you've dragged me away from my concert tonight."

In rapid German, Johann briefed the judge about Matty's arrest at the university. Judge Richter sat with his hands together in front of him. He drummed his fingertips in a rhythmic pattern as he listened. When Johann had finished, the judge sat in silence, still tapping his fingertips together. After several minutes he spoke.

"Herr Delingpole. How well do you know your son?"

"I've known him a little over a year," Dominic replied. "And I trust him to tell me the truth."

"Why?"

It was not a question Dominic had thought about. He automatically trusted his son. But it was a paternal loyalty without a basis in hard evidence. They had known each other for little more than a year and had met only three times during that period. He tried to think of his recent conversations with Matty. Might they show why he was confident to trust his son? He concluded it was not words that mattered, but Matty's actions.

"He's not an actor," Dominic replied. "When he saw the news report that Alex was a suspect for the attack on the Prinzknecht Bar, he was genuinely shocked. When he couldn't get in touch with Alex, he was genuinely upset. I know it sounds naïve, but I'm confident Matty's not been colluding with Alex."

Judge Richter shook his head.

"You'll have to do better than that, Herr Delingpole," he said. "A parent's love for his child is heart-warming. But it's insufficient grounds for me to argue with my fellow judges that they should release a potential terrorist collaborator from police custody."

"You're forgetting a fundamental fact," interjected Johann. "Matty is gay. So is Alex. Why would either of them plot to murder innocent gay men in a bar? They're not closeted gay with some kind of internalised homophobia." He turned to Dominic for confirmation.

"It's true," Dominic said. "It doesn't make sense."

Judge Richter nodded. "Unless their relationship is an elaborate hoax."

Dominic laughed. "Impossible. Matty braved the wrath and homophobia of his stepfather to come out. He's not straight. I know he's not."

"The difficulty is," replied the judge. "Is that if you argue Matty couldn't be involved in an attack on a gay bar because he's gay, you must use the same argument for Alex. Now, as I understand it, the police say they have video evidence connecting Alex with the attack. Therefore, if he's responsible for the attack on a gay bar, even though he's gay, Matty could be implicated through the same reasoning."

Dominic sighed. "I've only met Alex once, but I have to say I don't believe he's a terrorist. Certainly not an anti-gay terrorist." His mind went back to the night in Alex's apartment. An idea came to him. "I do remember something. We were watching the television, and there was some right-wing politician being interviewed. He said the gay men in the gas attack deserved to die. Matty was furious and so was Alex. I think he was genuinely angry. He's not a terrorist. I'm convinced of that."

Judge Richter stood up and flexed his leg muscles. Dominic was momentarily distracted as he admired the man's physique. The judge smiled, clearly aware of the impression he was having on Dominic.

"Thank you, Herr Delingpole," he said. "I trust you completely. As I said when we met a few minutes ago, your reputation precedes you. But, if I am to do what you and Johann ask me, I must have confidence in your judgement."

Johann stood, and the two men spoke in German for a few moments. At the end of their conversation they shook hands. Judge Richter extended his hand to Dominic, who stood up hastily and shook it.

"I must return to the concert, Herr Delingpole." Judge Richter smiled and released his grip on Dominic's hand. "My public will be waiting." He walked back to the church and went inside.

"What happens now?" Dominic asked Johann.

"Manfred's going to make some calls to the prosecutor involved in the case and possibly the police hierarchy," Johann replied. "He'll get us an emergency court hearing for tomorrow. I think he may have Matty released by lunchtime." He gestured towards the church. "Would you like to watch a group of good-looking men dressed in skin-tight leather play Beethoven? It's very sexy."

11

THE PEWS of the Church of the Twelve Apostles were full. Every person in the audience wore some kind of fetish clothing. Dominic felt underdressed in his khaki chinos and T-shirt. At least he was wearing a leather jacket. Although it was one more suited to a university lecturer trying to appear hip than a cool guy hanging out at a fetish event.

The music was surprisingly well performed. Judge Richter, now with his cello, sat with a leather-clad violinist and pianist on a makeshift stage at the front of the church. For the next twenty-five minutes they played a series of Beethoven piano trios. Dominic closed his eyes to eliminate the distraction of the fancy dress around him and allowed the beauty of the trio's playing to penetrate his soul. For the first time that day he sensed his body relaxing. His breathing dropped to a slower, deeper rhythm. As it did, his brain replayed the events of the last few days back to him, and he tried to make sense of what had happened.

The moment that Matty had showed him Alex's face in the news report on his phone kept returning to the front of his mind. The journalist had lifted Alex's photograph from his biography page on the university website. Farther down the article had been a grainy enlarged image taken from a security camera in the street outside the Prinzknecht Bar. A police statement said it showed the man responsible for the gas attack on the bar. Dominic and Matty had scrutinised the picture for some time, but had found it impossible to see much similarity between the man in the security camera image and Alex.

Then there was the comment Johann had made to Judge Richter. He was right. It made no sense for an out gay man to attack a gay bar. As far as Dominic was concerned, Alex's affection for Matty was genuine. True, he was still worried that Matty was, if not in love, then certainly infatuated with a much older man. A man that could be compromising his professional status at the university. But that was another issue entirely.

But if Alex was innocent, why had he disappeared? And why had he made no attempt to contact Matty or anyone else? The flight records obtained by Johann's friend showed Alex had arrived in Finland on the flight he had been scheduled to take. Perhaps something had happened to him at the airport. Or perhaps he had fallen ill and was in hospital somewhere in Finland.

But if that were the case, the authorities would have made attempts to contact his next of kin. Who would they contact? It was unlikely to be Matty. He and Alex had only been going out for seven months. It was more likely to be someone in Russia. Matty might know who that person was. If Dominic managed to speak to him tomorrow, it was one of the questions he needed to ask. Whether Matty was freed was a big if. It depended on the leather-clad judge now performing on stage, and Johann, sat next to him.

Dominic opened his eyes and turned his head to look at

Johann. He also had his eyes shut, apparently lost in the beauty of Beethoven's passion. The profile of his face was uncannily like Dominic's late husband. Dominic was both unnerved and fascinated by the similarity. Johann was very good-looking. He sat with a straight back, perfectly still, his head slightly tilted to one side as he listened intently. It was almost exactly Jonathan's pose when he and Dominic had gone to see opera together. Under different circumstances, and in a different time, Dominic imagined he would have been highly tempted to take things further with Johann.

But the circumstances were wrong. Johann was effectively acting as Matty's lawyer. It was a professional relationship. And if Dominic compromised it then there was a risk Matty's potential freedom could be jeopardised.

And besides, the timing was wrong. For all Jonathan's faults, Dominic ached to be reunited with his late husband. Not a day went by without Dominic feeling a longing, an emptiness within the depths of him. Maybe one day he might feel the courage to hook up with another man again. But not yet. It was too soon, and he felt guilty even thinking about it.

Johann opened his eyes. Dominic hastily looked away. Then, realising how guilty his move must have appeared, he looked back. Johann smiled, lifted his hand and gently patted Dominic's knee, before he closed his eyes to listen to the three leather-clad men performing Beethoven.

———

"That was very impressive." Dominic stood with Johann outside the church at the end of the concert. "I can truthfully say I've never been to a concert quite like that in all my life."

"My dear man, it's unique." Johann laughed. "Which is a great shame. I think an idea like *Fetish Meets Classic* would liven up some of your dreary opera immeasurably."

Dominic smiled. "If they revive the Royal Opera's production of *Elektra* I'll happily buy you tickets for it. You'd love it. Men dressed in leather, simulated sex on stage, and a major BDSM scene in Act Two."

Johann placed an arm affectionately on Dominic's shoulder. "My dear Dominic. That sounds like an opera I would love to see." He pulled Dominic towards him and kissed him. On the side of his mouth. Dominic tensed and held his arms at his side. After a brief, awkward moment, Johann dropped his arm from Dominic's shoulder. He regarded at Dominic with a quizzical look.

"Can I buy you a drink?" he asked. "There's a club down in Schöneberg where they're all probably heading now."

"No," Dominic replied. "I should go back to my B & B and thank my hosts for letting me stay for longer. Anyway, it's been a long day."

Johann smiled.

"Of course. In fact, there are several documents Manfred wants me to have ready for him before the emergency court hearing he's organising tomorrow. But maybe I'll go to the club with the guys and have a drink."

Dominic tried to make up for the awkwardness of the moment. "Can I help you with any of the documents?"

Johann shook his head. "The hearing isn't until midday. If there's anything I need I can check the final details with you in the morning before the hearing." He held out his arms in an offer of embrace. "I will bid you goodnight and sleep well."

Perhaps Dominic hesitated for a split second too long. But, as he was about to raise his arms to accept Johann's offer of embrace, the German dropped his arms to his sides. He nodded a brief, formal acknowledgement and strode away from the church.

Damn, thought Dominic.

―――――――――

After witnessing the man jump into the concrete-making tower, Hodan had fled the construction site and spent the rest of Friday fruitlessly trying to find a place in a hostel. Late that evening she reluctantly returned to the makeshift encampment of tents in the Tiergarten.

Two Somali women had agreed to share their tent with her for the night.

"But only one night," the older of the two women had said firmly.

It was a small tent. Too small for three women and their belongings. And the older woman snored. Very loudly. Hodan tried to get to sleep. But she was kept awake by both the snoring and her fear of sleeping in an open space like the Tiergarten. She knew they were vulnerable. Either to an attack or being moved on by the police.

In the early hours of Saturday morning her fears were justified.

As she lay staring up at the dirty orange fabric of the improvised tent, she heard shouts of racist abuse in the distance. Then she heard some of the other temporary shelters around them being smashed. Hodan grabbed her few possessions and helped the other two women flee the confines of the tent.

Hodan ran through the park in the opposite direction to the noise of the attackers until she came to a main street. At a bus shelter she found the right way to walk back into the central part of Berlin. Once again, she was without a place to sleep in the city.

A church clock showed it was nearly five o'clock. Hodan was very hungry. She had scavenged little to eat the day before. She began to recognise where she was and headed towards the district where she knew there were several large hotels. There was bound to be waste food waiting to be collected later that morning. She would find something, anything, to eat there.

It was fortunate she had run into Samira around the back of the Palace Hotel. Like Hodan, Samira was also from Somalia. She had been a refugee in Berlin for less time than Hodan, but she was already far better informed about how to survive in the city. Together, the two women carefully inspected the pile of surplus food thrown out by the hotel and pieced together a makeshift meal. As they ate, Samira explained that she had an appointment at the women's refuge that morning. It had been made earlier in the week. She invited Hodan to join her.

"We can tell them what happened to you in the Tiergarten last night," she said. "Surely they will see this is an emergency and that you need protection now?"

Hodan was not as confident as Samira that the refuge could help her, but she jumped at the chance. Perhaps finally she could get some sleep.

***

Dominic slept fitfully that night. He felt very alone and longed for the comforting arms of his late husband.

His had no complaints about his rented room in the B & B. It was nearly perfect in every detail. The gay couple that owned it shared Dominic's passion for art deco design.

Their large, third-floor apartment was exquisitely furnished with antiques and ornaments. They would have fitted in perfectly in Dominic's Oxfordshire apartment he had returned to after Jonathan's death. Everything was just right.

Except for the king-size bed.

Dominic felt lost in its giant expanse. At home he had a modest double bed. Even when Jonathan was alive, they had avoided buying a larger one. It had been early on in their relationship that they had realised how comfortable they had felt sleeping in each other's arms. They had cosied up together in the compact bed. Now, as Dominic lay in the semi-darkness and watched the start of the dawn through the closed slats of the Venetian blinds, the giant bed emphasised his feeling of loneliness.

He checked the time on his phone again. Almost six thirty. There were several hours to go before Matty's emergency court hearing. Dominic hauled himself to the side of the bed and returned the phone to its place on the black lacquered cabinet. Then he lay back on the pillows and closed his eyes.

There was little prospect of further sleep that morning. Even so, a sense of inertia and lethargy held him back from starting the day. He was reluctant to return to sleep, given the bizarre dreams that had dogged his unsettled night. Each one of them had featured Jonathan. And one of them in particular had been very disturbing.

In it, he and Jonathan had been flying to San Francisco for their honeymoon. They had been seated in first class, and a steward had served them champagne. Dominic had turned to toast Jonathan.

That was when he had seen his husband was holding a baby.

"Isn't he beautiful?" said the dream-bound Jonathan. "Let's call him Matthias. It's the perfect name."

Dominic could still recall the sense of horror he had felt. Jonathan had wanted to call their child by the same name as Dominic's own son. He had looked from the baby to Jonathan. But now, instead of Jonathan holding the baby, it was Johann. What had been more disturbing was that the lawyer had worn Jonathan's clothes. Dominic had tried to wrestle the baby from his arms.

"Don't touch him," Dominic had shouted in the dream to Johann. "You mustn't touch him. He's not yours."

That was the moment Dominic had woken up. His heart had been pounding, and there had been the damp of perspiration on his chest. As the details of the dream faded, he was left with an overwhelming sense of guilt.

He felt responsible for Jonathan's death. The pervading sense of guilt frequently dogged his waking hours. He knew it was common for people that were grieving to feel misplaced guilt, but that knowledge did nothing to dispel the actual emotion.

Dominic also felt guilty for having been absent from the first nineteen years of his son's life. Again, an irrational feeling, given he had had no knowledge of Matty's existence until a few years ago. Nevertheless, the feeling had resurfaced since Matty's arrest.

Finally, he felt guilty for the attraction he had experienced towards Johann the night before. No, it was more than simply attraction. Why should he be guilty about that? It was unreasonable and unfair. Dominic was now an eligible, reasonably attractive gay man in his late thirties. But since Jonathan's death he had lost all interest in men. Or dating. Or sex. More than once in the past year he had wondered whether bereavement had made him impotent.

The time he had spent last evening with Johann had dispelled that possibility. Dominic felt definite stirrings for Johann. Was it because the man reminded him so much of Jonathan? What were the chances of Dominic meeting someone who was almost the identical twin of his late husband?

And was it healthy for him to contemplate hooking up with the living embodiment of his dead husband? If Dominic were to belatedly accept the advance Johann had made last night, would it ultimately lead to years of psycho-analysis? He could imagine the conversation.

"So, Mr Delingpole. Do you not think that your break-up with Johann Hartmann was precipitated by your profound disappointment that, unlike your late husband, he was neither interested in landscape gardening nor in the operas of Strauss and Wagner?"

Dominic lies back on the couch in the darkened consulting room.

"Not at all, Dr Freud. The thought had crossed my mind at the start of the relationship, but I felt confident I could be won over by his keen legal mind and his love for Rodgers and Hammerstein."

Dominic sighed. Why poke the relationship hornets' nest now? There was enough going on, what with Matty spending the night in a Berlin jail cell. Dominic reprimanded himself. He must keep a respectful, professional distance from Johann and concentrate on clearing Matty's name.

His phone rang.

"Hi, Dominic."

It was Johann. His voice sounded bright and chirpy. "Sorry to call you so early on a Saturday morning, but I have some interesting information. Can we meet for breakfast?"

Dominic checked the time on his phone again to make sure he had not misread it. No. It was now six forty-five.

"It's very early," he said. "I thought you were out clubbing last night?"

"No," replied Johann. "But I went for a drink. Don't worry. I can get by on remarkably little sleep. So, my friend. Will I see you in Café Motz at nine?"

Dominic sighed and lay back on the pillow. "Can't you ask me the questions over the phone?"

There was a pause before Johann answered. "Dominic, this is a more complicated matter than I first thought. Let's say, I'd rather we avoid electronic communications. Just in case."

12

HODAN CARRIED her tray of food over to the long wooden table. She slid onto the bench next to her friend Samira, who had already started eating,

"Couldn't you wait two minutes?" Hodan asked.

The dining hall of the women's refuge was full. There were over sixty women seated at five long tables in the low-ceilinged room. The majority, like Hodan and Samira, covered their heads with a hijab. The woman who sat at the end of their table was noticeably pregnant. Most of the women appeared to be in their late twenties or early thirties. But a few were much older. The older women were always accompanied by a younger woman, who helped them to eat.

"I was ravenous," Samira replied. Her mouth was full of food, and she held her hand in front of it as she spoke. "So, come on. Tell me what happened at the building site. We've got ages before your second interview with the admissions woman."

Saturday was turning out to be a good day for Hodan. But, in her view, it seemed only fair that fate should deal her a lucky card after the series of bad events that had happened in the past few days.

Samira had been right. News of the vicious attack on the encampment in the Tiergarten had quickly reached the people that ran the women's refuge. When Hodan had explained she had been sheltering in the camp, the admissions staff offered to do all they could to help her. Samira's place in the refuge was confirmed, and the admissions clerk promised to try to find somewhere to sleep for Hodan. Certainly over the weekend, and maybe for a longer period.

Which was how they both came to be eating in the dining hall that morning.

"Come on," Samira said again. "Tell me what you saw."

Hodan did not answer immediately. She was very hungry. And the rice dish, whatever it was, tasted surprisingly good. She ate quickly for several minutes, until the warm glow of a sleep coma threatened to embrace her. She heaved a sigh of satisfaction and began to recount her story to Samira.

"I'm sure it was the man who woke me up," she explained.

"And he jumped inside the concrete-making tower?" Samira asked.

"It was dawn," Hodan continued. "And I couldn't see very clearly in the morning light. But I tell you. The man jumped inside."

"And he didn't come out again?"

Hodan shook her head. "I waited for ages. Even though I was frightened. I thought he might come out again from somewhere lower down the tower."

"Did you go to get a closer look?"

"No. Like I say. I was terrified he might find a way out lower down the tower and be waiting for me." Hodan picked up a piece of naan bread and used it to mop up the remains of the food on her plate.

"Perhaps he was one of the workers fixing the machine."

"No," Hodan replied. "I'm sure he wasn't. He wasn't wearing the right clothing. Or a hard hat." An image of the brown leather holdall came into her head. "He looked more like someone who was going to catch a bus or a train. Except he was on a building site. He was definitely not a construction worker."

Samira leaned across to Hodan. She glanced around her before she spoke quietly.

"You must tell someone. He might have been like us, searching for somewhere to sleep, and fell into the machine by accident."

"No. I cannot." Hodan was frightened. Now she had found sanctuary, there was too much to lose. "They will ask why I was there. Then they will know that I broke in through the fence. That I slept in the empty office. It would be very bad for me."

"But what if he's still trapped in the machine?" asked Samira. "He could die."

Hodan sighed. "But he jumped into it without hesitation. He didn't fall. That's the problem. I think he wanted to kill himself."

Dominic stepped out of the shower and reached for his towel. He dried himself off and turned to the full-length mirror fixed to the wall of the bathroom. He rubbed a face-sized hole in the mist on the mirror's surface and saw with dismay the image that stared back at him.

Haggard.

He would have preferred it if the adjectives *handsome* or *rugged* had sprung to mind. But instead, a word that was almost a conflation of the two adjectives popped into his mind.

Haggard.

Even after the supposedly rejuvenating shower, the skin on his face seemed to have surrendered to the inevitable pull of gravity. He dared not rub a larger hole in the mirror mist to inspect the rest of his body, for fear of what he might discover. He headed back into the bedroom. There were clinics in Berlin that could deal with a body-image crisis like his. Weren't there? Was it too early to call it a midlife crisis?

He reached for the remote control and turned on the television. It was tuned to an English language German news channel. Once again, the main headline was the attack on the Prinzknecht Bar. The death toll had increased to twelve, and six more people were in a critical condition in hospital. A picture of Alex flashed up on the screen while the reporter described him as "Berlin's most wanted."

Dominic dragged himself away from the TV and searched for some clean clothes in his suitcase. He had packed light, and now his supply was exhausted. Now that he was staying for longer, he would either have to ask his hosts if he could use their washing machine or buy some more clothes. He sniffed at a pair of socks, decided they were still reasonably fresh, and sat down on the end of the bed to put them on.

The news channel switched to a different story. Pictures of a construction site on the outskirts of Berlin appeared on the screen. A reporter at the scene described how the body of a man had been found in the site's cement-making machine the day before. Dominic paused to listen to the gruesome story. Apparently, a construction worker that had arrived early discovered that an inspection hatch on the machine had been tampered with. The worker had shone a touch into the interior of the machine and seen a man's arm protruding from the cement slurry inside.

It had taken the emergency services over three hours to recover the dead man from the machine. The reporter explained that the body was "in a number of pieces," and that it would take the police some time to confirm his identity. Meanwhile, they were working on the assumption that it was either an opportunist thief or a homeless person that had made the catastrophic error of climbing into the machine.

Dominic shuddered and got back to putting on his socks. Poor man. What an awful way to go. He recalled what Johann had said on the phone:

"I'd rather we avoid electronic communications. Just in case."

In case of what? And why did Johann say Matty's arrest was a more complicated matter? Dominic felt his heart rate quicken again. He lay back on the bed and took several long, slow, deep breaths. How he longed for this all to be over so he could return to his Oxfordshire home.

———

The waiter at Café Motz was still setting up the tables on the pavement outside when Dominic arrived shortly before nine. He went inside to check if Johann was waiting for him. The café was decorated in a grand baroque style with extravagant ruched curtains hanging at the windows and an ornate glass and gold chandelier suspended from the ceiling. On the back wall were five erotic sketches by the Finnish artist Touko Laaksonen, better known as Tom of Finland. The sketches were incongruously mounted in heavy, ornamented gold frames. Dominic spent some time examining the cartoon-like pencil drawings of men with impossibly large muscles and cocks.

"If you want to see more of his work," said a voice from behind him. "There's an exhibition three streets away from here."

Johann stood in the doorway.

"Such a wonderfully talented artist," Johann continued. "I'm sorry to drag you away from his work. But let's sit outside. It's a shame to waste this beautiful morning by staying here in the gloom."

Dominic followed Johann back outside. The waiter showed them to a table laid with a crisp white linen table-cloth, white napkins and heavy silver tableware. They took their seats, and Johann ordered orange juice, a pot of coffee, and toast for them both. The café was in a quiet side street, a hundred yards from Fuggerstraße, the gay thoroughfare. Across the street an elderly couple walked past, followed by a woman walking her dog. Apart from them, the street was deserted.

"In a few hours this café will be packed with sexy men in leather from the Folsom Street party today," Johann said. "But nine o'clock in the morning is much too early for the gays. They'll still be recovering from their clubbing last night."

"And there was no clubbing for you last night?" Johann's blue eyes were bright and alert and his hair was perfectly groomed.

"Of course not." Johann laughed. "I have an audience with the judge this lunchtime. If I wasn't fully prepared for his questions, he'd make mincemeat of me, as you English say. That's why I was up at six this morning."

"That's a relief to hear." Dominic sat back to allow the

waiter to set a plate of granary toast and marmalade down in front of him. "So, what was this information you had for me, and why couldn't we talk about it over the phone?"

Johann picked up his coffee cup. "I must ask you the same question Judge Richter asked you last night: how well do you know your son?"

"And I'll answer the same way I did last night. I've known him a little over a year, and I trust him to tell me the truth."

"Good. And what do you think of his choice in men?"

Dominic smiled. "That's another matter altogether. Alex seems like a nice enough chap. But I've only met him once. I can't vouch for him any more than that."

Johann leaned forward.

"I know someone who's well-placed in the Bundespolizei. I bumped into him at Mutschmann's last night when I went for a drink after the concert."

"Another contact on your pink network?" asked Dominic.

"Of course," replied Johann. "It's an essential one to be plugged into in this city. He told me some interesting information about Professor Alexeyev Krovopuskov. I'm hoping that Matty isn't involved in it as well. If he is, it may complicate his release from police detention."

Johann sat back in his chair and toyed with the handle of his coffee cup. He seemed lost in thought.

"So are you going to tell me what 'it' is?" asked Dominic.

"In a moment." Johann paused until the waiter had walked past them back into the café.

"The Bundespolizei began watching Professor Krovopuskov – Alex – shortly after he arrived at the university from St Petersburg nearly a year ago. They received a tip-off from Russia's FSB that he was suspected of industrial espionage."

Dominic frowned. He was deeply suspicious of Russia's secret service. On more than one occasion it had been shown they had used highly toxic poisons on British streets to eliminate enemies of the Russian State. "Can intelligence from the FSB really be trusted?" he asked.

Johann shrugged. "I know what you're implying, but the Bundespolizei are very thorough. They'll have carried out their own surveillance. My contact says there's sufficient evidence to indicate he was slipping information to the Chinese about the West's development of biomechatronics technology."

"How reliable is your contact?" asked Dominic.

"Let's say, I've known him for a lot longer than you've known your son, and I trust him completely to tell me the truth."

Dominic sat back in his chair and tried to absorb what Johann had said. If Alex was involved in industrial espionage, and he knew he was under suspicion, it might explain why he had suddenly disappeared. But it was not enough to explain why he was a suspect in the attack on the Prinzknecht Bar. Unless—

"Do you think he's being framed by the Russian or German authorities for the gas attack?"

Johann looked surprised and shook his head. "Even for me, a lifelong fighter of corruption and injustices by unscrupulous authorities, that's a conspiracy theory too far. On the other hand, my contact in the Bundespolizei says the security camera video is far from conclusive. He believes the investigating officers simply made a premature match with their database because Alex was already being watched."

Dominic poured himself some more coffee and took a long drink from his cup.

"Where does this leave Matty?"

"Don't worry, my friend." Johann reached across and patted Dominic's arm. "I'm feeling confident that by lunchtime he'll be freed, and you'll be able to give him a big welcome hug." He tilted his head back to bathe in the warmth of the early morning sunshine.

"And then I'll have some questions to ask him," Johann added.

13

MATTY'S SPECIAL court hearing was held in one of the many courtrooms of Berlin's criminal court building. Dominic and Johann stood on the steps outside the neo-baroque building at ten to twelve that Saturday morning. It was very quiet, and only a few people wandered past them as they talked.

"I'm afraid that members of the public won't be allowed in," Johann told him. "You'll have to wait outside. It's going to be an interesting meeting. There'll be the State prosecutor and an investigating judge. Probably your friend Kriminalkommissar Schutz or his boss, maybe somebody from the Bundespolizei, and me."

"What about Judge Richter?"

"Only the investigating judge can be there," Johann replied. "It's not Manfred's case."

"And what about Matty?" Dominic asked.

"Oh, he won't be in the hearing. But he'll probably be in the building. I think the police will have transferred him to one of the cells, anticipating that the judge will say he's free to go."

"Aren't the police going to object?"

"Of course they will," replied Johann. "But Manfred will have spoken to the judge last night, so he should be on our side. We'll be able to get any objections thrown out easily enough."

Dominic was puzzled. "Are you saying Manfred can lean on the investigating judge to set Matty free? Is that ethical?"

"Our German legal system's impartiality is beyond reproach, if that's what you're questioning." There was a cold edge to Johann's voice. "Manfred spoke to the judge after the concert last night. He reminded him that holding Matty is unreasonable and unnecessary when he's not a suspect. The law is clear. Matty's not a danger to the public. Schutz acted unreasonably. It will be difficult for the judge to argue against that."

Johann smiled and his manner softened. "I used the word 'we,' but I was in fact referring to myself. To my competence as Matty's legal representative. I think you British call it 'the Royal we.'"

Dominic smiled. "Only when it's the Queen speaking."

"Then maybe its usage can be extended to when *any* queen is speaking." Johann winked. He bade farewell to Dominic and strode up the steps into the criminal court building. Dominic was about to follow when his phone chirruped with a message from the Papi app: *Hey daddy.*

He clicked on the message to see the sender's profile. There was no picture, and there were few details. The person who had sent the message was called Boris. He was aged forty, had close-cropped hair and came from Berlin. The app also told Dominic that Boris was currently over a thousand miles away. Dominic shoved the phone back in his pocket.

The steps up to the criminal court building led Dominic to a cavernous entrance hall. He stopped and his mouth dropped open. It was one of the most beautiful spaces he had ever seen. It was like the interior of a cathedral. White marble pillars swept up to the ceiling. At the far end was a giant marble staircase, like something from an extravagant Hollywood musical. Everywhere Dominic could see exquisitely carved statues or finely carved detailing on windows and doorways.

Dominic wandered around the entrance hall for a long time, drinking in the beauty of the architecture. It occurred to him that he would have never had the opportunity to visit this building if Matty had not been arrested. At least one benefit had emerged from the disaster of the last twenty-four hours.

Finally, he sat down on one of the few benches and waited for Johann to return.

Nearly an hour passed. Very slowly. The hearing was running for longer than Johann had predicted. Dominic hoped it was not a bad sign. He thought about Matty's mother. Did she know about her son's arrest? It had crossed Dominic's mind she should be told. But he decided to wait for Matty's permission before he told her. Even then, he felt confident Matty would argue against letting her know.

At least not for a while.

All the same, Dominic felt guilty he had not taken the role of responsible adult/parent and picked up the phone to Amélie. On the other hand, he was confident she would blame him for Matty's incarceration. He knew Matty had told her of Dominic's exploits with the Natural Family Association and the Charter 99 group. Matty made no secret of the pride he felt for his father's role in defeating both organisations. Dominic recalled the comment made by both his college friend Miles and his personal assistant when he had told them what had happened to Matty:

"Like father, like son."

Doubtless Amélie would say something similar once she learned what had happened, even though Dominic was in no way responsible.

The sound of a familiar voice from behind him roused him from his musings.

"Hey, Dad."

The brightly painted tables and chairs outside the Pavilion Café were bathed in sunshine that afternoon. Johann led Dominic and Matty to the table that was farthest away from the little kiosk, where a large, jolly woman wearing a white blouse and bright green Austrian dirndl-style dress served snacks and drinks.

"We can be reasonably confident we won't be overheard here," Johann said. "I'll go and get us celebratory beers and one of those giant pretzel breads to sustain us." He turned to Matty. "You certainly look like you could do with a drink. And I think your father needs one as well."

He headed off to the kiosk. Dominic rested a hand on Matty's arm.

"It's good to have you back. How are you feeling?"

Matty sighed. "Surreal. It all happened so fast. That's the frightening bit. One minute you're a free man. The next, you're locked up in a small room with no windows. It was terrifying. Especially last night." He shuffled his chair closer to Dominic and rested his head on Dominic's shoulder. "Thank you for getting me a lawyer so quickly."

Dominic watched Johann patiently waiting in line at the kiosk. "What was he like in the hearing?"

Matty lifted his head from Dominic's shoulder.

"He was incredible. Inspiring. If I wasn't already doing mathematics, I'd be tempted to switch to law instead." He smiled at Dominic. "I bet you're as good as him too."

Dominic shook his head. "It's different for me. For one thing, I don't do criminal law. And for another, I'm not an advocate like Johann. I'm called a solicitor in English law. Which means I rarely stand up in front of a judge. We solicitors leave that to the lawyers they call barristers."

"Isn't that frustrating?"

"Some lawyers are born performers, which is why they become advocates. And in England they can specialise. But it's not my skill. I don't get any enjoyment out of it. As a solicitor, I do all the work with the client. The preparation. That's where I get my job satisfaction."

Matty sat back in his seat. "Johann's certainly a born performer. He made mincemeat of the police. He destroyed their argument."

"Johann doesn't think they had a strong argument to begin with," Dominic said. "They seemed to be holding you simply because you're Alex's boyfriend. Granted he's suspected of terrorism—"

"Which is absurd." Matty was suddenly angry. "Why on earth do they think he'd attack a gay bar? He's a gay man himself. I know you've only met him once, but surely you can see he's not the type of man to have some kind of internalised homophobia. He's happily out, which is why he was so keen to get out of Russia. It was much harder for him to be an out gay man when he was there."

"I agree. And of course, you know him better than me. But the police have got the surveillance camera evidence—"

"And we need to review that," Johann interrupted. He had returned with a tray of beers and a pretzel for each of them He placed the tray on the table and handed out the glasses of beer. "But first, let's drink a toast to Matty's release." He raised his glass in the air.

"To Rechtsanwalt Johann Hartmann," Matty said. "The man who rescued me from the evil clutches of the German police."

The three men drank from their beers, and Johann sat down at the table.

"I would be careful not to brand the whole of the Bundeskriminalamt with the label 'evil,'" Johann cautioned. He placed his glass on the table, picked up the pretzel and tore a large piece off. "It's true Kriminalkommissar Schutz is not a great advertisement for their fairness or intelligence, but they're not all like him."

Johann took a bite of pretzel and checked his watch. "I can only stay a few minutes. I'm meeting friends at the party in Folsom Straße. I don't want to spend my whole Saturday working."

Matty's eyes opened wide.

"You're going to Folsom? You mean you're—"

"Yes, my friend." Johann laughed. "In an hour's time I will no longer be wearing a sober suit and tie. It's time to liven up the weekend with some leather."

Matty shook his head. "I would never have guessed it."

"What if I were to tell you that I met a judge yesterday, dressed in full Tom of Finland leathers?" Dominic asked him.

"You've got to be joking me?" Matty nearly knocked his glass over.

"Welcome to Berlin's pink network," Johann said. "And all I can say is, thank God it exists. Otherwise, who would moderate the extremist excesses of people like Kriminalkommissar Schutz?" He reached into his black shoulder bag and pulled out his tablet computer. He tapped the screen and rapidly flicked through several pages of an internet news site.

"Now," Johann said briskly. "I'll take five minutes and then I must go. We can talk again after the weekend." He found the screen he was looking for and turned the tablet around for Matty to see. "I have two questions for you, Herr Matthias Lange. The first one: is this the face of Professor Alexeyev Krovopuskov?"

On the computer screen was a surveillance camera image released by the police that morning. It showed a man wearing a leather jacket, leather jeans and boots, carrying a motorcycle helmet. A pair of mirrored sunglasses obscured his eyes.

Matty peered at the screen intently. "It's difficult to say."

Dominic peered over his shoulder at the image on the screen. The man in the picture did bear a strong resemblance to Alex, even though he wore sunglasses. "It looks a lot like him."

"You've only met him once," Matty said. "How can you be so sure?" He stared closely at the image. "There's something not right. If I could see his eyes I could tell you immediately."

"Why?" Dominic asked.

Matty turned back to him with a look of incredulity on his face. "You didn't take much in that night, did you."

Dominic began to feel uncomfortable with Matty's hostility towards him. "You don't have to be so—"

"His left eye, Dominic," Matty said. He was clearly annoyed because he had stopped calling Dominic "Dad." "Come on. Don't you remember? Or were you more concerned about his advanced age? My boyfriend has amblyopia in his left eye," Matty said to Johann. "He had it as a child and they never fixed it."

Only then did Dominic recall how Alex's left eye turned inwards instead of tracking in unison with his right eye. It was a condition also known as "lazy eye."

Johann flicked through several more internet pages. He found a photograph of Alex from his biography page on the university website and lay it alongside the image from the security camera.

"Yes," Johann mused. "You can see the fault in the left eye in his college photo. Although it's not very pronounced."

"It gets much worse when he's stressed," Matty replied.

Dominic studied the two photos side by side on the computer screen. The two men looked very similar. The hair was different, and the man in the surveillance photograph wore sunglasses, but they both had similar long-shaped faces.

"Is this all the evidence they've got? Matty shook his head. "And I spent a night in the cells for this? I ought to get compensation."

Johann smiled. "We'd need to see all the surveillance camera video before we could conclusively say whether this was or wasn't Professor Krovopuskov."

Matty opened his mouth to protest, and Johann raised his hand to silence him. "But this wasn't the only reason the police suspected Alex." He drained his beer and put the glass on the table. "Which brings me to my second question, Matty. Did you know Alex was spying for the Chinese?"

The shocked reaction on Matty's face was, as far as Dominic could tell, entirely genuine. He slumped back in his seat, apparently stunned into silence.

"Before you dismiss that too quickly," Johann continued.

"I must tell you that I have the information from an extremely reliable source."

"Wait a moment," Dominic said. "Your source in Berlin might be reliable. But you told me the intelligence originated from Russia's FSB. That's not necessarily a reliable source."

Anger returned to Matty's eyes. "You know about this?" he asked Dominic. "What else do you know? Is the case against Alex sewn up already?"

"No, no." Dominic tried to rest a reassuring hand on Matty's arm, but it was shrugged away. "Matty, we're trying to help you. But there are a lot of unanswered questions about Alex. And we're going to need your help as well."

"Your father's right," Johann said. "If there's anyone you know who might be able to shed light on where Alex has disappeared to, you need to tell us. At the moment, what he's doing is very suspicious."

He turned to Dominic.

"I'm happy to keep helping you, if you like. I have contacts here as you've now discovered. I'll ask some more discreet questions on your behalf. Meanwhile, Matty must try to help us track down Alex."

He stood up.

"Right. I'm going now. I don't want to miss out on the action down at Folsom. I'm planning to meet up with some friends at the KitKatClub later." He winked at Matty, who ignored him.

Dominic smiled.

"That's the club featured in *Cabaret*, isn't it?"

"Yes," replied Johann. "But that one was fictional. This one actually exists. It's in Köpernicker Straße. They opened it in the nineties. It's always very popular, so we're going to get there in good time."

At that moment, Dominic's phone chirruped with a new message from the Papi app.

"Goodness," said Johann. "It seems you're getting some action yourself, Dominic. You are a dark horse."

14

AFTER JOHANN left, Dominic and Matty sat in silence for several minutes. Matty was angry, and Dominic was uncertain what to say to avoid upsetting him further. Eventually, Matty tapped Dominic's phone.

"Aren't you going to check who your hot date is?"

Dominic waved his hand at the phone dismissively.

"I'm in no hurry. I keep meaning to ask you to sort it out for me. Can you show me how to take that app off my phone? I'm really not interested."

"Oh, come on." Matty laughed. "I'm surprised it's not exploding with new messages from studs panting for a good-looking guy like you. Your profile picture is that great photo of you on the beach in Sitges."

"Not the one of me wearing—"

"Next to nothing?" There was a look of glee in Matty's eyes. "That's the one. What do you expect? You're not going to haul in the talent wearing a suit and tie." Matty chuckled. "On second thoughts, there are some guys with a suit fetish." He picked up Dominic's phone and looked at the screen.

"Boris?" He handed the phone back to Dominic. "I can't read the message unless you unlock your phone. You'll have to do that for me if you want the app deleted."

Dominic took his phone from Matty and put it back on the table.

"Later." He rested his hand on Matty's shoulder and gave it a paternal squeeze. "You must be exhausted. Why don't you go back to that nice studio apartment Eric rented for you and get a few hours' sleep? It will do you the power of good."

Matty's stepfather had used his contacts in the building trade to get his stepson a studio apartment for his second year at the university. Dominic knew that Matty enjoyed the independence the studio apartment gave him, but was conflicted by the privilege he felt as a result of his stepfather paying for it. Many of Matty's friends had struggled to find even shared accommodation at an affordable price. The rents in Berlin were soaring.

"You and Johann are right," Matty said. "I need to find out where Alex has gone."

"How are you going to do that?" Dominic asked. "If the police can't find him, I don't see what more you're going to be able to achieve."

"Were you always this defeatist when you fought the Natural Family Association with Jonathan? Oh my God." Matty's eyes opened wide and he stared at Dominic. "Now I know who Johann reminds me of."

Dominic held up his hand. "Now, before you say anything. He was recommended to me by—"

"By who?" Matty asked, a grin forming on his face. "Papi?"

"By that lawyer friend of mine Miles Torrington,"

Dominic replied. "And given that you're sitting here now, he gave me good advice."

"But you must admit, he looks a lot like Jonathan."

"How do you know? You never met Jonathan."

Matty had picked up his phone and was flicking through the photos. Dominic steeled himself for what he suspected was coming.

"There." Matty shoved the phone in front of Dominic's face. It was one of the best pictures taken of Jonathan. It was a publicity still from the Glyndebourne Opera and showed him wearing a coal-black suit with a white fedora during a production of *The Mikado*. He was strikingly handsome in the photograph.

"They could be twins." Matty was triumphant. Dominic studied the picture of his late husband. Of all the pictures Matty could have chosen, this publicity shot was the one image that captured the essence of Jonathan's exuberant personality. He sighed.

Matty took the phone away and shoved it back in his pocket. The triumphant grin had disappeared from his face. "I'm sorry, Dad," he said. "I guess that was pretty insensitive."

Dominic shook his head. "No, it's not. And you're right. Johann does look a lot like Jonathan. But they're very different."

"In what way?"

"Well, for a start, Johann doesn't like opera."

Matty raised his eyebrows. "So you've got to know each other pretty quickly?"

"We chatted a bit, that's all." Dominic was uncomfortable with the direction the conversation was taking. "Let's talk about Alex. You said you were going to find out where he's gone. Have you thought how you'd do that?"

"I'll start by going back to Alex's apartment. Perhaps I can find something there."

Dominic shook his head. "I doubt you'll be able to get into it. The police will have searched it already. They've probably locked it down while they continue the search for Alex."

"Well. The best thing I can do is go and find out if that's true." Matty stood up. "Are you coming?"

The streets around Berlin's Schöneberg district were crowded with men heading for the Folsom fetish party that afternoon. Groups of men dressed in skin-tight leather or rubber clothing meandered along the pavements. They mingled with local residents who seemed unperturbed by what was on display.

Dominic found himself frequently distracted as he followed Matty through the maze of streets as they headed towards Alex's apartment. Three beefy men dressed in leather shorts and chest harnesses sat at a table outside a café, drinking tea and eating chocolate cake. They smiled in greeting to him, and he hurried past to catch up with Matty.

"You can go back to them if you'd prefer." There was a hint of sarcasm in Matty's voice. "I don't want to ruin your afternoon."

"Don't be like that," Dominic said. "Of course I'm coming with you. I've only just managed to spring you from jail. I'm not risking you being arrested again so quickly."

Matty smiled. "Thanks, Dad."

Ten minutes later, they arrived at the apartment building in Nollendorfstraße. There was a police car parked on the opposite side of the street.

"I thought that might be the case." Dominic sighed. He saw no reason to continue.

"There are lots of police around this afternoon." Matty, undeterred, headed for the entrance door of the apartment building. "It's because of what happened at the Prinzknecht Bar. We passed several police cars on the way here." Matty stopped at the entrance to the apartment building. There was a cheeky grin on his face. "You didn't notice because you were too distracted by...other things."

To Dominic's surprise, there was no police tape across the front door to Alex's apartment. Neither was there a police officer on duty outside, and no signs of a forced entry to the apartment. Matty inserted his key in the lock and pushed the door open. He hesitated on the threshold of the darkened hallway.

"Hello?"

Dominic peered past his son into the gloom. There was no answer to Matty's call. Matty reached in through the doorway and switched on the hall lamp. Its light spilled into the living room beyond. Matty gasped.

"*Scheiße*." He strode into the living room. It was a mess. The entire contents of the bookshelves were thrown onto the floor. A few books remained neatly piled up, but the majority of Alex's papers were scattered across the room. The television had been torn away from the wall, and the couch had been ripped apart. Matty sat on the edge of the couch and put his head in his hands. Dominic stood beside him and rested an arm on his shoulder.

"I thought this would happen," Dominic said. "I should have prepared you better. They're searching for evidence. They've probably taken some things away."

Matty stood and headed for the bedroom. A moment later Dominic heard him shout the same expletive:

"*Scheiße.*"

If it was possible, the bedroom was in even more of a mess than the living room. The mattress had been slashed open, all the clothes from the wardrobes had been thrown into untidy piles on the floor, and a large glass lamp had been smashed. Dominic stepped into the room and sat on the end of the bedframe. Matty was kneeling on the floor sifting through the contents of an upended drawer.

"Perhaps we should leave?" Dominic suggested.

Tears glistened on Matty's cheeks. He shook his head. Without a word, he looked away and carefully continued to sort the contents of the drawer into neat piles.

There was the creak of a door from the hallway.

Matty's hand froze in mid-air, clutching a broken photo frame. He turned his head to Dominic and then towards the open bedroom door. The bulky figure of a middle-aged man appeared, silhouetted by the light of the hallway.

"Herr Lange," said Kriminalkommissar Schutz. "And Herr Delingpole. Good afternoon, gentlemen. You wasted no time in getting back here." He folded his arms and slouched against the doorframe. "Why are you here?"

"Are your gorillas responsible for this?" Matty scrambled to his feet.

Dominic stood and walked over to his son. He was worried Matty was ready to punch the police officer, and he wondered if he had the strength to restrain him. Kriminalkommissar Schutz smiled. He made it appear like an expression he struggled with.

"I will answer your question, Herr Lange. And then you will answer mine. My officers have thoroughly searched this apartment belonging to the suspect Alexeyev Krovopuskov. Do not refer to them as 'gorillas' again, or I will re-arrest you for your contempt of the law." He unfolded his arms and advanced into the room. His presence was intimidating. "Now tell me. What are you looking for?"

"Nothing." Dominic stepped forward. "Kriminalkommissar Schutz. I warned my son that you would most probably search Alex's apartment." He waved an arm at the chaos in the bedroom. "And I also warned him you might not leave it as you found it. We're tidying up your mess."

The police officer said nothing. He reached into his pocket and took out a packet of cigarettes. He tapped one out of the packet and put it to his lips. Dominic spoke before he could light it.

"Don't smoke in here, Officer. It's a disgusting habit, and my son suffers from asthma."

Kriminalkommissar Schutz paused, his hand reaching into his pocket. Slowly, he removed the cigarette from his lips and used it to point at Dominic.

"You are trying my patience, Herr Delingpole. Be careful I don't arrest you as well as your son." Schutz carefully put the cigarette back in its packet. "And you are mistaken. It was not my officers who made this mess. When we came to search the apartment the front door was open, and the place was already in this state. I would go so far as to say that my officers may have tidied it somewhat while they carried out their search."

"You're saying someone else broke in?" Dominic asked.

"No." The police officer clicked his tongue dismissively. "There was no sign of a break-in. It appears to be somebody with a key." Apart from you, Herr Lange, who else has a key to this apartment?"

Matty shrugged. "I don't know. Alex has a cleaner who comes once a week."

"Name?"

"Frau Koch. She cleans the other apartments here as well."

Kriminalkommissar Schutz took out a small notebook and wrote in it. "Anyone else?"

"Not that I can think of," Matty replied. "But I wouldn't know. It's not the sort of thing Alex would tell me."

"Has Professor Krovopuskov tried to contact you yet?"

Matty sniffed. "How could he? You only released me from jail a little over an hour ago. I haven't had a chance to recharge my phone yet."

The police officer put the notebook back in his pocket and walked towards the hallway. He stopped in the doorway and turned to face them.

"If he does, or if you find anything here that might lead us to him, you must contact us immediately. He's still the principal suspect in a murder investigation."

"That's absurd." Matty took a step forward and Dominic laid a restraining hand on his arm.

"You don't have any evidence," Matty continued. "All you have is that ridiculous security camera photograph. And you can't be sure that the man in it is Alex. You can't even see his eyes. Then you'd know."

Kriminalkommissar Schutz raised his arm and pointed at Matty. "Wrong, Herr Lange. We have other evidence connecting Professor Krovopuskov to the attack on the Prinzknecht Bar. If you withhold any information about his whereabouts from us, you will be charged with accessory to murder. We will be watching you, Matthias." He dropped his hand and walked out of the apartment.

Matty turned to Dominic.

"How do you know I suffer from asthma? I've never told you."

Dominic smiled. "I don't. But he didn't, and I was damned if he was going to smoke in front of us."

His phone chirruped with another message from the Papi app. "It's a good job that didn't go off while Schutz was here," he said.

"Why?" Matty asked. "You don't seriously think he's on it as well?"

Dominic shrugged. "Who knows? But he's certainly not my type." He pulled his phone from his pocket and checked the message. "It's that one called Boris again. I'll say this for him, he's persistent."

He used his thumbprint to unlock the phone and clicked on the new message.

"I don't like the sound of this guy at all. He's sending very strange messages. I really wish you'd delete the app."

Matty took the phone from Dominic and read what was on the screen:

I am Let Blood. But Boris is my hero.

Matty whistled. "*Mein Gott.* Awesome."

"Delete it," Dominic said. "He sounds like some kind of pervert. I don't want any more messages like that popping up on the screen."

"Hang on a minute, Dominic – I mean, Dad," Matty replied. "Sorry. I'm still getting used to calling you that, I guess." He looked down at the screen. Before Dominic could stop him, he had typed a reply to the message.

"What are you doing?" Dominic tried to grab the phone back from Matty, who deftly moved it out of his reach. "I don't want you encouraging creeps like that. Get rid of the thing."

"No, Dad," said Matty. His face lit up with a huge, beaming smile. "It's okay. I know who this is."

15

FROM THE outside, there was little to suggest the real nature of the imposing building at the head of Arsenal'naya Ulitsa in St Petersburg. True, the perimeter wall was high, topped with barbed wire and surveyed by security cameras every fifty yards or so. The only interruption in the smooth line of the wall was an archway, into which was set a steel door. Alongside the door was a keypad, the grille of an intercom and a green button. Professor Michael Zimmermann stood in front of the door. He wore a pair of loose-fitting jeans and a shabby check jacket with leather patches on the elbows. He pushed the button and waited.

"Hello," said a woman's voice in Russian. "Who is it?"

He cleared his throat.

"My name is Zimmermann. Professor Michael Zimmermann. I'm here to see—"

Before he could finish his sentence, there was the thump of an electronic lock and the door fell open.

"Yes, Professor. You're expected. Please enter the holding zone and close the outer door behind you. We'll admit you to the hospital lobby. Someone will meet you there."

Professor Zimmermann pushed hard on the door to open it sufficiently wide enough for him to step into the dimly lit area beyond. He turned and again pushed hard against the door to close it. As the last of the daylight disappeared, he heard the electronic lock secure him inside the holding area. In front of him he could vaguely see a pair of smoked-glass doors. He pushed against one of them, but it failed to yield.

"Please wait for scanning to complete."

He looked up. The voice seemed to come from a speaker set into the low ceiling above his head. There was a faint click, and bright, white light flooded the space. He screwed up his eyes against the dazzling light.

"Please stand with your feet on the marks on the floor and face the camera to your right."

Professor Zimmermann opened his eyes and squinted as he searched for the camera.

"Keep your head still."

Professor Zimmermann stopped moving and held his breath. The experience was proving very intimidating. He could see a camera lens behind a glass plate slide up and down. It stopped moving for several seconds. Professor Zimmermann was aware he was still holding his breath.

There was the hiss of compressed air, and the two smoked-glass doors ahead of him slid open. He exhaled with relief and stepped forward into the entrance lobby of the hospital. To his left were three glass-fronted booths, like the immigration booths at an airport. A woman in the middle booth beckoned him forward.

"I've come to see—"

"We know," the woman interrupted. "She's on her way down. Please sit over there." She pointed to a line of chairs set against the opposite wall.

Professor Zimmermann crossed the floor of the lobby, sat on one of the chairs and looked around him. Even now, there was little to indicate he was in the most secure psychiatric hospital in Russia. There were no signs on the light green walls, nor were there any leaflets on the low table next to the chairs. While he waited, he prepared his arguments for the meeting that was about to take place.

It was two days since Professor Katerina Patrikova had come to his apartment on University Embankment. Her visit had caused him two nights of lost sleep as he had struggled to resolve the problem she had presented him with.

It was nothing short of blackmail.

Even now, with only a few minutes left before the start of the meeting, he desperately tried to think of an alternative to complying with her demands. Certainly, what she offered would make him rich, and he would be able to retire in comfort. The work would be fascinating, and it would help him test out theories he had spent many years refining.

But she was forcing him to breach both his academic and moral principles. And that made him deeply conflicted. If it were not for the inevitable, catastrophic consequences his refusal to comply would cause, he would have said no immediately on the evening she had come to visit. He sighed. There was no other option.

"Professor Zimmermann?"

He looked up. It was Professor Patrikova. Professor Zimmermann stood and Patrikova extended her hand in greeting. He took it reluctantly.

"Thank you for coming today, Professor," she said. "It's fortunate you did. There's been a complication. We urgently need your help. Please come this way."

Dominic had to wait until he and Matty were back out in the street before his son would explain the reason for his excitement with the message on Dominic's phone.

"Anyone could have been listening," Matty explained as they emerged into the sunlight. "And what I'm going to tell you mustn't go any further." He turned to Dominic. "Promise me?"

"It depends what—"

"Promise me." Matty stared hard at his father. "If you go telling your new friend Johann, or worse, that bastard Schutz, I swear I'll—"

"Okay, okay." Dominic held up a hand in surrender. "I promise." He lowered his hand. "But I don't want you dropping me, or, for that matter, Johann, in it. Especially after we gave the judge assurances and undertakings about your good character."

Matty laughed. "Are you suddenly saying I'm dodgy?"

"Not you," Dominic replied. "But I think I know what you're going to tell me about that message. And it's the provenance of the message I'm worried about." He lowered his voice and brought his head closer to Matty. "It's from Alex, isn't it?"

"How did you know?"

"Lucky guess, maybe." Dominic smiled. "Plus he's the one person who makes you react like that. Why do you think it's him?"

"I know it's him." Matty seemed surprised that his judgement was being questioned. "Here. Give me your phone again."

Dominic reached into his pocket and pulled out the phone. He unlocked it and handed it to Matty, who quickly brought up the Papi message on the screen.

"See here. He says 'I am Let Blood.' Alex's last name,

Krovopuskov, means *let blood* in Russian. Kind of sinister isn't it? We joked about it a few weeks ago when he was teaching me some Russian."

"Clever." Dominic was impressed. "And what about 'Boris is my friend'? He's called himself Boris on the app as well."

"I'm pretty sure he means Boris Pasternak. The author of *Doctor Zhivago*. We were talking about the book on Thursday night while he was packing." Matty flicked through the messages on the Papi app. "That's what I asked him when I sent the message while we were upstairs. He hasn't replied yet."

Matty glanced around furtively and then lifted his sweatshirt to reveal a book tucked into the waistband of his jeans.

"Voila."

It was a copy of *Doctor Zhivago*.

"Alex gave it to me the night before he left. It's in Russian. I was going to get an English copy so I could start reading it. I thought I might learn a bit more Russian."

"Good luck with that," said Dominic. "I read it years ago. It's pretty heavy going in parts."

"Oh, sure," said Matty. He dropped his sweatshirt down again to cover the book. "But you know what I think?"

"What?"

"Alex is going to use this to communicate with me."

"How?"

Matty shrugged. "Page numbers, word counts. I don't know. Something like that. At least, that's what I'd do if I was undercover."

Dominic felt a glow of admiration for his son. "That's really impressive. Do you think that's why he gave it to you? Do you think he'd already planned to disappear?"

"I've no idea. Maybe we'll find out now."

"Are you sure it's him? What if it's someone masquerading as him?"

Matty grinned. "It'll be easy enough to check. There are a couple of things I know about Alex that I'm pretty sure no one else knows. A few searching questions should confirm if it's him or not."

"And how are you going to keep this secret?"

"What do you mean?"

Dominic gestured back at Alex's apartment. "That encounter with Schutz unnerved me."

Matty waved a hand dismissively. "Oh, I think his bark is worse than his bite. He's all old-fashioned Teutonic pomposity and bluster—"

"I don't mean him. You heard what he said, didn't you? The front door was already open when they came to search the apartment. That means someone had got there before the police. Someone else with an interest in Alex. Or maybe someone working for Alex."

"What do you mean 'working for Alex?'" Matty's voice grew louder. "You still don't trust him, do you? What's this all about? Because he's older than me?"

Dominic moved to put a reassuring arm on Matty's shoulder. But Matty shrugged it off.

"And don't try that caring dad shit again." He folded his arms defiantly across his chest. "You surely don't believe that crap Johann spouted about working for the Chinese, do you? Even you questioned it when he admitted the source was the Russian secret service. Christ, Dad. Did you know Alex's father spent six years in a Russian jail simply for thinking differently? Alex was ten by the time he was let out again. Alex is an academic. Not political. He's passionate about his work, and he's bloody good at it too."

"I know." Dominic spoke quietly. He glanced up the

street. He could see a police car parked almost out of view. "Let's go and pay Marlene Dietrich a visit in Friedenau Cemetery. We can carry on talking there. The police are still around. And who knows who else might be listening in to what we're saying."

"How can they?" Matty asked.

"Oh, don't be so naïve." Dominic was losing patience with Matty's contrariness. "Look. I honestly thought Alex was dead until ten minutes ago. And I felt for you." Matty rolled his eyes. "No, really I did. I know what it's like. So don't go laying some uncaring nonsense on me. I don't want you to get hurt. By whatever happens." He held out his hand. "Can you give me my phone, please?"

Matty meekly handed the phone back to Dominic.

"I've learned not to trust these things too much." Dominic held his phone up in front of him. "And I suggest you don't trust yours either." He spoke in a low voice. "Let's turn them off first."

Matty frowned, but obediently reached into his pocket. He took out his phone and switched it off. Dominic did the same.

"Good," Dominic said. "That reduces the risk of them either listening in to us or tracking us. Before we go and pay our respects to Marlene, can you take us to the nearest phone store so we can buy a couple of cheap disposables?"

"*Scheiße*, Dad." Matty looked shocked. "Aren't you over-reacting?"

"After what I've been through in the past few years?" Dominic asked. "Not a bit. To be honest, I'm not sure if it's enough. But we'll do the best we can. Right now, we don't know if Alex has been abducted, or if he's in hiding, or if he's actually dead and somebody's masquerading as him. We don't know if he carried out the attack on the

Prinzknecht Bar." He held up his hand to silence Matty who opened his mouth to speak. "Although personally, I don't think he did. What we do know is that he's disappeared, that somebody who could be him has got in touch with me through a dodgy dating app, and that some people other than the police have searched his apartment."

Again, Matty tried to speak, and again Dominic held up his hand. "I still haven't finished. We also know that Miles recommended a German human rights lawyer to us who got you out of police custody. That lawyer says Alex was spying for the Chinese. I've got every reason to think that Johann is a good lawyer. But I don't know what his political affiliations are. I do know he's plugged into the pink network here in Berlin, and he could be bloody useful to us." Dominic saw the alarmed expression on Matty's face. "Don't worry. I'm not going to start confiding in him. All I'm saying is that he could be a useful ally."

Dominic shoved his phone into his pocket.

"Right. Which way to the phone store?"

Marlene Dietrich's grave was covered with written tributes, flowers, and some bizarre trinkets from adoring fans. The strangest of the tributes was a miniature square tapestry of the movie legend, framed and protected from the elements under glass. According to a small label on the bottom of the frame, it was made entirely from human hair.

"Do you think Marlene would have appreciated it?" Matty asked when Dominic pointed out the tapestry.

"I doubt it." Dominic wrinkled his nose. "According to her daughter's memoirs, Marlene cared nothing for ordinary people. She found them vulgar and common."

"Not a very nice person." Matty gestured to the flowers and tributes on the grave. "Then why's she loved so much today?"

Dominic sat on a wooden bench opposite the grave and stretched out his legs. "There've been lots of stars over the years who weren't particularly nice in their private lives. But they're still worshipped today. Marlene was incredible because she kept reinventing herself. She had a career that lasted over sixty years. And she did an enormous amount to help refugees from Europe in the Second World War."

"So you were a fan?"

Dominic laughed. "I was eleven when she died, Matty. So don't make any more comments about my age. All I've really seen are her old movies. Some of them were as camp as Christmas. You should watch them some time."

He handed Matty the bag they had been given at the phone store on the way to the cemetery. "Here. Take one of the phones and load that dating app onto it. Then we can see if there's anything more from our friend Boris."

Matty sat on the bench next to him. For the next few minutes he worked studiously on the phone. Dominic stared at the inscription on the headstone in front of him and struggled to translate it:

Hier steh ich an den Marken meiner Tage

It seemed to say *here I stand at the marker of my days*. It made little sense to him. Finally, he relented and asked Matty.

"Ah, I remember that from my German literature lessons." Matty looked smug. "It's a line from a poem by Körner. He wrote it when he was dying at the end of the First World War. I think it translates as *reaching now the limit of my life*, or something."

"So, you're more than a mathematician, then?" Dominic

smiled. "I'm glad you've retained some of your artistic side."
He pointed at the phone in Matty's hand. "Any luck?"

"Yup." He handed it to Dominic. "See for yourself."

Dominic looked at the message on the screen and
handed it back to Matty. "Yet more cryptic messages. Does it
mean anything to you?"

There was a broad grin on Matty's face. "Of course it
does. I knew I was right." He pulled the copy of *Doctor
Zhivago* from his waistband and handed it to Dominic. "He's
using the book to send a message. Listen: *Boris loves reading.
Se137 Li34 St4 La10. Enjoy!*"

Dominic was still puzzled. "Come on, Dad. It's a simple
code. 'Se' stands for *Seite*, that's *page* in English. And 'Li'
stands for *Linie*, the German word for *line*."

"And what about St4 and La10?"

"'St' means *start*," replied Matty. "It's the same word in
German or English. And 'La' means *Länge* in German, or
length in English." He gestured to the book in Dominic's
hand. "Well, go on, then. Go to page one hundred and
thirty-seven and line thirty-four."

Dominic obediently opened the copy of *Doctor Zhivago*
and turned to page one hundred and thirty-seven. "But it's
in Cyrillic."

"Well of course it is." Matty laughed and held out his
hand. "Give me the book back."

"You can read Cyrillic?"

Matty shrugged. "A few words, maybe. But Alex also sent
me a link to a German translation of *Doctor Zhivago* online. I
bet he's using that for this message. Give me a moment."

For several minutes he said nothing, engrossed in
painstakingly decrypting the message in the online copy of
Doctor Zhivago. Finally, he looked up at Dominic.

"Oh *Scheiße*."

16

Dominic craned his head to see the phone.

"What is it? What does he say?"

Matty angled the screen towards his father and read the message out loud:

Pasha is particularly vulnerable. He is in very great danger, but sends love.

"Who's Pasha?" asked Dominic.

Matty sighed. "Alex. It's his second name."

The two men sat for several minutes absorbing the new information. It was Dominic who broke the silence.

"At least we know he's alive."

Matty slumped back on the bench. He had the air of a man defeated. His head rolled forward, and he stared disconsolately at the phone screen.

"Yeah, maybe," he said. "But you're right, Dad. How do I even know it's him? The message talks about 'Pasha' in the third person. And it says he's in great danger." There was a look of despair in his eyes. "It's hardly reassuring."

Dominic put an arm around his son's shoulder.

"It's only written in the third person because it's a quote

from the book. I imagine it was the nearest quote Alex could find to get his message across." Dominic removed his arm from Matty's shoulder. "I thought Alex lost his phone? How is he sending these messages?"

"He must've done what he said he was going to do and buy a cheap replacement at the airport. At least with a different number no one can trace him through the phone." Matty sighed. "It's going to take ages searching through *Doctor Zhivago* for a phrase which is vaguely close to what I want to say."

"Will it be any easier if you work on a laptop?"

"Sure, it will." Matty flicked through the pages of Boris Pasternak's masterpiece on his phone. "On a big screen, it will be much easier. It wouldn't take me long at all."

Dominic stood up. "Then the sooner you get started the better. You should go back to your place and get working on it."

Matty stared at Dominic with the look of someone with an unspoken question on his lips.

"What's the matter?" asked Dominic.

"If I go and pick up the laptop from my place will it be okay if I come and work on it at your B & B?"

"Of course." Dominic sat down beside his son. "Any particular reason?"

Matty rested his head on Dominic's shoulder. "Seeing Alex's place messed up like that has got to me, I guess. I don't want to be on my own at the moment. You're sure that's okay?"

"If you want to stay over tonight, I'll ask the guys if they've got a spare bed or couch you can sleep on. Unless you want to share the bed with me."

"No way, Dad." Matty lifted his head from Dominic's

shoulder and sat back on the bench. "That would be seriously weird."

Dominic's hosts were out when he and Matty arrived at the B & B an hour later.

"I imagine they're at the Folsom Street party." Dominic led Matty into the living room of the third-floor apartment. It was a large space with white-painted walls and a polished wood-block floor. Floor-to-ceiling glass doors opened onto a wide terrace that overlooked a tranquil courtyard on the inside of the building. Dominic opened the doors, and the two men stepped out onto the terrace. The heat from the afternoon sunshine was intense. Dominic reached for a large metal lever fixed to the wall next to the glass doors.

"This is supposed to lower the awning and give us some shade." He fumbled with the lever, but nothing happened. "I've tried before and failed to make it work."

Matty took the lever from Dominic's hand and gave it a sharp twist. The end of the lever dropped into the shape of a crank handle. Matty rotated it, and a red and white awning expanded from the wall above them. Matty grinned at Dominic.

"There you go."

Dominic hated being defeated by technology. "I'll go and make us some coffee." He walked back into the living room.

"Have you got beer?" Matty called after him.

Dominic stopped. "I'll have to go down to the supermarket at the end of the street to get some. I haven't really asked the guys here if I can help myself to their drinks." He waited, hoping Matty would change his mind about the beer.

"Okay, cool."

Dominic closed the front door of the apartment behind him and headed towards the elevator. The apartment block was built along the same lines as a modern hotel, with apartments on both sides of a central corridor devoid of natural light. As Dominic passed the door of the neighbouring apartment, he noticed it was slightly open. He continued walking and heard the slam of a door behind him, followed by footsteps on the polished concrete floor.

He quickened his pace. Maybe it was because of the discussion with Matty, but somehow he felt vulnerable. He arrived at the elevator and pushed the call button. The doors opened immediately. Dominic stepped in and pushed the button for the entrance lobby. As the doors started to close, a chubby hand reached in to open them again.

A large man in dark glasses, wearing a suit that was too tight for him, stepped into the elevator. Dominic moved to the back of the cramped cabin to make room for the man's bulk.

"Good day." The man had a strong accent. Possibly Russian.

Dominic nodded back. The man stood in front of the doors as they closed. The elevator juddered and began its slow descent to the lobby. Dominic glanced between the man standing silent and motionless in front of him and the floor indicator above the man's head.

The floor numbers counted down agonisingly slowly. As they were about to reach the end of their journey, the man reached out to the control panel. Dominic tensed. What if the man was about to press the emergency stop button? He was an imposing figure. Several inches taller than Dominic, and a bulky combination of muscle and fat.

The elevator juddered to a halt, and the man hit the door open button. At the same time, he pressed himself back against the wall of the elevator to allow Dominic to squeeze past him.

"Please, *mein Herr*," he said. "After you."

Dominic stepped into the entrance lobby and took a deep breath. He felt ridiculous for his unjustified suspicion of the man. It was clear recent events were making him overly paranoid. Nevertheless, he glanced back over his shoulder several times as he walked the short distance down the street to the supermarket. The large man in the suit and dark glasses was following him.

Ten minutes later, Dominic emerged from the supermarket with a selection of German lagers, several packets of snacks, and an assortment of chocolate. They both had a sweet tooth.

A tram clattered to a halt at the stop outside, and its doors hissed open. A few people got off and several more got on. The man in the suit and dark glasses was leaning against the wall of the tram shelter. Because of his dark glasses it was impossible to be certain, but he seemed to be watching Dominic. Nervously, Dominic headed back to the apartment.

"How are you getting on?" Dominic called from the hallway of the apartment when he got back from the supermarket. There was no answer from Matty. He closed the front door and crossed the living room to the terrace. Matty was sat at a round table in front of his laptop. He was wearing headphones. Dominic set down his bag of groceries on the table, and Matty looked up from his laptop.

Dominic gestured to the bag. "I got us some essential supplies. Beer, pretzels and chocolate."

Matty grinned.

"How are you getting on?" Dominic pulled two bottles of beer from the bag, opened them and handed one to Matty.

"*Pröst.*" Matty took the bottle and tipped its neck towards Dominic.

"Cheers." Dominic took a mouthful of beer and sat down next to his son. He could see the text of *Doctor Zhivago* on Matty's laptop screen. "Have you finished reading it yet?"

"Are you kidding?" Matty drank from his bottle and wiped his mouth with the back of his hand. "It's nearly six hundred pages. But that does make it a lot easier to find phrases to send to Alex."

"Are you sure it's him?"

"Oh, yes."

"How do you know?"

Matty looked sideways at Dominic.

"I'm not going to tell you precisely. But there's something we did on our first date that no one else could possibly know about."

"Are you sure Alex won't have told anyone?" asked Dominic.

"I'm certain." Matty laughed. "And I'm sure as hell not going to tell you."

Dominic smiled. "So what have you found out?" He took another drink of his beer.

Matty scanned the terrace and the apartments opposite. "Are you sure we're not going to be overheard? After what you said earlier, I'm feeling paranoid now."

"Me too," Dominic replied. He told Matty about the man in the suit and dark glasses.

"And you say he's from next door? Did he follow you back here?"

"No." Dominic shook his head. "I checked several times on the way. I was so paranoid about him. But I think it was entirely coincidental he happened to come out of his apartment at virtually the same time."

"But you said he was staring at you when you came out of the supermarket." Matty took another swig of his beer and grinned. "Wearing a suit was he? And there you are, dressed in the suit you wore to meet me at the court today." He winked. "What did I tell you about men with a suit fetish, Dad? You shouldn't play so hard to get."

"You think I missed all the signs?" Dominic sat back in his chair and sighed. "You're probably right. Jonathan always said I was the most innocent gay he'd ever met." He stood up. "I'll go and get a pen and some paper."

"Why?"

"Because if you're going to reveal some crucial evidence to me, it's best we keep it from prying ears." He indicated the terrace of the next-door apartment. "Who knows who's listening."

Dominic went to his bedroom, collected his notebook and a pen, and brought them back to the terrace. He ripped a few blank sheets of paper from the notebook and handed them with the pen to Matty.

"I hope your handwriting's legible."

Matty raised his eyebrows, took the pen and paper, and began to write. Dominic peered over his shoulder as the pen skated across the page.

"*Alex is in Russia*," he read. "*He flew to Finland, but he saw the news and managed to cross the border. We need to speak to the guy he exchanged with at the university. I think he's called Professor Michael Zimmermann.*"

"Does he say how we can contact this professor?" asked Dominic.

"No," Matty replied. "It's too dangerous for Pasha to send me the details, even using the book code. But I can probably find the professor's details in Pasha's apartment somewhere."

"What do we need to ask him?"

Matty shrugged. "I haven't got that far with Pasha yet." He pointed at the *Doctor Zhivago* text on the screen. "It's a slow process."

"Does he say where he's staying?"

There was a banging on the front door. They both turned to look into the apartment.

"Are you going to see who it is?" asked Matty.

"It doesn't make sense," Dominic replied. "There's an intercom system on the main entrance door. If it was someone calling for the guys who live here, the intercom in the hallway would have buzzed."

"Do you think it's that guy you said was following you?"

The banging on the door happened again. This time it continued for longer. A voice shouted from outside in the corridor.

"Herr Delingpole. Please open this door."

"Damn. That sounds like Schutz." Dominic stood up. "I'll have to answer it." He pointed to the scraps of paper and the laptop on the table. "Do something with all that, can you?" he whispered.

As he crossed the floor of the living room, the banging on the front door started again.

"I'm coming, I'm coming," he shouted. There was no

spyhole in the front door, but there was a security chain on the doorframe. He unhooked it and attached it securely.

"Who is it?" he called through the closed door.

"Herr Delingpole. This is Kriminalkommissar Schutz. Will you open this door immediately, please?"

Dominic unhooked the security chain and opened the door. The German chief inspector was in the corridor. Next to him stood the uniformed police officer that had been at the university when they had arrested Matty.

"May we come in?"

17

"Where is your son, Herr Delingpole?"

Kriminalkommissar Schutz's tone was curt. Dominic closed the door behind the two officers. He paused and considered his response.

"He's not answering his phone," Schutz continued. "So we went to his apartment, but he wasn't there. Can you tell us where he is?"

"I thought you'd finished with him after the court hearing this lunchtime," Dominic replied. "Why do you need to talk to him again so soon?"

Schutz crossed to the large television set hanging on the wall of the living room. "Haven't you heard the news?" He gestured to the TV screen. "Why don't you turn it on and see for yourself? There's been another attack."

Dominic picked up the TV remote from the coffee table and switched on the television. It was already tuned to a German twenty-four-hour news channel. His landlords were obsessed with the news. A studio presenter was interviewing a journalist standing in front of police tape.

"You'll have to translate for me, Kriminalkommissar," Dominic said to Schutz. "My German is rudimentary."

"Of course it is," said the chief inspector. Video of the aftermath of an explosion appeared on the screen. "It was a bomb this time. A nail bomb. At the KitKatClub. A gay club. Have you heard of it?"

Dominic's stomach churned and his mouth went dry. Johann had said he was going to the KitKatClub.

"It was closed when the bomb exploded," the chief inspector continued. "We think it was a mistake by the bomber. Although some people were waiting outside for it to open. Ten people were injured. Mostly staff from the club. One of them seriously. It would have been packed tonight. If the bomb had gone off later, hundreds of people would have been killed."

Dominic watched the images on the television. He felt numb. The camera closed in on huge nails embedded into the wall of the club. Once again, it reminded him of the horrific attack by a right-wing terrorist in London in 1999, when three people had been killed by a nail bomb in the Admiral Duncan pub in Soho.

"Ah, Herr Lange," said Kriminalkommissar Schutz. "Good of you to join us."

Matty stood by the doors to the terrace. His face was ashen. He gazed wide-eyed at the television news report. Dominic walked across to his son and put an arm around his shoulder. He turned to Schutz.

"Matty has nothing more to say to you," Dominic said to Schutz. "If you want to question him, you'll have to wait until there's a lawyer present." Schutz opened his mouth to speak, but Dominic got in first. "A proper, German lawyer, as you might say."

The Kriminalkommissar's thin lips split into the semblance of a smile. "Very good, Herr Delingpole. But be careful you don't allow your son to implicate himself through silence. If he knows the whereabouts of Professor Krovopuskov, and he's withholding that information from us, he will be charged." Schutz attempted one more smile. "I'm sure even you, as an English lawyer, are aware of that."

Dominic dropped his arm from Matty's shoulder, pulled out his phone, and called a number.

"What are you doing?" Schutz was annoyed.

Dominic gave no reply. Instead, he held up his hand to the chief inspector and waited for an answer.

"Johann? Oh, thank God. It's Dominic."

"Hi, Dominic." Johann was shouting into his phone. There was the sound of music and a party atmosphere behind him. "Is everything okay?"

"Haven't you seen the news?" Dominic asked. "It's terrible. There's been another attack. This time at the KitKatClub."

Johann made no reply. All Dominic could hear was people laughing.

"Johann?"

"Yes. Yes, I'm still here." Johann was no longer shouting. Dominic strained to hear his voice. "My God. That's terrible. When did it happen? We've heard nothing about it."

Dominic turned to Schutz.

"When was the attack, Kriminalkommissar?"

The chief inspector checked at his watch. "Two hours ago. Around two thirty."

"My God, Dominic," Johann said. "Is Schutz there?"

"Yes, he is. With that police officer who was at the university. That's the other reason I'm calling you."

"Fuck them."

Dominic regarded the chief inspector nervously. Johann had shouted the expletive into his phone. But if Schutz had heard it, he betrayed no reaction to the insult.

"Give me your address," Johann continued. "I'll be right over."

"I don't want to—"

"*Scheiße*, Dominic. Give me your fucking address."

Chastened, Dominic gave Johann the address of the B & B.

"I'll be there in twenty minutes." The party sounds ended abruptly in Dominic's ear.

"He's coming over," he told Matty. "Why don't you go back on the terrace while we wait?" He switched off the television. "I think we've seen enough for the moment." He began to walk with Matty towards the terrace.

"Herr Delingpole." Kriminalkommissar Schutz's voice was almost plaintive behind them. "Herr Lange. Be aware we are still here."

Dominic stopped.

"Of course," he replied quietly. "Let me see you out."

"But we haven't finished—"

"Oh, but you have, Kriminalkommissar." Dominic stepped forward and stood directly in front of the chief inspector and the police officer. They were both tall men. He felt very intimidated, but he refused to show it. He was so close to Schutz, he could feel the large man's hot breath on his face. "If you have any more questions, you must wait until our lawyer arrives. He'll be here in twenty minutes. In the meantime, I'd prefer that you wait outside." He glanced at the other police officer. "Both of you. There's no reason for you to wait in here. Matthias has done nothing wrong, and the judge made clear this lunchtime that you've no right to hold my son."

Dominic crossed to the hallway. He opened the front door, held it open, and turned to the police officers standing in the living room.

"Good day, Kriminalkommissar. Good day, Polizeimeister."

Schutz sniffed, and his head twitched as though affected by a momentary, involuntary spasm.

"Herr Lange," he called after the retreating figure of Matty. "From now on, don't switch your phone off, young man."

He turned and, together with Polizeimeister Weiß, walked into the hallway. Schutz paused in front of Dominic.

"Don't get so cocky, Herr Delingpole." Schutz's eyes narrowed, and he jabbed Dominic in the shoulder with his finger. "We'll be back. And next time, we'll arrest both of you."

"*Scheiße*, Dad. You were fucking brilliant."

Matty beamed at him. "You fucking slayed them."

Dominic walked back into the living room and reached for the back of an armchair. His hands were shaking, and he desperately needed to steady them. He could feel a rapid pounding in his ears, and he forced himself to take long, slow breaths.

"No wonder everyone thinks you're a hero. If you took on the Natural Family Association like that, they must have been screaming for mercy."

"Who says I'm a hero?" Dominic asked. The pounding in his head was reducing, and he was no longer aware of his heart thudding in his chest. "Because I'm really not. And a couple of years ago I certainly couldn't have done that."

"My friends in the gay politics group at university think you're a hero," Matty answered. "When I told them who you were, they practically orgasmed. You've got a helluva reputation." He walked over to Dominic. "Are you okay? You've gone a strange shade of ashen."

Instead of the pounding in his head, Dominic now felt distinctly lightheaded. "I'll be fine," he replied. He straightened up. "Let's go outside and enjoy the good weather. Johann will be here soon."

They walked out to the terrace and resumed their seats at the table. Dominic sat back in his chair and basked in the warmth of the sun on his face.

"Here." Matty handed him his bottle of beer and raised his own in salute. "Here's to smashing the oppressive police state."

"Whoa there, Matty." Dominic was alarmed by his son's words. "Were they the result of your night in a police cell? I'd tone it down a bit if I were you. Otherwise they'll be arresting you again."

"Oh, come on, Dad," Matty protested. "You stood up to them. There's far too much police oppression in this country. We're in danger of losing our human rights if we allow them to behave like Schutz and his men."

Dominic set down his beer bottle in front of him.

"Is this what you talk about with Alex?" he asked. "I didn't realise you were so political. No wonder the police are trying to keep tabs on you." Dominic raised an eyebrow at Matty. "Have you been in trouble with the police before?"

"No." Matty banged his beer down on the table. "It wasn't until you arrived that I got arrested."

Dominic was taken aback by Matty's words. "Hey, hang on—"

"And as for Alex," Matty continued. "He's almost as apathetic as you. If you must know, it's Mama who's got the balls."

"Amélie?" Dominic thought back to the time twenty years ago when he had first met the woman who became the mother of his son. Amélie had been a fiery seventeen-year-old. Her passion for justice and for living a principled life had been very attractive to Dominic. "Is she still angry at the injustices of the world?" he asked.

"Of course," Matty said indignantly. "Mama is always angry. Only now all she does is talk about injustice. But she takes no action. She's too busy helping Dad – Eric that is – to make his money."

"And do you take political action?"

Matty folded his arms and stared at Dominic defiantly. "And what if I do?"

Dominic sighed. "It might explain why the police aren't leaving you alone. What sort of action?"

Matty lowered his head. "I thought you'd be proud of me. I thought you valued standing up for what's right in this world."

"I do." Dominic reached forward to put his hand on Matty's shoulder, but Matty shrugged it off. "Matty, you've got to pick your battles. You can't do anything if you're locked away behind bars."

Matty glowered at him. "Oh yes you can. Nelson Mandela did. Václav Havel did."

Dominic laughed. "Are you seriously comparing yourself to—"

Matty stood up suddenly. His chair toppled over behind him. "Are you laughing at me?"

"I'm sorry." Dominic held up his hands in what he hoped was a gesture of surrender. Or peace. Or something placatory. He realised he was not very experienced at dealing with passionate teenagers. "I'm sorry. That was very clumsy of me. I'm worried about you. You've been arrested once already—"

"Wrongly."

"Yes, wrongly. And I don't disagree with you that the police – well – certain individuals in the police can be heavy-handed. But that's all the more reason for choosing your battles carefully."

Matty picked up his chair from where it had fallen and set it straight again. He sat down and reached for his beer. "I still don't understand. You stood up to that *Scheiße* Schutz. What's the difference?"

Dominic smiled. Before he could answer, the front door buzzer sounded.

"That'll be Johann."

"You're not going to tell him anything about...Boris?" Matty asked. "You promised."

Dominic stood. "I won't. But you need to think carefully about who you're going to trust in all this. Johann might be a valuable ally."

Matty said nothing. He raised the beer bottle to his lips and took a long drink. Dominic walked through the living room to the hallway and picked up the intercom handset. A small video panel showed Johann standing at the main entrance to the apartment block. Dominic pushed the door-release button.

"Come on up, Johann." He replaced the handset, opened the front door and waited.

A few minutes later Johann appeared in the corridor. His appearance was striking. He wore skin-tight black leather breeches, tall boots, a leather harness, a black leather waist-coat, and a black leather police cap. Dominic was speechless.

Johann grinned. "I didn't have time to change." He nodded to the inside of the apartment. "Is Schutz still here?"

Dominic shook his head. He continued to scan the handsome, leather-clad man in front of him. The harness enhanced his gym-sculpted torso. Dominic made an effort to stop himself from staring.

"I'm very glad you're here. When I saw the news report, and Schutz said it was the KitKatClub." Dominic sighed. "Dammit, Johann. You'd told me you were going there."

Johann removed his leather cap. Dominic continued to stare. The man was even more like Jonathan. It was uncanny.

"Were you worried about me?" Johann asked. "I'm sorry. Are you okay?"

He stepped forward, kissed Dominic on the lips, and wrapped his arms around him in a strong, bear-like hug.

"Oh, yeah?"

The voice came from inside the apartment. Johann relaxed his arms. Dominic saw Matty walk away from the hallway and back into the living room. He turned back to Johann. "You'd better come in. Matty's a bit worked up at the moment, but it's fine. Come on in."

He stood aside, and Johann walked into the living room. Dominic closed the door and followed him. Matty emerged from the terrace. He struggled to put on his jacket with his laptop bag in one hand.

"I'm going back to my place," he said. "I'll leave you two to talk."

"Matty," said Dominic. "Johann's here for your benefit."

"Oh yeah?" said Matty. He strode past Dominic into the

hallway. Dominic hurried after him. Matty opened the door. "You know where I'll be."

"And what if Schutz comes for you again?"

Matty shrugged. "I'll give you a call," he said and left the apartment.

18

THE CHIMPANZEE lounged on a pile of bedding at the back of its glass-fronted cage, eating a banana. It lazily reached for a TV remote control and pointed it at a screen on the opposite side of its eight-foot square cell. Images from a Bugs Bunny cartoon appeared on the screen. The chimpanzee tossed the remote control to one side, finished the banana, and lay back against the wall of the enclosure, its head resting on the palms of its hands.

Professor Michael Zimmermann watched with fascination. It had been over six months since he had last seen a research animal. That was when he had still worked at the Technische Universität in Berlin. His work in St Petersburg since the academic exchange with Professor Alexeyev Krovopuskov was purely deskbound research, combined with a little teaching. He was pleased to have an opportunity to get back into a research laboratory again.

On either side of the chimpanzee's enclosure were three other cages. Two of them were empty. Inside the one to the right was another chimpanzee. It lay on its bedding, apparently asleep. The animals' cages were ranged along the back wall of the lab. Professor Zimmermann sat on a stool at a marble-topped bench on the opposite side of the lab. Behind him was a whiteboard. Scrawled across it were lines and lines of closely packed Cyrillic text interspersed with mathematical calculations.

A door opened, and Professor Katerina Patrikova walked in. She placed the laptop she had carried into the lab onto the bench and sat opposite Zimmermann. She gestured towards the animal cages on the far wall.

"I see you've met Harpo and Zeppo."

"You named them after the Marx Brothers?"

Professor Patrikova smiled. "My grandfather was a big fan. Ironic, when you learn that Harpo was spying for the Americans during his visit to the Soviet Union."

"But there were four Marx Brothers." Zimmermann pointed at the cages. "You only have two."

"There were five," corrected Professor Patrikova. "The other three were Groucho, Chico and Gummo." She shrugged. "I'm afraid they didn't survive our earlier tests." She opened up the laptop. "Harpo there has been our most consistent subject in his responses. She continues to behave in exactly the way we predicted."

She turned the screen around for Zimmermann, clicked on a document and scrolled to a video embedded in the text. "Here. I'll show you the progress we've made. Then we can talk about how you can best contribute towards the work."

An image of Harpo the chimpanzee appeared on the screen. She was cuddling a soft toy. Professor Patrikova pointed at the image with a pen. "You see this toy bear she's holding? Harpo bonded with it when she was an infant."

Zimmermann was puzzled.

"Yes, she's a female," Professor Patrikova continued. "But I still named her after one of the Marx Brothers." She typed on the laptop again. "That toy bear never left her grasp. She showed very strong nurturing instincts. She is by nature a very passive animal."

The video changed to violent images of chimpanzees fighting in the wild. Patrikova pointed at the screen again. "We attempted to develop her aggression. We used many techniques, including these videos. The technique has sometimes been successful with other passive primates. But in the case of Harpo it wasn't. She was resistant because her instinct was very deep-seated."

The image on the screen changed again. This time to a close-up of surgery on an animal in progress. "We then considered an undeveloped aspect of your work on brain implants. You, Professor Zimmermann, primarily use brain implants to trigger motor functions in the subjects. Moving limbs. But in one of your papers, you gave details of an operation that went wrong, and the implant was wrongly placed. Instead of directly stimulating motor functions, it affected the subject's free will."

"That was a very interesting case," Zimmermann said. "I wanted to pursue it further, but the university's board of ethics forbade me from continuing with the research."

Professor Patrikova's eyes glinted with excitement. "And as I told you last time we met, we continued that research here." She pointed to the video on the screen. "We put implants in chimpanzee's brains specifically to stimulate the areas of the brain governing free will. They were complex operations because the implants needed to stimulate not only the frontal cortex but also the basal ganglia, deep within the brain."

"And you said you succeeded?"

Professor Patrikova wrinkled her nose. "Partially. Harpo, as I say, has been our most successful chimpanzee subject.

After the implant was adjusted, we restarted the mood modification techniques. This time, the results were dramatically different."

Zimmermann watched the video again. It showed Harpo methodically destroying her soft toy and attempting to eat it.

"Did you have the same success with the other chimpanzees?"

"No," Patrikova replied. "Zeppo has been partially successful. But, as I said, the other three died."

"What were the causes of death?"

"In all three cases, the animals killed themselves."

Zimmermann was shocked. "That's impossible. Animals don't do that. Are you sure they weren't depressed, and the depression may have contributed to their deaths?"

Patrikova stopped the video. "No. Each one killed themselves through deliberate acts. Violent acts. When we discovered the body of Groucho – he was the first – we thought perhaps one of the other chimpanzees had broken into his enclosure and attacked him. But sadly it wasn't the case."

Zimmermann watched the placid figure of Harpo. She lay contentedly in her cage watching television. He stood and walked across to peer through the glass at her. He pointed at a small black box strapped to the side of her head.

"What's that?"

Patrikova joined him at the glass screen that separated them from the chimpanzee. "A radio pack. That was a major development in the project. We're able to remotely monitor the subject's brain function, as well as stimulate the implants."

Her eyes were once again bright with excitement. "In effect, we're able to turn her training on or off. Watch."

Professor Patrikova took a small soft toy from a shelf alongside the animal enclosures. She opened a hatch in the front of Harpo's cage and dropped in the toy. After a few moments, Harpo rolled down from her bedding and ambled across to the toy. She picked it up and examined it for several minutes. After sniffing it closely all over, she hugged the toy close to her body and returned to her bedding. She gazed tenderly at the soft toy, as though it was an infant chimpanzee cradled in her arm.

"Now watch."

Patrikova went back to the bench where they had been sitting. Her long, bright red fingernails clattered across the keyboard of her laptop. Zimmermann was startled by an angry sound from the enclosure behind him. Harpo bared her teeth and made loud aggressive sounds. She threw the soft toy to the ground, jumped down from her bedding and attacked it. Within a few minutes the toy was destroyed. The chimpanzee nonchalantly climbed back onto her bedding, picked up a banana and began to eat.

"My God," said Zimmermann. "You've created a split personality."

"No." There was a self-satisfied smile on Patrikova's face. "Oh, much more than that. Harpo is a sleeping soldier. A placid, apparently non-aggressive, member of the group who can be triggered into action when we choose."

Professor Zimmermann took one last look at the reclining figure of Harpo. There was a serene expression on her face as she methodically ate her banana. Torn shreds of the soft toy she had destroyed a moment ago lay all around her. Zimmermann was fascinated and repulsed in equal measure.

These experiments originated from his own work. For that he was flattered. And it was carried out here, in the basement of the so-called "Correctional Hospital." An institution whose notorious patients were branded criminally insane. But what Professor Patrikova had demonstrated confused him. She had led him to believe their research work on brain implants was designed to control patients with a criminal tendency. To manage their aggression.

But why was the demonstration in reverse? A placid creature turned criminal? Why had they not taken an aggressive animal and attempted to modify it to be more socially acceptable?

He walked back to Professor Patrikova and resumed his seat at the bench.

"Can you achieve the reverse?" he asked.

The professor shrugged. "Oh yes. We know we can reduce levels of aggression in a person. But while we were developing that work, the basis for our funding changed." She gestured towards the animal cages. "What you see here is more important."

Zimmermann was confused by her answer. "But surely, with your work based here in this hospital. And after what you said to me the other day when you visited my apartment—"

"Don't be such an idealist, Professor Zimmermann." Her voice was raised in tone and sounded almost contemptuous. "Our work is expensive, as I'm sure you know. By contrast, it costs the government very little to keep the relatively small number of patients locked up here. If we could reduce the cost of the procedures and the monitoring that would be required for each patient, they might consider using brain implants as an alternative way to manage those who are criminally insane. But not for the moment."

"Then what's your intention with this work?" Even as he asked the question, he guessed the answer.

"I said it a moment ago, Michael," replied Professor Patrikova. Her voice had dropped to its familiar, even tone. "Sleeping soldiers. The FSB has experienced repeated failures with agents in the field who fail, despite rigorous recruitment screening and extensive training. They become too...independent. Detached from their original briefing. They have to be recalled, replaced. And that takes time and money."

Zimmermann knew that several governments around the world pumped millions into research to create so-called "robotically enhanced" soldiers. The work was not only in Russia. But this was the first time he had seen evidence of it first-hand. When Professor Patrikova had visited him two days before, she had talked about how they might research techniques to manage the levels of aggression in patients at the hospital who were classified as criminally insane. It had taken him a great deal of time to reconcile how he could work on that project, given the ethical framework he had spent a lifetime refining at the Technische Universität in Berlin. This was something entirely different.

"No." Zimmermann stood up. "What you're suggesting is out of the question. The work you've done here." He gestured towards Harpo who was now asleep in her cage. "The issues involved in translating those to a human subject are monumental. The risks involved would be immense. I really don't think you've thought this through."

Professor Patrikova placed her hands together as though in prayer. She put her elbows on the bench and rested her forehead on her clenched hands.

"Michael, you don't understand. We've already been successful with a human subject."

Zimmermann had walked away from the bench and had been about to leave the lab. He stopped. He was angry with himself for his curiosity. He should have stood firm by his principles, refused to hear more, and left this woman and her dangerous military research behind. But he was intrigued.

"When?"

Patrikova lifted her head and unclasped her hands. She pulled the laptop towards her and typed rapidly. "We carried out the procedure some time ago. But we were only able to test it for the first time this week. Come sit here. I'll show you what we did."

Reluctantly, Zimmermann returned to the bench and sat on the uncomfortable metal stool. Patrikova showed him a video of another operation. This time on a human brain.

"The operation was a great success. As with Harpo, the implant stimulated both the frontal cortex and the basal ganglia. We were also able to bury the communication device beneath the skin, so that it wasn't visible from the outside. Once the operation has healed, all that's left is a small scar."

The video switched from the operation to shots of a man sat at a computer screen.

"As with the chimpanzees, we then began the mood modification. Because it was a human subject, we could make this much more sophisticated. It took time to develop the techniques, but you can see that the subject responded well."

Zimmermann stared in horror at the face on the screen. The subject was someone he knew very well indeed. It was the face of Alex.

"Professor Alexeyev Krovopuskov is the human subject?" he asked. "And he agreed to do this?"

Patrikova glanced at the screen, threw back her head and laughed. Zimmermann was both alarmed and furious.

"I don't see what there is to laugh—"

"No, no, I'm sorry," replied Professor Patrikova. She cleared her throat. "I can see how the confusion has arisen."

She closed the laptop and stood.

"Come with me. I have more to show you. Then you will understand."

19

"BAD TIMING?" asked Johann.

Dominic turned from the retreating figure of Matty to the leather-clad lawyer that stood in front of him. A shaft of sunlight shone through the doorway to the terrace and reflected off Johann's face. His features were almost too perfect. From his angular high cheekbones to the curve of his lips and the vivid blue of his eyes.

"Something like that."

"Should I leave?"

Dominic folded his arms. It was too late to undo the hug that had clearly upset Matty a moment ago. But he decided it was prudent to maintain a distance with Johann. For his own sake as much as Matty's.

"No, no. It's my fault. I'm not very experienced at handling teenage jealousy. Even though you're here to help him he's jealous of you and me. I think he wants me to himself at the moment."

"Perhaps he has reason to be." There was a twinkle in Johann's eyes. "You're a very attractive man."

He stepped forward, but Dominic walked away towards

the kitchen.

"I'll go and make us some tea." He stopped in the doorway. "I'm sorry, Johann. Let's not complicate things further. There's too much going on at the moment." He nodded towards the television. "Perhaps you can translate the news for me. I know very little about the bombing. Schutz didn't give much away."

Dominic entered the kitchen and began to make tea. While the kettle boiled he opened the chocolate he had just bought. He had an urgent need for extra sugar.

Johann appeared at the doorway to the kitchen. His eyes had lost their lustre and he was on the verge of tears.

"It's terrible," he said. "No one's been killed, but the injuries are very bad. Some of the injured may not survive."

"Do they think it's the same person who attacked the Prinzknecht Bar?"

"The TV reporter is trying to link them," Johann replied. "But the police have said nothing. For me, it makes no sense. These are two completely different modus operandi. The only thing the same is the type of target."

He gestured towards the television. "And anyway. Despite the horrific injuries, the person who did this must be incompetent. Not like the one who attacked the Prinzknecht Bar. From what I understand, that was a far more sophisticated device. This is a nail bomb, not some kind of poison gas. And this bomb went off too early. I almost think it's a – what you say? – a copycat attacker."

Dominic filled a bone china teapot with boiling water from the kettle.

"Honey?"

"How civilised." Johann smiled. "The world is turning upside down outside. But in here, everything is made normal. By tea. Yes, please."

Dominic set down the kettle and took a step back. He waved at Johann, like a couturier showing off a fashion model's outfit.

"Tea and leather," he said. "So very normal."

Johann opened wide his arms and bowed.

"You like?"

Dominic turned away and searched the kitchen for a lemon.

"Of course. On the right person it's very…sexy." He reached for a knife and sliced the lemon in two. "But there are some very unattractive bodies out there in the street party this afternoon. And many of them are wearing very little apart from leather harnesses and shorts. I'm not sure it's right for everyone."

"Body shaming?" Johann wagged a finger at Dominic. "I'm surprised at you. So what if they don't have flat stomachs and gym-expanded chests? The Berlin Folsom party has a long and proud history of being open to everyone. And that means everyone, whoever they may be and whatever their size or shape. What unites everyone here should be their unashamed love of fetish. If these people can't walk around dressed like that here, where else can they do it?"

Dominic immediately regretted his words. He knew they had made him sound like a shallow, gay snob. Perhaps it was because he remembered how awkward he had felt when he had visited Folsom with his late husband. He had envied the hundreds of men, mostly very ordinary people, that paraded the streets dressed in outrageous fetish gear. Jonathan had confidently mingled with them, dressed in his leather biker gear and harness. And he had looked good in it. Very much like Johann did now.

"You're right. Perhaps I'm projecting my own sense of shame on them."

Johann laughed. "Come on. You don't have to be so heavy. What have you got to be ashamed of?"

Dominic tried to concentrate on making the tea. What was he ashamed of? It was a question he often asked himself. Shame had dogged him for much of his life. From his years in school when he had tried desperately to fit in with the other boys, to his early working life in a corporate law firm in the heart of London.

It was only when he had met Jonathan that he had begun to feel more at ease with himself. Dominic had envied the way Jonathan had been comfortable and always open with his sexuality. He had challenged Dominic frequently about his choice to be "discreet" in his working life. But being challenged was no use to Dominic.

He wanted help. Not challenging. He wanted someone who could help him understand why he still felt the urge to run away from who he was.

Johann leaned forward and kissed him.

It was a brief kiss. On his forehead. And it took Dominic by surprise. Johann smiled. His face was only a few inches in front of Dominic. He could feel his warm breath on his skin.

"No complication," Johann said quietly. "Honestly. You went away for a minute. Is everything all right?"

No, thought Dominic. Everything was wrong. He was helplessly confused. It was worse than confusion. He felt guilty. And he knew it was absurd. After all, Jonathan was dead. Why should he not be allowed to have emotions for another man? When Jonathan had been alive, he had often asked Dominic for an open relationship. Something Dominic had never been comfortable with.

So why did he still feel obligated to Jonathan? Johann

was a very attractive man. Not only that, he made it clear he was attracted to Dominic. It would be so easy.

And yet, it was so difficult.

Dominic's stomach spun somersaults to mark time with his confusion.

Johann straightened up, folded his arms and rested against the doorframe of the kitchen. "You're thinking of Matty, no?"

"No, it was someone else." Dominic handed Johann a dainty bone china cup of tea and the chocolate. "Go and sit on the terrace. I'll bring the teapot."

The moment was gone.

When Dominic emerged onto the terrace a few minutes later, he found Johann had shifted the table and chairs. The sun had moved around, and most of the terrace was in shade. Johann sat in the last remaining sunny spot. "I like the sun," he said.

Dominic pulled his own chair back a foot to sit in the shade and sat down. "Did the news say anything about Alex being a suspect?"

"Not in so many words." Johann hooked his hand around his neck and stretched. His bicep swelled impressively. "At the end of the report on the KitKatClub bombing, they mentioned the Prinzknecht attack. And they showed that picture of Alex again. It was sort of guilt by association. The media can be very good at that kind of snap judgement."

He released his neck, reached for his cup and took a drink.

"Earl Grey with honey," he said. "How perfectly English." He waved at the packet of chocolate on the table. "But where are the cucumber sandwiches? I thought they were essential at an English tea party?"

Dominic shrugged. "I gave cook the afternoon off." He opened the packet. "Chocolate?"

"Thank you." Johann helped himself. "What are you going to do about Matty?"

"I've no idea. I'm sure he'll call me in a while, once he's cooled down. Otherwise, I'll call him."

"Has he heard from Alex?"

Dominic said nothing. He took a drink of his tea. Johann pulled a sheet of paper from the pocket of his leather waistcoat.

"Can you explain this, please?"

It was the paper Matty had used to write his note to Dominic. He must have left it behind in his haste to leave the apartment. Johann had discovered it. Dominic sighed. He had made a promise to Matty, but that was now undermined by Matty's carelessness. He shrugged.

"I was worried someone might hear what we were saying when Matty and I were sitting here. So I told him to write those notes for me. And we're trying to avoid using our phones." He held up the cheap phone they had bought earlier.

Johann looked across the terrace to the apartments opposite. "Very sensible, given what we're learning about all this. I think there are sophisticated forces at work. Do you have a pen?"

Dominic went back into the apartment and returned with a pen. For the next few minutes he wrote down a summary of how Matty had discovered the code that Alex was using to communicate with him. Johann sat back, rested his elbows on the arms of the chair, and put the tips of his fingers together. He said nothing for several minutes.

"May I have the pen?"

Dominic handed it to him, and Johann wrote rapidly on

the reverse of the paper:

You must continue this dialogue with Alex. He contacted your Papi account to communicate and obviously needs your help. Remember, if you discover significant information relating to the attack on the Prinzknecht Bar, you have an obligation to tell the police.

"I need to keep Matty involved." Dominic shook his head. "After all, he's the one who worked out how to use the online copy of—" He was about to say *Doctor Zhivago*, but he stopped himself in time. "The book," he continued. "And anyway. If I start messaging Pasha without talking to Matty first, it will create confusion."

"Then call him." Johann picked up his teacup. "You can't let a teenage tantrum hold us up. Remember that this is a murder investigation. The latest report is that twelve people have died from the effects of the poison gas at the Prinzknecht Bar."

"You're right," replied Dominic. "I'll use the safe phone we bought earlier instead of mine."

"I wouldn't worry about that. You're simply a concerned father calling his wayward son." Johann smiled. "I do envy you that."

"What?"

"Having a son."

The comment surprised Dominic. "You've got plenty of time."

"I'm nearly forty."

"Join the club."

"Yes, but Matty's – how old – nineteen?"

Dominic nodded.

"See? You've got a head start on me." Johann stood. "My time is running out. Go on. Call your headstrong son. I need your bathroom."

He walked back into the living room.

Dominic switched on his phone and called Matty. The voicemail answered. Dominic left a message, hung up, and also sent a text in the hope Matty would respond to one or both of them.

Johann reappeared on the terrace.

"Now I understand."

"Understand what?" Dominic asked.

"Why you're being so...elusive."

"Elusive?"

Johann walked to the perimeter wall of the terrace. He leaned with his back against it and rested his hands on the wall either side of him. The sun highlighted the deep curves of his chest and the thin downy coverage of hair on his otherwise smooth skin.

"I took a wrong turning when I went to find the bathroom," Johann explained. "I opened the door of your bedroom by mistake."

Dominic raised his eyebrows.

"Honestly I did. I was about to close the door when I saw the photograph by the side of your bed. It's your husband Jonathan, isn't it?"

"Yes, it is."

"He looks exactly like me," Johann said. "Or I look exactly like him. Why didn't you tell me? I must be like a ghost standing in front of you. Do I resemble him in any other way?"

Dominic stood and walked over to Johann.

"He loved opera and you hate it. He was a landscape gardener and you're a lawyer. He was English and you're German—"

"You know what I mean. You were obviously in love with him. You married him. What was it about him that..."

He stopped speaking as Dominic rested a hand on Johann's waist and kissed him on the lips.

"He was different." Dominic kissed Johann again. He leaned back and stared upwards. Johann followed his gaze.

"What are you doing?"

Dominic smiled. "Oh, I wondered if the sky has fallen in yet."

Johann looked puzzled.

"It doesn't matter," Dominic said. He dropped his hand from the waistband of Johann's leather breeches. "Yes. I was shocked when I first met you. But no, you're not the ghost of Jonathan. He was a beautiful man in so many ways. But he's gone. I have to get over that."

"Believe me, you don't get over it."

Dominic was taken aback by the reply. "I'm sorry. I didn't realise that you—"

"My twin brother," replied Johann. "Twenty years ago. A motorcycle accident. You don't get over it. But you find ways to stop it dominating your life." He sighed. "I was eighteen at the time."

"You must miss him terribly."

"It's better these days. But it took me a long time. A very long time." Johann reached out to rest his hand on Dominic's shoulder. "You poor man."

He pulled Dominic towards him, and they kissed again. A long, slow, tender kiss. Dominic felt a huge sense of relief. Something had gone right in the world for a change.

His phone rang. He glanced across the terrace to where it rested on the table.

"Answer it." Johann released his hand from Dominic's shoulder. "It could be Matty."

Dominic crossed to the table and picked up the phone.

"Hello, Dominic? It's Amélie. Where are you?"

20

MATTY LAY back on the brown leather couch and drummed his fingers on one of the growing piles of notebooks and papers beside him. He had spent nearly an hour going through Alex's things, but the name and address he was looking for eluded him.

His search was hindered by the mess left behind by the police, or whoever it was that had turned the apartment upside down. Matty had managed to bring some organisation to the chaos, but his obsession with order was far from satisfied. So far he had methodically searched the contents of Alex's desk, where he had found several computer hard drives. He knew Alex distrusted cloud storage for his work and used hard drives for backups. None of them yielded what Matty was searching for.

When he had arrived at Alex's apartment an hour earlier, he had used the rear entrance to the block. He had remembered what Dominic had said about the possibility of the police watching the apartment, and he wanted to avoid being seen entering the building. The rear entrance was hidden away in a dingy alleyway next to the kitchens of a

Turkish restaurant. If the police were watching, he hoped they were only watching the front entrance.

At the end of the alleyway was a steep flight of stone steps that led into the basement of the apartment block. The top of the steps was usually scattered with the overspill of kitchen waste from the restaurant. Alex had once told Matty that the entrance was hardly used.

Matty had avoided the elevator and had walked up the stairs to Alex's top floor apartment. He had met no other residents on the way. Once inside he had kept low and away from the windows. He was probably being unnecessarily cautious, but he wanted to avoid another confrontation with Kriminalkommissar Schutz.

From his vantage point of the couch, Matty surveyed the living room once more. He had searched Alex's desk and a large floor-to-ceiling cupboard in the bedroom that was stuffed full of papers. Several of them were written in Cyrillic, and Matty realised he risked missing what he was looking for because of his inability to read Russian. Nevertheless, it was time to press on.

He scanned the large wooden bookcase beside him. Scattered across the floor in front of it was an untidy mess of notebooks and papers that had been swept from the shelves. He slipped down from the couch and crawled on his hands and knees across the floor to the bookcase.

Sat cross-legged in front of the bookcase, he picked up one of the notebooks and thumbed through it. Each page was covered in Alex's handwriting in a mix of Russian and German. Periodically there was a date at the top of one of the pages. Matty went through the other notebooks and sorted them into date order. He selected one that contained notes from before Alex's arrival in Berlin and flicked through its pages.

After ten minutes he found what he was searching for. The address, email and phone number for Professor Michael Zimmermann in Russia. He took a picture of it with his phone and carefully put it back where he had found it. Feeling satisfied with his efforts, he lay back on the floor and studied the latest message he had deciphered from Alex:

I send all my love, but keep away. It is not safe. I have something I must do. All my love. Pasha.

Matty dropped the phone onto his chest and stared up at the ceiling. He thought back to the moment when he had seen Dominic and Johann in their cosy embrace. Something had snapped inside him. He had known his father might one day start meeting men again. But why did he have to do it right now? When Matty was in the middle of a crisis.

And why did he have to pick Johann? Surely there was supposed to be something called client confidentiality between him and Matty? His father had made a solemn promise not to tell anyone about the messages he was receiving from Alex. But how could he trust him? His paranoia forced him to conclude that Dominic would tell Johann everything. It would then only be a matter of time before Johann informed the police. He considered warning Alex that the code might be compromised. But if he did that, Alex might stop using it, and he would hear nothing more from him.

Matty rolled onto his side and curled up into a foetal position. His time with Alex had been the happiest in his life. So far. Alex was an inventive and passionate lover, and Matty had learned a great deal about giving and receiving pleasure.

But their relationship was much more than that. Alex was the first older man with whom Matty could have a heated, intellectual discussion without feeling patronised. It was obvious Alex knew far more than Matty, that he had more life experience than Matty. But he never handed it down with the air of a superior, older man. For the first time in his life, Matty felt like an equal.

Dominic, by contrast, seemed desperate to adopt the patriarchal role for which he was only biologically qualified. It seemed he wanted Matty to adopt the position of a dutiful son, a mythical ideal that must have existed somewhere in his father's head.

It was true there were times when Matty had felt he had been able to talk to his recently discovered father as an equal. The support he had given when Dominic had talked about the death of his husband, for example. Even then, Dominic had cut him short by saying, "Of course, you wouldn't know. You've not experienced the death of a loved one."

Well, that was untrue. Matty had been very close to his grandfather. Opa, as he had called him. He had been heart-broken when Opa had died. He still was. The man had played an essential role in Matty's life when he was growing up. Despite being weakened by his heart condition, Opa had been a constant source of emotional strength. He had been Matty's refuge from his bullying stepfather.

Matty sat up. He knew what he had to do. He checked his phone for flight timetables. If he moved quickly, he could still make it today. He stood up, collected his laptop and its bag and walked over to the bedroom. He found a large backpack in the top cupboard, laid it on the bed, and hastily packed a few of Alex's clothes into it. Back in the living room he found his passport where Alex had left it with the ticket to Helsinki neatly wrapped around it. He shoved it in the backpack and looked around the room as he went through a checklist in his head.

Finally, he slung the backpack over his shoulder and set off for the airport.

Tegel airport was quiet when Matty arrived at six that evening. He collected his boarding card from a gloomy-faced man at the Finnair check-in desk and headed for security. He joined the end of the line of people waiting at X-ray and dropped his backpack at his feet.

He looked around and allowed himself a moment of self-satisfaction. His subterfuge at Alex's apartment had worked. Despite the heavy presence of police on the check-in concourse, they had showed no interest in him. On the other hand, an official was about to scan his passport into a machine and register his exit from Germany. If the police still wanted him, his covert efforts would have been for nothing.

His phone vibrated to announce the arrival of yet another new message. Who wanted him this time? Since he had left Dominic with Johann, he had received half a dozen messages. A few from Dominic, the rest from his mother. He checked the phone. It was from Johann.

Matty angrily switched it off. So Dominic even had Johann chasing him now? For Matty, the message was confirmation he had made the right decision to fly to Finland. Once he got there, he could work out how to cross the border into Russia and find a way to St Petersburg.

A security official beckoned him to step forward. He dropped his backpack onto the conveyor belt and glanced nervously at the security cameras watching him.

Amélie appeared older than Dominic remembered her. It was nearly a year since they had last met.

She and Matty had flown to London for Jonathan's funeral. It had not been the best of circumstances for their first face-to-face meeting in twenty years. But he had been grateful to her for making the journey. After the funeral, he had talked to Amélie for nearly an hour. She may have added a few pounds in the intervening years, but the elegant black dress she had worn had enhanced her curves. She had still been beautiful, still the same fun, lively person he had first met in Munich.

But now, standing with him on the terrace of the B & B apartment, she seemed tired and careworn. Her face was gaunt and pale. Her long black hair was tied back in an untidy ponytail. Wisps of it floated in front of her face, and she nervously stroked them back behind her ears.

"Has he answered yet?" she asked Johann, who leaned against the perimeter wall of the balcony.

Johann shook his head. "I'm not expecting him to. If he won't reply to you or Dominic, he certainly won't reply to me."

"Then something must have happened to him." Amélie resumed her seat at the table with Dominic. "It's time I called the police and reported him missing."

"No it's not," said Dominic. "It's been less than three hours since he left here. They'll say it's too early for him to be considered a missing person."

"I also don't think you should alert the police about him. Not yet, anyway," said Johann. "Especially to say he's gone missing so soon after we got him released. I'm sure he'll get in touch when he's ready."

Amélie glowered at Dominic. "It's difficult to believe you chose this man to be Matty's lawyer when he's"—she gestured towards Johann—"dressed like that. Is there some kind of fancy-dress party in Berlin this weekend?"

"You're forgetting it was Johann who got Matty released from police custody today," Dominic replied. "And on a Saturday. And despite the fact he was being held under anti-terrorism legislation. Johann is one of the best human rights lawyers in Germany."

"Then why doesn't he dress like one?" Amélie retorted. "He looks like a second-rate extra from a porn film."

Johann walked towards the glass doors to the living room. "I think maybe I should leave."

"No." Dominic stood up from the table and laid his hand on Johann's shoulder. "I'd rather you remained here." He turned to Amélie. "Where are you staying in Berlin?"

"My sister's. She lives a little way outside the city. It's a town called Falkensee."

"Then why don't you go back there for the moment?" Dominic asked. "We can keep in touch by phone. If he's not contacted either of us by tomorrow we can talk again about reporting his disappearance to the police."

Amélie reached down and fumbled with a large cloth bag at her feet.

"I see," she said. "Well, I'm not going back to Anna's straight away. I'm going to Matty's place first. Just in case he's gone back there." She slung the bag over her shoulder and stood up. "If he's not, I'll think about calling the police. One of us has to be responsible here."

A few moments later the front door slammed.

"Do you think she *will* call the police?" Johann asked.

Dominic shrugged. "I honestly don't know her that well. But, yes, probably."

"Oh dear." Johann sighed. "Maybe I will need to go back to court. So I'll have to put my suit back on very soon."

"What a shame." Dominic slid his hand over the surface of Johann's leather waistcoat appreciatively. "I was getting used to you walking around dressed like that."

"I'd prefer it if you did as well." Johann wrapped his arms around Dominic's waist and pulled him close. "Why don't I lend you some of my leather? We could go out together tonight?"

"For several reasons." Dominic laid his hands on Johann's shoulders and gently pushed him away. "Because my son is missing and I might hear from him at any time. And secondly, because there's someone bombing gay bars here in Berlin. I for one don't want to be his next victim."

Johann sighed. "You're right. I'm only teasing. I wouldn't be surprised if they haven't closed many of the bars already. There'll certainly be a much bigger police presence on the streets tonight." He smiled. "Which would at least give us something enjoyable for our eyes if we went out."

Dominic unhooked Johann's arms from his waist and headed for the kitchen.

"I'll make some tea. It's what we British do in moments of crisis."

"You can do something else," Johann added as he followed Dominic to the living room. "You can check on that Papi app to see if there are any more messages from Alex."

Dominic emerged from the kitchen. "But what if Matty's on it? Surely it won't let me in?"

Johann shrugged. "You won't know until you try. If you do manage to see the messages, you'll see the ones from Alex as well."

"That's a good idea." Dominic headed back towards the terrace. "I'll get my phone." He stopped. "But the messages will be in German. Alex only used English the very first time he made contact with me. Now Matty's talking to him they're in German. So I'll have to use a German online copy of *Doctor Zhivago*. I'm not fluent you know."

Johann smiled. "I hear what you're saying. I'll do it for you. Give me your phone and your laptop, and I'll see what I can find while you make the tea."

Dominic put an arm around Johann's waist and kissed him. "Thank you," he said. "Here's to Anglo–German relationships."

21

HODAN SAT patiently in the noisy waiting area of the police station. It was early Saturday evening, and there was a lot going on. An elderly woman shouted through a grille in the thick glass that protected the police officer at the reception desk. In the middle of the waiting area, two men sat on chairs and sang loudly. On the bench opposite Hodan, a man sat handcuffed to a police officer. When she had first taken her seat in the waiting area she had made the mistake of glancing at him. The man had bared his teeth at her and then laughed.

She glanced at the clock. More than half an hour had passed since she had given her details to the officer at the reception desk. She wondered if she could slip out of the door and forget about the whole thing. Hodan stared down at the floor again, trying to avoid the gaze of the scary man sat opposite.

"Fräulein Dahir?"

Hodan got to her feet quickly. A young woman police officer stood in front of her. Hodan nodded to confirm her name.

"Do you understand German?" asked the police officer.

"A little."

"Do you need a translator?"

Hodan shook her head. "Is okay."

"Come with me," said the police officer.

They were let through a set of glass security doors, and the noise of the waiting area receded behind them. The police officer took her down a long white corridor. It smelled of stale food and men's sweat. The police officer walked briskly, and Hodan found it difficult to keep up. The women's refuge had promised to find some replacement shoes for her. The ones she was wearing were broken and slipped from her feet as she hurried behind the police officer.

Halfway down the corridor they arrived at a green-painted door. The police officer took a set of keys from her pocket, opened the door and stood to one side.

"Please."

Hodan entered the room. There was a table next to a wall with two chairs on either side of the table. The police officer gestured to one of the chairs.

"Please. Sit."

Hodan sat on the hard, uncomfortable chair, and the police officer sat opposite her. She operated some electronic equipment on the wall and a red light began to flash.

"Polizeimeister Juli Müller. Interview with Hodan Dahir at eighteen thirty hours."

She turned to Hodan.

"Thank you for coming into the police station this afternoon, Hodan," Polizeimeister Müller began. "It is all right to call you Hodan?"

Hodan nodded.

"Please say 'yes' or 'no.'"

"Yes." Hodan's voice was subdued.

"Louder, please."

"Yes."

"Good. Please tell me about what you saw two nights ago at the Bouman construction site."

"But I told the man at the desk when I arrived."

"Now you tell me. Again." Müller pointed to the equipment on the wall. "We need a record of your statement."

Hodan recounted how she had discovered the hole in the perimeter fence of the construction site. How she had slept on the floor of the offices and woken to see a man climb the tower of the concrete maker. Finally, she described how she had seen the man climb inside the concrete maker and disappear. As Hodan spoke, Polizeimeister Müller interrupted with a few questions, or to help when Hodan struggled to give her explanation in German. But for the rest of the time the officer simply made notes.

"Why didn't you tell someone about this as soon as you saw it happen?" Müller asked.

Hodan stared down into her lap and was silent. This had been a bad idea. She was beginning to regret coming here. But Samira had been very persuasive, especially after she had seen that man's face on television.

Müller flicked through her notes.

"You told my colleague at the desk that you knew the man. Please. Tell me his name."

"I don't know," Hodan said quietly.

"Speak up, please."

Hodan looked up at the officer. "I don't know," she repeated. "But I saw him on television. I'm sure it's him."

"Who?"

"The man on the news."

Polizeimeister Müller frowned.

"The man from the bombings," Hodan explained. "I saw him on the television at the refuge today."

Müller looked down at her notes. "This is the women's refuge in Martin-Buber Straße?"

"Yes," Hodan replied. "I don't see television. But I was with the welfare officer this afternoon. She had a television, and I saw the man's face. I know it's him."

Polizeimeister Müller swivelled around to a computer screen and typed on the keyboard. A man's face appeared on the screen.

"This man?"

Hodan peered closely at the image. The man was much smarter than the one she had seen at the construction site. He was smiling at the camera. But there was no doubt. It was the same person. She nodded.

"Please say yes or no."

"Yes."

Polizeimeister Müller picked up a telephone handset from the wall. Hodan rested against the hard back of her chair and listened.

"Hello?" Müller said. "I need to speak to an investigating officer at the Bundespolizei." She paused and listened. "Someone working on the Prinzknecht Bar attack. We've got a positive sighting of the suspect." She paused again. "Yes, that's right. Here in Berlin. Professor Krovopuskov."

Dominic leaned over the balcony to see into the street below. It was hard to see what was happening. The street was shaded from daylight for much of the day, and now the sun was almost set. He could hear cheers and laughing.

Men's voices shouted in German. In the distance a siren sounded. Periodically, the muffled, rhythmic thud of music became louder as the door of a club at the end of the street swung open to admit more partygoers. He sighed.

"Feel like you're missing out?" Johann was behind him.

Dominic smiled.

"Not really," he replied. "I'm curious to see what's going on. But my mind's on too many other things at the moment." The open laptop was on the table. "Those messages, for instance."

"But they are good news," replied Johann. "At least, partly good news. It means Matty has been sending messages in the last few hours. But they're not to you."

"Yes, but I'm still not clear what they all mean."

It had taken Johann a long time of patient work to decipher the messages on the Papi app on Dominic's phone. The coded messages often contained up to thirty different page, line and word references to the *Doctor Zhivago* book. When these were put together, they formed a sentence. Even then, the sender had clearly had to compromise their choice of words to accommodate the vocabulary in Pasternak's novel. After Johann had translated the results into English, he had given them to Dominic to decipher their possible meaning.

"For example," continued Dominic. "What about that last one Matty sent to Alex? *The visit is vital. How across the divide to travel?* What's 'the divide?'"

Johann shrugged. "It's clearly not the right word. Whether in English or German. *Kluft* also means gap in English."

"Either way, it still makes no sense. Matty said Alex was in St Petersburg. What would be the divide or gap in St Petersburg?"

"The Neva River, perhaps?" Johann suggested. "Isn't that

the main river in St Petersburg?" He rested his back against the balcony alongside Dominic and folded his arms. "Are you certain the messages are coming from Alex? Is Matty sure it's him?"

"He says he checked him out with a question." Dominic smiled. "It was about what he and Alex did on their first date. Apparently only Alex would know the answer."

"I like that." Johann nudged Dominic with his elbow. "Did you and Jonathan have secrets like that between you?"

"Oh, yes."

When Johann nudged him again Dominic pulled a face of mock horror. "What? You're surely not expecting me to tell you? Why do you think they're called secrets?"

Johann pursed his lips. Dominic had seen him do it before. It was very sexy. He might have been considering what to say next, but it looked like he was preparing for a kiss. A kiss on those very attractive lips.

Neither of them spoke. The sounds of partying funnelled up from the street below. It was Johann who broke the silence between them first.

"Here's a deal. I'll tell you one of my secrets if you tell me one of yours."

"Go on, then."

"I want to go to bed with you."

Dominic laughed. "That's hardly a secret. You've been flirting with me ever since we met in your offices. You'll have to do better than that."

"And don't you?"

Yes, thought Dominic. *I do.*

It was the first time in over a year he had felt attracted to another man. And yet, he was wracked with guilt. Right now his conscience told him he ought to be worrying about Matty. Amélie had further fuelled that guilt.

But why? There was nothing to say Matty was in any danger. He had simply stormed out because he was jealous of Johann. The messages he had sent on the Papi app showed he was alive and well. And if he was communicating with Alex, it would only be a matter of time before Matty got back in touch with Dominic with more information about where Alex was hiding. Meanwhile, that unpleasant police officer Schutz had been sent packing. First by Johann and the judge this lunchtime and then by Dominic himself. He had done everything he could. Why should he feel guilty?

"Well?" asked Johann.

A sudden, cold breeze disturbed the stillness of the evening air. It brushed across Dominic's neck and shoulders, and he shivered.

"Are you cold?"

Dominic looked down at Johann's naked chest. Johann unfolded his arms and placed his hands on Dominic's waist.

"Surely you're the one who should be cold? You're not wearing very much."

Johann said nothing, but placed his lips on Dominic's. They were moist and full, and tasted good. He kissed Dominic gently and pulled away to stare intently at him.

"Is that okay?"

Dominic nodded.

"No feelings of guilt?"

"How did you know?" Dominic was taken aback by Johann's question.

"I didn't." Johann continued to stare at Dominic. "But I guessed. You're recently widowed. You miss your man terribly. And I'm not surprised, when he was clearly as handsome as me."

Dominic laughed.

"That's good." Johann smiled. "You need to laugh.

There's a lot happening in your life. Thanks to your son. And it can't have helped for his mother to come visit."

"It was bad timing, wasn't it?" Dominic sighed. "And she's expecting me to jump into action and get a search party out for Matty. When he's probably—"

"When he's probably sulking in his studio apartment listening to some awful teenage trash metal music. Or worse."

"Oh, no." Dominic rested his forehead on Johann's. "Matty has very good taste in music."

"You mean he's a fan of musicals?"

"Not really." Dominic smiled. "But he likes quite a few solo female singers."

"Ugh, ballads with angst." Johann wrinkled his nose. "I think there's quite enough angst in the world today. We don't have to add to it."

He kissed Dominic on the lips again. This time for much longer.

Their tongues met. It was a delicious moment, and Dominic felt a thrill like electricity course through his body. He put his arms around Johann's torso, and his hands made contact with the leather back of his waistcoat. He slid his hands down the smooth leather and slipped them under its lower edge. Johann's back was warm against his palms.

The charge of electricity coursing through Dominic's body strengthened as Johann explored the inside of his mouth with his tongue. He moved his hands part way up Johann's back. They connected with the leather harness Johann was wearing under his waistcoat, and Dominic gripped the straps. The stiff leather front of Johann's jeans pushed hard against his chinos and reawakened sensations Dominic thought had long ago disappeared.

Images of Jonathan flashed through his mind. The first

time they had met at Glyndebourne. Their furtive, impatient embraces hidden away from the rest of the operagoers in the rose garden. Their honeymoon in Spain, when they had sunbathed naked on the beach in Sitges, or walked hand in hand along the promenade, stopping occasionally to wrap their arms around each other and kiss.

And then there had been that moment in northern California when the gun had fired, and Jonathan had fallen to the ground. The agonising journey to the hospital in the helicopter. The days waiting by Jonathan's bedside. Watching and waiting.

He relaxed his mouth and gently pulled away from Johann.

"Are you okay?"

Dominic breathed deeply. He had thought everything was okay. But now he was not so sure. He wanted to control his thoughts, the memories in his memory bank. But it was impossible. They would always be there, ready to pop up when he least expected.

"I want it to be okay," he said to Johann. "Let's go to the bedroom."

22

DOMINIC LED Johann down the long, unlit corridor that led to his bedroom. He had the strangest mix of emotions churning in his head.

On the one hand he was elated and excited that a man like Johann was so interested in him. Interested enough to want to have sex with him. But it had been over a year since Dominic and his late husband had made love. He felt nervous and apprehensive at the prospect. It was almost like it was his very first time all over again.

And it worried him.

What if he failed to perform? What if he was unable to satisfy Johann? What if Johann was unable to satisfy him? Dominic doubted the latter would be the case. His cock was rock hard at the prospect of being intimate with the sexy German. More likely was the risk that Dominic would cum in the first thirty seconds, and it would all be over in a fountain of long-suppressed semen.

Dominic thought back to the very first time he had ever had sex with a man.

It was also the first time he had visited Berlin. The man

had been Bernhardt Freude. The man whose grave he had visited only a few days ago. Dominic remembered every detail of that first night in Bernhardt's apartment as if it was yesterday. Bernhardt had been patient with Dominic's virginity. Patient with his very obvious first-night nerves.

"No need to rush things," Bernhardt had said as Dominic had begun thrusting like the pistons of a runaway steam train. "Slow it down. Vary the pace. Bring yourself to the edge of orgasm and then pull back. That way, you prolong the pleasure. For both of us."

In the sixteen days Dominic had stayed at Bernhardt's loft apartment in Schöneberg, he had learned a great deal about pleasure. Bernhardt had revealed to him the sensuous regions of his body he had never known about before. He had learned the joy of giving sexual pleasure to another person. He had discovered the thrill of spending an entire afternoon in bed together. Of enjoying mutual, hedonistic pleasure while the rest of the world beyond the bedroom door scurried about pursuing matters of exaggerated importance.

But that had been twenty years ago.

Dominic stopped at the door at the end of the corridor.

"What's the matter?" Johann asked.

"Nothing." Dominic smiled. "I guess. Really. Everything's good."

"Is this what you want?"

"Oh, yes." Dominic ran his hand over Johann's chest. "It's what I want. More than anything right now." He smiled again. "I'm just...strangely—"

"Nervous?"

Dominic nodded.

Johann lifted Dominic's hand from his chest. He raised it to his cheek and kissed the palm. "Don't be nervous," he whispered. "I'll start by giving you a massage. It'll relax you. Do you have any oils?"

"I don't," replied Dominic. "They're not top of my packing list."

"You should."

Johann released Dominic's hand and pushed steadily against his chest. They moved back into the bedroom and Dominic felt the edge of the bed against his calves. Johann held on to the waistband of Dominic's chinos and reached behind him. He dragged the duvet from the bed and discarded it on the floor. Dominic placed his hands behind Johann's head and attempted to pull him towards him. But Johann resisted.

"Don't do anything," he said. "Relax."

He unbuttoned Dominic's shirt and slipped it from his shoulders. He kneeled down, unbuttoned the fly of Dominic's chinos, and slipped his hands inside his briefs. As he tugged them down, Dominic's cock stood erect like an old-fashioned railway signal. Johann leaned forward and licked the tip.

"Precum." Johann looked up at Dominic. "You *do* want this, don't you?"

Johann got to his feet. He went as if to kiss Dominic on his lips, but instead he gently pushed, and Dominic fell back onto the bed. Johann kneeled again and rapidly removed the remainder of Dominic's clothes.

"Roll over, lie on your front, and don't move," Johann commanded. "I'll be back in a moment. I'm going to raid the bathroom."

Dominic shuffled up the bed to the pillows and did as he was told. He lay with his eyes closed, his head cradled on his arms. He was grateful to Johann for taking command of the situation. It was a pleasurable moment to simply let his anxieties and fears slip from him and disappear into the coolness of the sheet beneath him.

He sighed and reopened his eyes. In the half-light of the room he could see the framed photograph of Jonathan watching him from the nightstand. He reached out and laid the frame on its front.

"Good idea."

The voice came from behind him. Dominic pushed himself up on his elbows and saw Johann standing naked at the foot of the bed. In his hand was a glass pot containing something white.

"I found this in the kitchen. I'm sure your landlords won't mind us using some of it. Lie down again."

Dominic rested his head back on the pillow. He felt Johann climb across the bed and straddle his back. A moment later his nostrils were filled with the distinctive aroma of coconut. Johann's broad hands smeared a creamy substance across Dominic's back and began to massage.

"In the absence of aromatic oils, I find that coconut butter is equally effective. And maybe more erotic."

The tension in Dominic's back dissipated as Johann's fingertips massaged the coconut butter up and down his spine. He slid his fingertips across Dominic's buttocks and massaged firmly into his gluteus muscles. Dominic stretched out his arms and sighed contentedly.

Johann worked the inside of Dominic's thighs with his hands. Dominic arched his back and allowed Johann to reach underneath him. While Johann manipulated Dominic's cock with one hand, he used the other to massage the length of Dominic's spine. A wave of erotic pleasure swept through Dominic's body, and he shivered with the thrill it gave him. Johann released Dominic's cock and slid up his back to whisper in Dominic's ear.

"Do you want to fuck me?"

Dominic grunted his affirmation.

"Good," whispered Johann. "I want to feel you deep inside me. Roll over, and I'll ride you."

"Have you got protection?" Dominic asked. "Only, like massage oil, I don't carry any with me these days." He sighed. "I'm a bit out of practice I'm afraid."

"Yes, I have." Johann laughed. "And don't worry about being out of practice. I'm confident you'll remember pretty quickly."

He dismounted to let Dominic roll onto his back and took up a position astride him again. He smeared more coconut butter over Dominic's chest, massaged across his shoulders and around the curve of his pectoral muscles. He worked his hands down towards Dominic's navel and embraced both their cocks with his palms. Dominic closed his eyes and exhaled deeply as a further wave of pleasure swept up his body.

The coconut butter was a sensual lubricant, and Johann moved his hands constantly. They worked around the base of Dominic's cock, slid up to its tip, and then back down to its base in an urgent, unceasing rhythm. At the moment Dominic felt an orgasm about to explode from him, Johann released his hands and placed them on Dominic's chest. He then placed them on either side of Dominic's torso and pushed up on the mattress. His face was only inches away from Dominic's.

"You beautiful man," he breathed. "I so want you inside me."

His lips moved across the features of Dominic's face, kissing them gently as they passed. He tucked his hands behind Dominic's neck and pulled their faces close. Their lips connected, and their tongues explored deep into each other's mouths. Johann gyrated his groin against Dominic's. The lubrication of the coconut butter heightened the stimulation.

Johann released his hands from the back of Dominic's neck and pushed himself up until he sat astride him. With his knees on either side, and his palms on Dominic's abdomen, Johann gently squeezed Dominic's cock with his buttocks. Dominic reached down and grasped Johann's cock. He squeezed it and manipulated it in the way he remembered had given so much pleasure to Jonathan. Johann closed his eyes and groaned appreciatively.

At the same time he continued to manipulate Dominic's cock with his buttocks and massaged its base with his fingertips. Dominic felt the muscles in his chest tighten, and his breathing quickened. Johann stopped and lowered himself to bring his mouth close to Dominic's ear.

"Not yet," he whispered. "We've got all night. That's unless you've got it in you to cum more than once tonight."

Dominic opened his eyes. "It's been a long time. I think I could cum all night."

Dominic woke to find Johann sitting on his side of the bed looking down at him. A hint of daylight glowed around the edges of the closed curtains. Dominic blinked, rubbed his eyes and yawned.

"What time is it?" he asked.

"I'm sorry, Dominic," Johann replied. "It's early. Just after five. I've got to go."

"But it's Sunday." Dominic rolled over onto his back and hauled himself up to rest his head against the untidy pile of pillows behind him. "Why do you have to leave at this ungodly time? Are you off to church?"

Johann smiled. "They wouldn't let me in dressed like this."

Dominic squinted at Johann in the half-light of the bedroom. He was wearing the leather breeches, boots, harness and waistcoat he had arrived in the evening before.

"I don't see why not," Dominic replied. "The Church of the Twelve Apostles was happy to welcome several hundred men dressed like you the other night."

Johann laughed. "I've got to hurry home and change. I'm needed down at the police station."

"What's happened?"

"A colleague of mine needs help with a human rights case."

"At this time of the morning?"

"I don't usually do on-call work." Johann shrugged. "But this one's different. Friedrich only gave me brief details, but the police are holding a Somali refugee. She came forward to identify that body they found at the construction site the other day. Instead of thanking her, they're holding her as a suspect. Friedrich thinks they want to use the fact she broke into the construction site to fast-track her deportation."

Dominic scanned Johann's bare chest beneath the leather waistcoat.

"Are you leaving dressed like that?"

"Why not? I arrived dressed like this."

"You'll be arrested for looking too sexy." Dominic rested his hand on Johann's leather-clad thigh. "Thanks for last night."

"No, no, Mr Delingpole." Johann kissed Dominic on the lips. "It's me who should thank you for last night. I don't know why you thought you were out of practice. I haven't had sex that lasted as long as that, and was as good as that, for years. I hope we can do it again some time."

Dominic sighed. "It was good for me too. Do you really have to rush off straight away?"

"I'm sorry, I do." Johann kissed Dominic again on the lips. "No time for sex now."

"No. I didn't mean that." Dominic hoisted himself farther up the bed. "I wondered if you had a few minutes to help me translate any new messages Matty might have sent."

"I really can't. I'm sorry. I have to go." Johann stood up. "Why don't you try? You understand a little German. I'll see how I get on at the police station this morning and call you later. I can help you then."

"Of course." Dominic lay back on the bed. "Off you go. Are you sure you don't want to borrow a jacket or something?"

Johann laughed. "I'm fine. I'll catch a cab downstairs. We'll speak later."

He walked to the door and was gone.

Dominic stretched and yawned. The light seeping in around the edge of the curtains was getting brighter. He got out of bed, crossed to the window and looked down into the street below. There was no one around. No vehicles passed by. Farther down the street he could see the normally tidy German recycling bins overflowing with empty bottles and wrappers from takeout food.

The room was at the front of the building. Dominic waited a while at the window and enjoyed the almost pre-dawn light and lack of noise from the street. Directly below him was the bright red-and-white canopy above the entrance door to the building. After five minutes he noticed Johann emerge and stand in the street.

He was with another man.

The two men chatted for a few moments and then crossed to the bus stop on the other side of the street. Several minutes later, a cab arrived and stopped beside them. They said their goodbyes and embraced. Johann climbed into the cab and it started off down the street. The other man continued to wait at the bus stop. Dominic could clearly see who he was.

He was the man in dark glasses from the neighbouring apartment who had followed Dominic to the supermarket the day before.

23

THE BLOND-HAIRED waiter with the miniscule waist and bad attitude finally acknowledged Dominic's attempts to attract his attention. He took the order for Dominic's third coffee of the morning, flared his nostrils and flounced away. Dominic half-expected the unsmiling youth to tell him he was taking up valuable table space and should leave.

It was nearly midday. The Café Mozart had filled up with bleary-eyed men, finally surfacing from their bacchanalian parties of the night before. They sat at tables in groups of four, or five, or six. The majority of them were still dressed head-to-toe in leather. The large, bear-like men among them loudly recounted lurid tales of their sexual exploits, laughed a lot, and ate full English breakfasts, German style.

Dominic sat alone at a table in the shade of the awning outside the café. His open laptop screen glowed at him from across the table. The English translation of Matty's most recent message was clearly visible, despite the glare of the September sun reflecting from the screen:

At border on Helsinki train. See you St Petersburg.

He had checked his decoding and translation several times before being forced to admit he had got it right. The context of the sentences also made it easy for Dominic to understand one of Matty's earlier messages. The word *divide,* that he and Johann had decoded yesterday, was actually *border*.

Dominic's phone buzzed with a new message, and he checked the screen. Amélie was on her way.

When he had decoded the message a little under half an hour ago, Dominic's first instinct had been to call Johann. When the phone had switched to voicemail, he had left Johann a message, thought for a few minutes, considered calling the police, rejected the idea, and finally called Matty's mother. He had chosen not to tell her what he had learned until they could meet. In some way, although he had no idea how, he thought he might be able to manage her reaction better if they were in a public place.

And how might she react?

In Dominic's experience since he had re-established contact with Amélie, her default emotion was anger. It was why it had taken him such a long time to get to meet Matty. When he had first re-established contact with Amélie, she had immediately been hostile to his request. She had refused to even consider the possibility of telling Matty that Dominic wanted to see him. It had taken a long and patient negotiation, partly with the help of Dominic's lawyer friend Bernhardt, before Amélie had acknowledged that Matty was now an adult and had the right to make the decision for himself.

Dominic tried hard to understand why Amélie had been so opposed to him meeting Matty. He could only presume Amélie had a long-held resentment against him for not getting back in touch sooner, even though it was she who had left him in Munich. It was a question he might put to her one day. But not yet.

He asked himself again: how might she react when he told her that Matty was on his way to St Petersburg?

Dominic rehearsed the conversation in his head. He would tell her that Matty had flown to Helsinki, and that he was now at the Finnish/Russian border, heading for St Petersburg. She would glower at him and then ask that awkward question: how did he know Matty was there? Dominic would be forced to tell her about the coded messages between Alex and Matty, and how he had known about them for several days.

Then she would get really mad.

She would tell him how she bitterly regretted ever letting Dominic into Matty's life. She would say that nothing like this had ever happened before Dominic came on the scene. That Matty was a conscientious, hard-working boy who already had a perfectly good father in the shape of Eric, and that he had no need for another one. She would add that Dominic was a bad influence on her son – "her" son and not "their" son – and it was time she took back control before Matty's studies at the Technische Universität were adversely affected.

One of the leather bears sat behind him leaned forward and asked to take the ashtray from his table for his cigar. Dominic willingly handed it to him.

Perhaps he had not chosen the best location to meet Amélie.

"Dominic."

It was not a question or a happy-sounding "Hello! How are you?" use of his name. It was a simple statement. He stood, cleared his laptop away, and motioned to the chair opposite him.

"Amélie. Good of you to meet me here."

She sat down and looked around her.

"Is the fancy-dress party still going on?"

Dominic smiled. "It's the tail end of it now. The big parties were last night. They're recovering from them this morning."

"And did you go to any?" Amélie's tone was disapproving.

"No." Dominic shook his head firmly. "We – I mean I – stayed in last night."

Amélie took off her sunglasses and raised her eyebrows. "I see."

"Would you like something to eat?" asked Dominic. The other tables were laden with plates of food and he felt hungry. "Or just a coffee?"

"No." Amélie wrinkled her nose. "I might have a coffee. But I won't stay long." She narrowed her eyes. "Why did you want to see me? Is there any news? I didn't call the police last night as you and your...friend." She hesitated for a fraction longer than was necessary on the word *friend*. "You and your friend advised me. I hope you have some good news."

Dominic took a deep breath. "Well."

Before he could continue, the blond-haired waiter with the narrow waist and no improvement in his attitude arrived with a coffee for him. Dominic offered it to Amélie, who accepted it graciously.

The waiter turned his scornful eyes on Dominic. "*Wollen sie noch einen Kafee für sie?*"

Three cups were enough. Dominic shook his head. The waiter stalked off.

"Yes, I do have some news," Dominic began. This time he was interrupted by his phone ringing. Amélie rolled her eyes.

"Answer it, please," she said. "I'm sure I can wait another few minutes to find out what's happened to my son."

Dominic answered the call.

"Herr Delingpole? Kriminalkommissar Schutz here. I have news about your son."

Dominic pressed the phone to his ear. He put a finger in his other ear to deaden the sound of laughter from the table behind him.

"Kriminalkommissar," he replied. "Thank you for calling. What's happened?"

"Your son is in Finland," the chief inspector announced. "We believe he may be trying to make contact with Professor Krovopuskov. Is it possible you can come to the police station? I'd like to ask you some more questions."

Dominic looked across at Matty's mother. He was relieved. His side of the conversation he had rehearsed for Amélie was now redundant.

———

This time the waiting area of the police station was almost empty. Dominic sat next to Amélie on the hard, plastic chairs. He stared at a strange black-and-white poster on the opposite wall and tried to decipher what it said. Even though Amélie was a native German speaker, he had no intention of asking her to help him translate it. She was clearly in no mood.

"Why didn't you tell me you were already talking to the police?" she asked. "If I'd called them yesterday evening, I would have appeared very foolish. Can't we at least work together on this?"

Dominic sighed. "You knew Matty had been arrested. So

I thought you would have assumed we'd talked to the police."

"I don't assume anything with you," she snapped. "What else haven't you told me?"

Dominic paused to consider how to answer such an impossible question. There were things Matty had told him in confidence. Some of them were not to be passed on to his mother. Even with Matty missing in Russia, Dominic was reluctant to betray his son's confidences.

"Did you know about his relationship with Alex?" asked Dominic.

"Of course I did," Amélie replied. "Matthias told me. What's the matter? Don't you approve?"

"Well he is twice Matty's age. And he is a lecturer. I just think he needs to be careful."

"Is that why he's run off?" Amélie's voice was more strident. "Did you and your...friend say something to upset Matty?"

Dominic was becoming frustrated with Amélie's combative approach. "Johann is Matty's lawyer. He's been extremely helpful for Matty."

Amélie sniffed. "It's a strange lawyer who meets his client wearing that leather...fetish outfit of his."

"Amélie." Dominic was annoyed. "It's not helpful to pick a fight with me when we're about to meet Schutz. We ought to be presenting a united front. The man is..." Dominic saw Kriminalkommissar Schutz walking towards them. "Heading this way," he whispered.

Amélie stood and greeted Kriminalkommissar Schutz. They spoke together in rapid German, occasionally glancing in Dominic's direction. Schutz laughed and turned to Dominic.

"What a charming lady your ex-wife is, Herr Delingpole."

Dominic opened his mouth to correct Schutz's error, but the Kriminalkommissar continued before he could speak.

"Will you come with me, please? I have an interview room booked for us." He gestured towards a secure door at the far end of the waiting area. "*Bitte?*" Amélie walked with Schutz towards the door. They talked animatedly in German.

Dominic stood and followed them. As they approached the door it burst open and Johann emerged. Gone were his leathers and boots, and in their place he wore his business suit with a starched white shirt and tie.

"Herr Hartmann," said Schutz. He stopped and reached for the door Johann held open for him. "What a pleasant surprise." He turned to Dominic. "See? Even your lawyer is here for you. Again."

Johann clicked his heels together in a mock military salute to Schutz. The gesture clearly angered the chief inspector. The two men spoke in German, and both looked towards Dominic.

"It seems your lawyer is in urgent need of a case conference with you," Schutz said. "I suggest you talk here and call for me when you're finished." He turned back to Amélie. "Meanwhile I'll begin the meeting with your charming ex-wife."

Schutz and Amélie walked through the open doorway, and the door slammed shut behind them.

Johann laughed. "Ex-wife?"

Dominic shook his head. "I'm not sure if he's being deliberately provocative or simply ignorant."

"How did you get on with her?"

"I don't think we're a match made in heaven." Dominic

smiled at Johann. "It's good to see you. The memory of us last night kept me sane this morning."

"Me too." Johann grinned. "He pointed to two chairs near the door. "Come. Sit down. I'm afraid I have some worrying news."

Dominic sat down, and Johann sat next to him.

"Well?"

Johann cleared his throat. "Did you tell Amélie about the messages we've been decoding?"

"No," replied Dominic. "I was about to tell her when we were at the café. But then Schutz called. He saved me. I thought she'd be furious when she found out we'd been withholding the information from her. As it was—"

"Good. It would have caused difficulties with Schutz if it was her and not us who told him about the messages. But we've got a bigger problem to worry about."

"What?"

Johann cleared his throat again. He seemed strangely nervous. "I came here this morning to help a Somalian refugee called Hodan Dahir. They're threatening to deport her tonight. The joke of it is, she came in to help them. She knows the identity of the man whose body was found at the Bouman construction site yesterday."

"And?"

"It was Alex."

Dominic stared at him. He realised immediately the implications of the news.

"Which means," continued Johann. "If Alex died on that construction site, he never went to Helsinki. And it also means he's not in St Petersburg."

Dominic nodded. "So, who's Matty talking to in those messages?"

24

"MATTY'S CONVINCED the man in the security video image isn't Alex." Dominic struggled to piece together the new information. "He says something's not right, and he'd know for certain if the man wasn't wearing sunglasses because of Alex's lazy eye. I don't think the body at the construction site is Alex's."

"Don't you think Matty was clutching at straws?"

"No, I don't." Dominic stood up. "I think Matty's right. It is Alex sending the messages. I have to go. Schutz is waiting."

"Do you want me to come in with you?"

Dominic thought for a moment. It might be useful to have Johann with him. After all, Dominic was not a specialist in criminal law, let alone German criminal law. But he decided on balance there was no need.

"Thanks," he said. "But I don't want to risk antagonising Schutz by having you there. I'll keep calm and keep my answers as brief as possible."

Johann smiled. "The perfect lawyer's response."

Dominic reached for the button on the wall by the security door. Johann laid a hand on his arm. "One more thing."

"What?"

"You need to tell Schutz about the messages in the Papi app, and the *Doctor Zhivago* code."

"No." Dominic pressed the button. The strangely gentle chime of an electronic bell sounded behind the door.

"Why not?"

"Two reasons," replied Dominic. "I don't trust Schutz. He's persisted in pursuing Alex, even though Matty's convinced of his innocence. And, as you know, I think Matty's right. I think Schutz is yet another lazy police officer who convicts the first suspect he finds without taking the trouble to look further."

"And the second reason?"

Dominic shrugged. "I promised Matty I wouldn't tell anyone. It's bad enough that I told you. I'm certainly not going to breach his confidence and blurt it out to Schutz."

"I admire your familial loyalty," said Johann. "But you're wrong. If you withhold this evidence from him now, you could be endangering Matty's life."

It was the first time Dominic had found himself in conflict with Johann, and it made him feel uncomfortable. He was convinced his instinct to withhold the information from Schutz was right. But there was a nagging doubt in the back of his mind that his judgement was marred by both his distaste for the man and the promise he had given Matty. Perhaps he trusted his emotions too much. He should use his analytical mind more. But his gut instinct had proved to be right on many occasions in the past. He was not going to doubt it now.

"No," Dominic repeated. "I don't trust anything Schutz has done so far. From arresting Matty on a spurious terrorism charge, to hounding us at the B & B and demanding to know Alex's whereabouts. It only goes to confirm my belief that he's lazy and incompetent. He's unwilling and probably unable to pursue multiple lines of investigation."

"Thank you for that, Herr Delingpole."

Dominic spun around to find Kriminalkommissar Schutz standing at the open security door.

"I do hope your low opinion of me doesn't impede your willingness to cooperate with my investigation," Schutz continued. "As I understand it, you are a lawyer in England. And as such you are an officer of the English Supreme Court. You swear to uphold its law. Now, although that oath doesn't apply here in Germany, I hope you have the courtesy to respect our laws."

He stood to one side of the security door and held it open. "Please. Come this way."

Dominic could feel his face flush and cursed himself for his indiscretion. He turned to Johann. "Let's talk later."

"I'll wait for you here," Johann replied. "I'm sure the Kriminalkommissar won't keep you long." He smiled at Schutz.

Dominic stepped through the door and waited for Schutz.

"Follow me."

Schutz strode off down a long white corridor lit by overhead fluorescent lights. Dominic hurried behind. He thought about whether his clumsiness had put him at a disadvantage. Then again, there was no harm in Schutz knowing what Dominic thought of him. He probably knew it already.

Along the corridor they passed a series of steel doors on

either side with small panes of glass set into each one. Schutz stopped at the eighth door along.

"It will just be us," he said to Dominic. "My colleague Polizeimeister Müller is talking to Frau Lange." He smiled. "Frau Lange is being very helpful. And she has corrected me about your relationship. My apologies. I was unaware your son was born out of wedlock."

Schutz opened the door, entered the interview room, and stood aside for Dominic.

The walls of the room had once been white, but now they were dirty and scuffed. There was no window. Light came from a single, naked fluorescent tube hanging crookedly from the ceiling. There was a metal table set against one wall with a battered metal chair on one side of it and a padded swivel chair on the other. Schutz closed the door behind Dominic and gestured to the metal chair.

"Please. Sit."

Schutz sat opposite Dominic at the table. A microphone hung a few inches above their heads. Schutz switched on the recording equipment set into the wall.

"I'm sure you understand the need for me to record this conversation, Herr Delingpole. It helps our investigation if we can refer to it later."

Dominic shrugged. He thought about taking out his phone and insisting on recording the interview for himself. But he felt that, on balance, it would be pointless to annoy Schutz further.

"Frau Lange told me that your son went missing yesterday afternoon and that you persuaded her not to report his disappearance to the police. Why was that?"

Amélie had already fired the opening shot, and Schutz was quick to pick up on it. Dominic sighed.

"Yesterday, Matty and I..." He thought carefully before

he continued. "Had a difference of opinion, and he left to return to his apartment. He wasn't answering his calls. It was little more than an hour later when Amélie arrived. Of course I was concerned about Matty, but I thought he was simply upset and needed a bit of time to cool down. I never dreamed he'd fly off to Helsinki."

"So his mother was right and you were wrong." Schutz sat back in his chair. "How long have you known your estranged son, Herr Delingpole?"

"A little over a year."

"His mother has known him all his life. And yet you thought you knew better." He leaned in close to Dominic. "Or had he, in fact, told you about his plans and persuaded you to lie to his mother?"

"No, of course not." Dominic was irritated by the question. "Why are you so keen to pursue Matty, anyway? He studied that image you have from the security video and he's convinced it's not Alex."

"Your son is impressive in his loyalty to his boyfriend—"

"It's more than that. Did you know that Alex has a lazy eye? It's a condition called amblyopia. In his left eye. You should check for that."

Schutz waved his hand dismissively.

"It's irrelevant now. We received new information yesterday about your son's boyfriend." He nodded towards the door. "I presume Herr Hartmann has already told you. We've had a visual identification of the body discovered at the Bouman construction site. A witness claims she saw the man before he climbed into the cement-making machine. She says the man is Professor Krovopuskov. We're attempting to use DNA testing now, but it will take time."

"Are you simply going to ignore what Matty's saying?" Dominic asked. "Dismiss what he's saying as misguided loyalty to Alex? And anyway, if you think Alex is dead, why are you still looking for Matty?"

"Don't you think it's strange that your son is heading for Russia?" asked Schutz. "There's been a gas attack on a bar here in Berlin. People killed and injured. A man's body, possibly your son's boyfriend, is found on a construction site." He smiled. It was an emotionless smile. "Herr Lange has questions to answer. Many questions."

"How can you be sure you know where Matty is?"

Schutz tapped the side of his nose conspiratorially.

"It wasn't difficult to track him, once we were alerted that he was on a flight to Helsinki yesterday evening at eight twenty."

"And where exactly is he now?"

"The last we heard, he was in a Finnish town called Muurikkala, a few kilometres from the Russian border. But that was nearly three hours ago."

Dominic shook his head. "What on earth is he doing there?"

Schutz leaned back in his chair and put his fingertips together. "I thought *you* might be able to tell *me* that, Herr Delingpole. Have you heard nothing more from Matthias since his disappearance yesterday afternoon?"

"No," Dominic replied. "He's not returned my calls or messaged me since he left my apartment." It was the truth. The message Dominic had read on the Papi app, which showed Matty was heading for St Petersburg, had been intended for Alex, not for him. He was still determined not to tell Schutz about the messages. There was something about Schutz that did not make sense.

"If you're convinced Alex killed himself on a construction site in Berlin," Dominic continued. "Why are you so interested in tracking Matty to St Petersburg? Surely you should be hunting the man who attacked the Prinzknecht Bar?"

Schutz rocked forward onto his elbows. His face was inches away from Dominic's.

"How do you know he's going to St Petersburg?"

"I don't." Dominic sat back and cleared his throat. "But if Matty intended to meet Alex at the conference in Helsinki, and he arrived to find him not there, he probably decided to go on to St Petersburg. It's where Alex lived before he came here. And it's not that far away from Helsinki."

Schutz glared at him. Dominic held his stare. He refused to break the silence first.

At last, Schutz spoke. "I'm sure you're right." He switched off the recording equipment.

"Is that it?"

Schutz stood up. "You're free to go."

Dominic remained in his seat. He was surprised at the abrupt way in which the interview had ended. He had been expecting much more. Schutz held out his hand. Dominic stood, and the two men shook hands. He pushed back his chair and headed towards the door.

"One more thing."

Dominic was about to open the door. He silently cursed Schutz for using an old police questioning technique.

"St Petersburg is three hundred and eighty-nine kilometres from Helsinki." Schutz had sat down again and was fiddling with the recording equipment. "Did you also know that Helsinki looks extremely similar to St Petersburg? It was used in several films that were made during the Cold War." He smiled. "One of them was *Doctor Zhivago*. Good day, Herr Delingpole."

"I thought you might need a drink after that."

A waiter put two small glasses of amber liquid down on the table between them. Johann paid the waiter, picked up one of the glasses and handed it to Dominic.

They were sitting outside a restaurant two streets away from the police station. The table was close to the street and the traffic was noisy, but Dominic was grateful to be away from the claustrophobia of the police station.

"*Pröst.*" Johann raised his glass to Dominic.

"What is it?" Dominic asked.

"Kräuterlikör. Herbal liquor," Johann translated. "It's very good. This one is from a small town in the eastern part of Germany, not far from where I was born."

Dominic clinked his glass against Johann's and tasted the liquor. It was almost medicinal in flavour and had a slightly bitter taste. It reminded him of an ingredient for a cocktail Jonathan used to make.

"You survived the interrogation, then?"

"I think Schutz knows more than he's letting on." Dominic placed his glass on the table and moved his chair closer to Johann to hear him better. The traffic noise seemed to be getting louder.

"Ah." Johann smiled. "So, you no longer think he is – what was it you said? – 'lazy and incompetent?'" Johann laughed. "How did you recover from that unfortunate moment before the interview?"

"I don't think I did." Dominic shook his head. "And no, I don't think he's lazy and incompetent. But I do think he's a devious little bugger."

"Good. So do I." Johann kissed Dominic on the lips. "And, for what it's worth, I think you might be right to be cautious in what you tell him."

Dominic took another sip of his Kräuterlikör and

savoured Johann's words. He waited for the apology that would surely follow.

"That's not to say I think your caution with Schutz is for the right reasons," Johann continued. It looked like the apology was not on its way. "For you to have blind faith in Professor Krovopuskov's innocence, merely based on Matty's loyalty to him, is not good judgement in my opinion."

Before Dominic could protest Johann continued in a low voice, despite the noise of the traffic. "But I think you might be right about your suspicions of the FSB. While you were in with Schutz, I called a friend of mine who might be able to help us."

"Another connection on Berlin's pink network?"

Johann laughed. "Of course. What else did you think? I should have called him before. He knows Mickey Zimmermann."

"Who?"

"Professor Zimmermann," Johann explained. "He's the man who Alex did the academic exchange with. He was at the Technische Universität and is now in St Petersburg at the ITMO University, where Alex used to be."

"How has this man persuaded you to change your mind in less than an hour?" Dominic asked. "Before I went in to be grilled by Schutz, you were adamant I should tell him all about the messages Matty was getting from Alex. Now you're admitting you were wrong—"

"No. I was right, given the limited information I had available then." Johann smiled. "But Pavel has given me fresh information, which made me reconsider."

"Pavel?"

Johann took another sip of the Kräuterlikör. "He's the friend I called. Pavel Strelnikov. I've asked him to join us here. I thought you should hear what he has to say first-hand." His gaze shifted to look beyond Dominic. "And here he is. Perfect timing."

Dominic turned. A large man was approaching their table. He wore a suit that was too tight for him and dark glasses.

It was the man that lived in the apartment next door to Dominic's B & B. The man that had tailed him to the super-market the day before.

25

PAVEL STRELNIKOV stood by their table. He clicked his heels together and bowed his head in greeting. His multiple chins compressed together as he did.

"Don't be so formal, Pavel." Johann stood and held out his arms. "Come. Give me that great Russian bear hug."

The two men embraced and kissed each other on the cheeks. Dominic managed to push back his chair in the cramped space and got to his feet awkwardly. Johann relaxed his grasp on Pavel and gestured towards Dominic.

"Allow me to introduce my English friend, Dominic Delingpole."

Pavel held out his right arm to Dominic, and the two men shook hands. Pavel's grip was strong, and the hand-shake was more of a wrestling contest than a friendly greeting.

"We've already met." Dominic extricated himself with difficulty from Pavel's chubby hand.

"You know each other?" Johann turned from Pavel to Dominic.

Dominic shook his head. "We don't know each other,

but we shared a journey to the supermarket yesterday." He looked at Pavel. "Didn't we, Mr Strelnikov?"

Strelnikov laughed. "Mr Delingpole is right, Johann. I was visiting a friend yesterday afternoon in Gleditschstraße. Mr Delingpole and I happened to leave the building at the same time when I went to catch the bus home." Strelnikov's accent was unmistakably Russian. His voice deep and booming.

"You were in that apartment block where Dominic's staying?" Johann asked.

"He was in the apartment next door," Dominic interjected.

"Who were you visiting?" asked Johann.

"It is of no matter." Strelnikov waved his hand dismissively. He looked at the crowded tables around them and frowned. "We must move. It's not safe to talk here. There are too many people. And the traffic is too noisy."

"Really?" Dominic asked. "I thought the traffic noise would be ideal if you're concerned about somebody listening in."

"*Niet*" Strelnikov shook his head vigorously. "It is loud. And as a result we will all speak too loud. And our voices will carry far. *Niet.* It is not good." He moved away from the table and beckoned them. "Come. There is a place I know not far from here."

Dominic looked at Johann and shook his head. He was unhappy at the prospect of following this mysterious Russian anywhere. Johann nodded in understanding.

"Where is this place, Pavel?" he asked.

Strelnikov whispered in Johann's ear. Johann smiled and turned to Dominic.

"Pavel's right," Johann said. "We should go there. There'll be far fewer people around. It's a short ride on the

U-Bahn from here. Probably only fifteen minutes." He patted Dominic's arm. "It'll be fine."

On the walk to the station, Strelnikov and Johann talked in German, sometimes dropping into Russian. Dominic was unaware Johann spoke another language apart from English. He felt excluded from the conversation. The entrance to the U-Bahn station was crowded with tourist groups and a large party of students. Strelnikov used his bulk to clear a path through the people milling around. Johann was close behind him followed by Dominic.

"Is everything all right, Dominic?" asked Johann when they got to the crowded platform.

"Who is he?" Dominic whispered. "A Russian spy? What was he really doing in the apartment next to me yesterday? And why did he follow me?"

Johann held a finger to his lips. "Best not to talk here." A growing number of passengers crowded around them. "I can tell you more about Pavel once we get to where we're going."

"And where's that?" Dominic asked.

"The Garden of Lust." Johann grinned. "Appropriate, don't you think?"

A rush of warm air and the clatter of metal wheels on the track announced the impending arrival of the train. Dominic felt people around him push forward, jostling to get into the right position to board the train when the doors opened. Strelnikov stood directly in front of him. He was at least four inches taller than Dominic, with a broad back, and a thick, squat neck.

Dominic felt a strong urge to break free from the crowd and get away from the platform. He wanted to leave Strelnikov behind with Johann. But Dominic was wedged between a large man in a thick overcoat on one side, Johann on the other, and a crowd of people behind him. He had no chance of making an exit without causing a major disturbance and drawing Johann's attention to what he was doing.

The train screeched to a halt. The doors opened with a hiss of compressed air. Dominic felt Johann grab his arm.

"It's busy, isn't it?" He clung onto Dominic's arm. "Don't worry. We'll soon be there."

***

The three men stood in the middle of a bridge over the river. Johann was right. It had only been one stop on the U-Bahn train to arrive at Unter den Linden station. From there it had been a two-minute walk to the bridge. Strelnikov leaned over the iron railing and looked down into the water below.

"It is surprisingly deep here, Mr Delingpole." Strelnikov straightened up. "Be careful you don't fall."

Strelnikov's laugh was deep and loud. It resonated in his broad chest. He slapped Dominic on the shoulder. "I'm joking of course." He headed off in the direction of a park on the far side of the bridge. "Come. Follow me. We are almost there."

Dominic massaged his shoulder. Strelnikov was a strong man, and the slap was much harder than Dominic had expected. He looked at Johann, who smiled and patted his arm.

"Don't worry about Pavel. He's a mad Russian with a heart of gold. And he's got some very interesting information you need to hear."

Johann slipped his arm under Dominic's, and they followed Strelnikov along the bridge. At the far end they turned off onto a wide, gravel path under a double line of densely packed trees. The avenue of trees extended for several hundred yards along the bank of the river.

After a few yards, Johann stopped and gestured to a large park with a domed cathedral on the opposite side of it.

"This is the Garden of Lust, as I like to call it," he said to Dominic. "It's called *Der Lustgarten,* which actually translates as 'The Pleasure Garden.' But it amuses me to call it 'Lust,' particularly when it's in the shadow of the grand Berlin Cathedral." Johann swept his arm in a full circle around them. "And of course, you know we are on an island now? An island in the middle of the city of Berlin. I can think of no better place to listen to secrets."

"Come over here." Strelnikov had walked on farther and stood in an open space on the edge of The Pleasure Garden. He beckoned to them. "This is perfect."

Johann walked over to join him. Dominic held back and fumbled in his coat for his phone. He tapped in the message code he had previously arranged with Gillian and waited for her response.

"Are you joining us, Dominic?" Johann called. A message flashed up from Gillian. Dominic held the phone and hurried over to join the other two. The rumble of city traffic was deadened by the densely planted trees that surrounded them. There was only a handful of visitors to the garden, and all of them were at least fifty yards away. Strelnikov clapped his hands together and smiled broadly at Dominic.

"Mr Delingpole," he began. "I hope that what I have to say to you will reassure you that your son is safe. And I also hope I can reassure you about his boyfriend, Alex Krovopuskov."

"Do you know where Matty is?" Dominic asked.

Strelnikov shook his head. "Not exactly. But I have a good idea where he's going. Tell me, have you heard of Professor Michael Zimmermann?"

"I have," replied Dominic. "Johann told me he was a professor at the Technische Universität that Alex exchanged with. He's in St Petersburg now."

"Good," Strelnikov replied. "But I have more information I need to tell you about him."

"Before you do," Dominic interrupted. "Could you tell me who you are, please?"

Strelnikov laughed again. A deep, rumbling, bear-like laugh. "I'm what you might call a security consultant. I work for whoever will pay me."

"And who's paying you at the moment?"

Again, the laugh. "Many people pay me, Mr Delingpole. But who they are is commercial confidential. However." He smiled at Johann. "I sometimes do work for my friends. For free of course."

"He's working for you?" Dominic asked Johann.

Johann shrugged. "In a manner of speaking. Pavel and I have been very good friends for several years now. We help each other out sometimes."

"Good friends?" Dominic asked.

Johann coughed. It was the first time Dominic had seen him embarrassed. "We were lovers once."

Strelnikov sighed. "It was a very good time. A very good time." He smiled at Johann. "Sadly no more. But we are good friends. Friends for life."

"Honestly, Dominic, you can trust Pavel," Johann said. "I know you're suspicious. And I understand why. But he can help us."

"Very well." Dominic nodded and turned to Strelnikov.

"Go on. You were about to tell me about Professor Zimmermann."

"Yes. Good." Strelnikov clapped his hands together enthusiastically. "Zimmermann was professor of biomechatronics here in Berlin at the Technische Universität. Eight months ago he made an academic exchange with Alex Krovopuskov."

"Which is how Alex came to be in Berlin," Johann explained.

Strelnikov waved his hand dismissively. "That was the mechanism for getting him to Berlin, but not the real reason he came here. Do you know about Alex's work?" He asked Dominic.

Dominic shrugged. "Matty did try to explain it to me, but I didn't really understand."

"I know it well," Strelnikov replied. "I will put it simply. Alex is working on ways for humans to control robotic extensions of themselves. It is of great value to stroke victims and other people who can no longer move parts of their body."

He looked around, lowered his voice to a whisper. Dominic strained to hear him.

"But Alex's work also has enormous potential for the military. When he came to Berlin and started work on this new project, there was suddenly a lot of interest in what he was doing." Strelnikov paused. "From Washington to Beijing."

"You mean he was actually working for the military?" Dominic asked. "Whose side is he on?"

"Nobody's but his own," said Strelnikov. "He doesn't want to work for the military at all. But you know, a lot of the work that academics do is of interest to the military, whether these professors like it or not."

"You see," Johann said to Dominic. "That's why Pavel told me Alex was spying for the Chinese. The Bundespolizei had been told that by the Russian secret service. The FSB."

"*Da, da.*" Strelnikov nodded his head vigorously. "The FSB wanted to discredit him in the West because he refused to work for the Russian military."

"And is that why they killed him?" Johann asked.

"But if that refugee's to be believed," Dominic interrupted before Strelnikov could open his mouth, "then Alex killed himself. She said she saw him climb into the cement maker voluntarily."

Strelnikov looked puzzled. "I don't know what you're talking about, but Alex isn't dead. He's in St Petersburg with Professor Zimmermann. He messaged me this morning."

Dominic felt vindicated by what Strelnikov said, but he needed to be certain. "How can you be sure it was Alex who messaged you?"

"We have a code," Strelnikov replied. "I have known Alex a long time. It was I who had a big part in getting him here to Berlin. He wanted to get out of Russia." He patted his chest proudly. "It was me who fixed it for him."

"Pavel and Alex were also good friends," Johann said to Dominic. He winked. "You understand?"

"I do," Dominic replied. It seemed there was a pink network in Russia as well.

"Why did Alex go back to St Petersburg if he wanted to escape Russia so badly in the first place?" Johann asked Strelnikov.

"I know what you mean," replied Strelnikov. "I thought it was strange at first, also. But for Alex, it was an instinctive thing to do."

"Instinctive?" Dominic repeated. "What on earth do you mean?"

"Let me explain." Strelnikov pulled out a large red handkerchief from his inside pocket and mopped his brow. "It is very hot today." He put the handkerchief back in his pocket and loosened his belt. His waistband seemed to grow several inches.

"When Alex arrived in Helsinki for the symposium, he got a taxi from the airport to the hotel. On the way there, he tested out the new phone he had bought at Helsinki airport. He checked the news on it. That's when he saw the photograph of the suspect for the Prinzknecht Bar attack. He realised immediately what had happened and called Zimmermann in St Petersburg. Zimmermann told him he should get to St Petersburg as quickly as possible. Alex managed to get a train from Helsinki to a small town close to the Russian border. Meanwhile, Zimmermann drove from St Petersburg to meet him in Finland. He was able to hide Alex in the car and drive him back to St Petersburg."

"I still don't understand," Dominic said. "What's Zimmermann got to do with all this?"

"No, no. I'm not explaining well," Strelnikov said impatiently. "It's not about Zimmermann. Alex was concerned about his brother."

"Alex has a brother?" Dominic thought back to the evening he first met Alex after the attack on the Prinzknecht Bar.

"He never mentioned he had a brother to me."

Strelnikov sighed. "It is very sad. His brother is not well. He has not been well for many years. He's in a psychiatric hospital in St Petersburg. When Alex decided to come to Berlin, it was a very difficult decision to leave his brother behind. But he realised there was nothing more he could do to help. Even so, he felt very guilty. And of course, when he saw the photograph in the news, he had to get back to St Petersburg to find out what had happened."

Dominic could not understand the logic connecting Strelnikov's sentences. "Why should the photograph make him decide to go back to St Petersburg?"

"I didn't tell you?" Strelnikov slapped his forehead. "I am so stupid. Karol is Alex's twin brother. They are identical twins."

26

"OH MY GOD."

A thousand thoughts collided in Dominic's head, and his legs felt weak. He glanced around for a bench or a low wall to sit on, but there was nothing nearby.

"Excuse me," he said to Johann and Strelnikov. He dropped down onto the gravel, pulled his knees up to his chin and hugged them. Johann squatted alongside him and rested his arm across Dominic's shoulder.

"Is this really true?" Dominic asked Strelnikov.

"Of course," replied Strelnikov. "I would not lie to you. Alex never said very much about his brother Karol. I think he's embarrassed. Karol is not a good man. He has done many bad things in his life. He is now in a psychiatric hospital for criminals. Alex is loyal to him. Of course. They are family. But you can understand why Alex would say nothing."

Dominic took several deep breaths.

"How long have you known about this?" he asked Johann.

"I told you," Johann said. "Pavel telephoned me while

you were being interviewed at the police station this afternoon."

"So, what happened?" Dominic asked Strelnikov. "Did Alex's brother Karol escape from the psychiatric hospital? And if he did, why did he travel all the way to Berlin and attack the Prinzknecht Bar? Surely he didn't act alone? I can't imagine how he could have got to Berlin without help."

Strelnikov held up his hands. "Too many questions, Mr Delingpole. I only learned this information this morning. That was when Alex messaged me. He is safe with Zimmermann. That I do know."

"And Matty?"

Strelnikov coughed and looked at Johann.

"Well?" Johann asked.

"He's safe," Strelnikov began. "But there's a problem."

"What problem?"

Strelnikov placed his hand on Dominic's shoulder. "The problem is, my friend, at this very moment, your son is crossing the border into Russia."

"How?" Johann asked. "Unless he's managed to get a visa in advance, they won't let him in."

"That's the problem," Strelnikov continued. "Zimmermann is smuggling him in. The same way he smuggled in Alex."

"What?" Dominic pushed Strelnikov's arm away. "Alex told you this morning, and you didn't think to let me know immediately? If you had, we could've let the police know, and they'd have stopped him."

Strelnikov shook his head. "Not a good idea. We didn't want to draw attention to where Matty was. Although the police might know by now. There's a risk that they might tell the Russian authorities that your son is a wanted criminal. Then that would put Zimmermann in danger again. And put Alex at risk. The Russian authorities are very...unpredictable in how they react to such information. They don't cooperate with the German police. They might simply put all three men in a Russian jail."

Dominic was angry and frustrated. He knew where Matty was, but he was powerless to do anything about it.

"So that means you won't tell Schutz?" Dominic asked.

Strelnikov shrugged. "I have no confidence in Kriminalkommissar Gerhard Schutz." He waved his hand dismissively. "The German police can be very clumsy when it comes to matters of dispute between political states."

"How on earth is it that the German police don't know Alex has a twin brother?" Dominic asked. "Surely he's the obvious suspect for the Prinzknecht attack if he looks like Alex?"

"It is the enigma that is Russia." Strelnikov held up his hands as if the idea defeated him. "He is in a psychiatric hospital for criminals. Technically Russia has no psychiatric criminals. Therefore Karol Krovopuskov, Alex's brother, does not exist on any official records."

Strelnikov smiled. "At least you know that your son is safe."

"Safe?" Dominic's voice rose several decibels. "How the fuck is he safe? Schutz clearly has suspicions about Matty. What they are I don't know. Meanwhile, he's being smuggled across the Russian border as we speak."

Strelnikov looked around anxiously and raised a finger to his lips. "Shhh, please, Mr Delingpole. Do not draw attention to our meeting here."

Dominic took a deep breath and lowered his voice. "Can't you understand why I'm so angry? Matty's done something incredibly stupid. It's so stupid, Johann. Matty could get into a lot of trouble. I'm beginning to think

Amélie's right. Alex is old enough to know better. He's a terrible influence on Matty."

Johann appeared surprised at Dominic's outburst. "I think you're being too hard on Matty. He's simply an impetuous young man in love. And think of all the dangerous things you did with Jonathan when you tackled the Natural Family Association. Perhaps Matty simply wants to be like his father."

Dominic said nothing. Was Johann right? It was true Matty had told him on more than one occasion how much he admired him. How he wished he had known him when he and Jonathan had uncovered the Natural Family Association conspiracy. Was Matty following his example as Johann suggested? If he was, Dominic felt very responsible.

A boat horn sounded from the river. As the echoes of its mournful blast faded away, the bells in the cathedral on the opposite side of the gardens began to toll. It was a hauntingly beautiful sound. Dominic closed his eyes and, with an effort, slowed his breathing to release the emotion built up inside him. He reopened his eyes to see Johann smiling at him.

"Let's concentrate on the present," Dominic said. "We have to tell Schutz about Alex's twin brother. Once he knows it was Karol and not Alex who attacked the Prinzknecht Bar, he'll call off the search for Alex. Then he'll be free to come back to Berlin."

"*Niet.*" Strelnikov's voice was quiet, but firm. "Alex says his brother was not mentally responsible for what he did. He believes he was forced to do it. Alex will stay in St Petersburg and clear Karol's name."

"But his brother's dead." Dominic was confused. "What does it matter now? Why can't he come back to Berlin? And bring Matty with him?"

Strelnikov shrugged. "It's a matter of family honour. Alex is angry about the death of his brother. He says he knows who organised the attack on the Prinzknecht Bar, and he plans to expose them."

"Expose them?" Dominic quickly thought through the implications of what Strelnikov was saying. "That's mad. Alex got into Russia illegally. Matty's about to join him, also illegally. And now Alex plans to singlehandedly expose the perpetrators of a murderous attack on a gay bar in Berlin?" Dominic shook his head. "He's mad. And he's putting Matty in a very dangerous position." He squared up to the Russian, his face a few inches away from Strelnikov's. "I need to speak directly to Alex. I need to tell him to send Matty back home."

"*Niet*," said Strelnikov.

"Fine." Dominic took out his phone. "I'll call Schutz and tell him about Alex's twin brother."

Strelnikov shrugged. "And how will that help you? If you tell Schutz, he'll tell the Russian authorities. I said already they can react...unpredictably. What if they arrest your son for entering the country illegally and put him in jail?" He shook his head. "*Niet*. I care less about your son, Mr Delingpole. But I will not allow you to jeopardise Alex's safety, or Mickey Zimmermann's for that matter. Russia is a dangerous country. And the German police, especially Schutz, are fools."

"Fuck you." The words exploded from Dominic's mouth. "If you won't help me then I'll go to St Petersburg myself to get Matty back."

Strelnikov laughed. "And how will you do that? You'll need a visa and an invitation to enter the country from someone in Russia."

"How will I do that?" Dominic repeated. He smiled at Strelnikov. "You're going to help me."

Strelnikov held out his hands. "And why should I do that?"

Dominic pulled out his phone. "Because if you don't, my personal assistant back in England will send this recording she's been making of our conversation to Schutz. And, given what you get up to, I'm damn certain he'll make sure you'll never set foot in Berlin again."

―――――――

The air inside the cramped compartment was stale and fetid. The car's suspension had been denied the care and attention it so urgently needed, and the potholes over which they drove were deep and frequent. Matty's joints ached, and he felt nauseous from the constant rolling and shaking of the car.

In the confines of the small space it was impossible to reach for his phone to check the time. It was probably only fifteen minutes since Professor Zimmermann had helped him into the cavity hollowed out beneath the rear seat of the car and secured the seat cushion back on top of him. Matty kept his eyes closed, breathed deeply, and tried to imagine the track around the Tiergarten where he ran every morning. It helped him avoid the dead hand of claustrophobia tightening its grip on his windpipe.

Professor Zimmermann had said it would be no longer than an hour before he could release Matty from his confinement. That was provided there was no hold up at the Russian border. But the professor had reassured him there had been no delay when he had brought Alex across two days before. He was confident the guards would recognise him with his battered old Volvo estate car and simply wave him through.

When Matty had first seen the hiding place under the long rear seat of the car, it had reminded him of the ingenious ways in which people had fled from East Berlin to the West during the Cold War. He had learned about them in his first year in Berlin, when he had gone with his friends to the Checkpoint Charlie Museum. One of the galleries had a Mini car on display. The owner had hollowed out the front seat to allow a person to hide inside and escape from East Berlin.

Now that Matty was trapped in his own hiding place in Professor Zimmermann's Volvo, his enthusiasm for this big adventure of being smuggled into Russia was waning.

The car slowed to a halt. Matty could hear the muffled sounds of men's voices speaking Russian outside. He heard an electric window being lowered, and the voices became louder. A man, presumably a border guard, asked Professor Zimmermann for his passport. Matty clenched and unclenched his fists and breathed in time to the rhythm to try to lower his quickening heart rate.

The engine stopped, and Matty heard a car door open. There was the sound of feet walking around to the back of the car followed by the creak of the rusty rear hatch opening. Earlier, Matty had noticed the back of the car was full of old newspapers and bags of clothes. He could hear these being moved about as a border guard searched the car.

Another of the car doors opened. A rush of fresh air filled Matty's nostrils. In different circumstances he would have welcomed it, but he knew that the rear passenger door was now open, and the guard was standing inches away from where Matty was hidden.

The seat cushion above him creaked, and he felt it

compress down on top of him. Even before the guard had rested his weight on the seat cushion, there had been very little room for Matty in the cramped space beneath it. Now, Matty struggled to breathe at all. He held his breath and resisted the impulse to cough as his chest cavity compressed.

Matty heard Professor Zimmermann shout something to the guard, and the weight was lifted from the seat cushion. A moment later the door slammed, and there was the sound of muffled conversation in Russian. Matty inhaled deeply and reflected on how calm he had been at this moment of crisis.

The car bounced as someone climbed back into the driver's seat and slammed the door. The engine restarted, and the car shuddered as it began to move.

"*Scheiße!*" Professor Zimmermann's expletive penetrated the rattling noises in the car. "Are you okay, Matthias?"

Matty opened his mouth to reply and inhaled a cloud of dirt and dust that had been released from the seat cushion when the guard had leaned on it. His body convulsed in a fit of choking. He feared he was going to throw up at any moment.

"Hold on," Professor Zimmermann shouted. "There's a safe place where I can let you out about five kilometres from here. We'll be there in a couple of minutes."

The car accelerated, and its wheels bounced violently in and out of potholes. The thudding of the car's broken shock absorbers threatened to regurgitate the contents of Matty's stomach. He gritted his teeth and tried to distract himself by picturing the wide-open spaces of the Tiergarten.

The pounding of the wheels became the pounding of his feet on the grass. His breathing dropped into the rhythm he adopted when he was running. The roar of the engine became the sound of the wind rushing in his ears. If he squeezed his eyes shut, tiny speckles of light appeared, like the early morning sunlight shining through the leaves of the trees. It was as though he had been running for an entire morning. He was dehydrated, and his stomach was in spasm. His legs felt exhausted, and he could run no farther. He staggered away from the track and into the dense foliage. He rested against a tree and fought for breath. But no air entered his lungs. He was overwhelmed by a sense of panic, and his body convulsed.

"Matthias. It's okay. I'm here."

Professor Zimmermann's voice came to him as though from high up in the tree above him. He blinked open his eyes. He could see the unfocused, yellowy glow of the car's interior light above his head. He inhaled the clean air coming in through the open door and breathed deeply.

"Are you okay? You look terrible. Are you going to throw up?"

It was not a reassuring voice. More the sound of a man worried about the upholstery of his car. Matty smiled feebly at the professor's concerned face staring in through the open doorway.

"I'm fine," he replied. "Are we there?"

Professor Zimmermann nodded. "We are. Welcome to Mother Russia."

Matty slept for most of the drive to St Petersburg. He lay curled up on the large rear seat cushion, which at the start of his journey had effectively been his jail door. His dreams were full of danger, with faceless guards chasing him through the streets of Berlin. He awoke several times during the journey to find beads of sweat on his forehead, and his palms cold and clammy.

A disturbing dream in which he was being thrown about inside a steampunk washing machine shook him awake. His neck ached, and the vibration of the car on a cobbled street bounced his head against the door panel. He twisted around to sit up and checked the clock on the car's dashboard. It was after midnight. The journey from the Finnish border had taken a little over three hours. The car drew to a halt in a dingy, unlit courtyard. Professor Zimmermann switched off the engine and looked around at Matty.

"Here we are," he said. "Welcome to St Petersburg. My apartment's a short distance from here. Alex will be waiting for you there."

He climbed out and walked to the back of the car. He opened the hatch and began to search for Matty's bag. "I borrowed this car from one of Alex's friends at the university," he said. "I'll return it to her tomorrow."

Matty sat up, rubbed his eyes and opened the passenger door. A flashlight shone in his face.

"Herr Lange," said a man's voice in German. "It's good to see you again. I hope your journey was not too unpleasant."

Matty held up his hands to shield the light from his eyes and slumped back in his seat.

The voice of Kriminalkommissar Schutz was unmistakeable.

27

Berlin's Tegel Airport was already busy at seven o'clock that Monday morning. Lines of people waited patiently to check-in for their flights. The businessmen and women without luggage glanced smugly at the slow-moving line, before going straight to the security area.

Dominic watched an elderly woman in blue overalls walk with a shuffling gait behind a giant floor-washing machine. As it crept across the floor, it was unclear whether the machine or the operator dictated its slow progress.

Johann picked up a newspaper from the kiosk and thumbed through it. Dominic glanced over his shoulder.

"You see?" Johann held up the paper. "The attacks are already history."

The front-page headline was about the continuing crisis in Europe. But news of the attacks on the Prinzknecht Bar and KitKatClub were relegated to a few column inches on page four. Dominic reached into his pocket and pulled out the documents Pavel had handed him half an hour earlier, before they had got into a taxi for the airport.

"Do you think Russian immigration will accept these?"

he asked Johann. "I'm not going to know until we get to St Petersburg. What will you do if security guards frog-march me away to a jail cell?"

"You'll be fine." Johann dismissed Dominic's concern with a wave of his hand. "I know you didn't trust Pavel initially—"

"Do you blame me?"

"No, I suppose not." Johann shook his head. "But I think you can trust him now. Especially after you spoke to Alex last night. And Pavel got those documents for you very quickly. He's done a lot."

"That's true."

Johann shoved the newspaper back in the rack. "I think you actually intimidated Pavel back at the Lustgarten. I never thought he'd offer you his secure line so that you could talk to Alex. But then, you threatened to remove the one privilege Pavel treasures. He would hate to be banned from his beloved Berlin."

"I sort of guessed it would be a good bargaining ploy." Dominic smiled. "It was good to speak to Alex. Up until then I thought Pavel was simply spinning me a yarn."

"*Bitte?*"

Dominic laughed. "An English expression for 'not telling the truth.' And I was relieved to hear Alex didn't want Matty to stay with him. I think he'll help us get Matty back to Berlin so he can get on with his studies."

Johann turned to Dominic and kissed him. "And that's the next problem. How?"

"The same way he came in, I suppose."

"Do you think Zimmermann will do it a third time?" Johann asked. "Won't it be risky for him to cross the border so frequently?"

Dominic shoved the documents back in his jacket

pocket. "Alex says Zimmermann knows someone who lives in Finland. If he's stopped, his story is that she's ill and he needs to visit her." He rested his arm on Johann's shoulder and kissed him again. "I'm very grateful to you for coming with me. I'm sure you've got a lot of work on."

Johann shrugged. "The only pressing matter was that Somalian refugee. But now we know they'll withdraw her deportation order today, my colleague can deal with her temporary residency application while I'm away. Everything else can wait." He smiled. "Anyway. I wouldn't miss a Dominic Delingpole adventure for the world."

He raised his hands to hold Dominic's head. Their lips connected, and they kissed slowly and comfortingly. Dominic sighed. For a few seconds, the daunting task that lay ahead disappeared from his mind.

His phone rang. He took it from his pocket, glanced at the screen and answered the call.

"Good morning, Amélie," he said. "Thanks for calling me back."

Johann rolled his eyes and dropped his arms away from Dominic.

"I was out with my sister last night." Amélie seemed surprisingly conciliatory. "I'm sorry I missed your call, but your message didn't come through until now for some reason. Has something happened? I've tried calling Kriminalkommissar Schutz a few times, but he hasn't got back to me."

"I'm at the airport," replied Dominic. "With Johann. We're going to St Petersburg to get Matty back."

"You're going to Russia?" Amélie's voice was suddenly much louder in the earpiece. "Why didn't the Kriminalkommissar tell me?"

"We're not going with the police. They don't know

anything about this." Before Amélie could respond, Dominic pressed on with the main reason he wanted to talk to her. "Listen. Have you heard anything from Matty? A message or a call? He's not responded to me for several days. Not since that Saturday when he walked out on us. I telephoned you to find out if he'd called you."

"I've heard nothing, and I've tried to call him many times," Amélie replied. "But what do you mean the police don't know about you going to St Petersburg? Why? What's happened?"

Dominic and Johann had argued for nearly an hour the night before about telling Amélie they were going to St Petersburg. Johann thought it was a bad idea. He feared she would immediately tell the police. Dominic felt he had an obligation to tell Amélie everything he knew about the danger her son was in. She needed to understand that Matty risked being thrown in jail if the Russian authorities discovered how he had entered the country. Dominic knew there was a risk she would ignore his request to keep quiet and tell the police anyway. It was fortunate Schutz appeared to be ignoring her phone calls.

Patiently, he told Amélie about his conversation with Alex the night before. He emphasised how Alex supported Matty's return to Berlin, but needed to stay in St Petersburg himself to find out exactly what had happened to his twin brother. Amélie interrupted frequently, and it was clear she had little faith in their plan.

After fifteen minutes of increasingly heated debate, Johann pointed to the flight departures screen above their heads.

"Listen, Amélie," Dominic interrupted her. "We've got to go. They're calling our flight. I'll message you when we get to St Petersburg, and I'll keep you updated on what's happening."

"I think you're a fool for going," Amélie said. The frustration in her voice was unmistakeable. "Whatever you say, I'm going to try to get hold of Kriminalkommissar Schutz. I trust him more than you to find Matty."

"I understand," Dominic replied. "But I think you're wrong about Schutz. And if you tell him, Matty could end up in jail. I'm doing my best to get him back for you safely."

"I know. But I think you're going about things the wrong way." Amélie sighed. "If you find him, please make sure Matty isn't hurt or put in jail."

"I will."

"And, Dominic?"

"Yes, Amélie?"

"Take care of yourself."

Dominic's fears about the immigration papers Strelnikov had supplied turned out to be baseless. After their two-and-a-half-hour flight, he and Johann had a tense, fifty-minute wait in the immigration line before their papers were stamped and they were waved through. Now they stood in another line to go through customs and finally enter the arrivals hall of Pulkovo Airport in St Petersburg.

"So, have your last doubts about Pavel gone now?" Johann asked.

"They have," Dominic replied. "He's quite a contact to have. Although I must say, I never thought he'd be your type." He raised an eyebrow at Johann. "You and Strelnikov were lovers?"

Johann smiled. "Pavel was much leaner and fitter in

those days. He had a body like a Greek god. Now he enjoys his German beer too much, and he's put on a lot of weight."

"And you still like men with bodies like Greek gods?"

"Of course," Johann replied. "I like you, don't I?"

Dominic laughed and went to kiss Johann. Just in time, he remembered how attitudes to men kissing each other in public were significantly different in Russia. He pulled back and looked around anxiously to see if anyone had noticed. He felt a flush of anger for deferring to Russia's anti-gay sentiment. After all, it was not yet illegal for gay men to kiss in public. But he knew they risked arrest for any actions that might draw attention to their sexuality. And that was the last thing they needed.

The line shuffled forward towards three Russian customs officers who would check their papers once again.

"It was good to talk to Alex." Dominic tried to move the conversation away from relationships, in case they were overheard. "I thought he was going to be hostile. But he was very supportive about Matty returning to Berlin. Alex is pleased I'm coming, and he says he's going to help me."

"Perhaps you didn't need to make this journey after all."

"Oh, but I do," replied Dominic. "I think Alex wanted me to be there, so he didn't look like the bad guy, throwing Matty out. And I understand that."

They reached the exit. A customs officer inspected their passports and papers once more, and the doors swung open. Dominic and Johann stepped into the busy arrivals hall and searched for the signs for the taxi stand.

Dominic felt a hand on his arm, and a hard metal object was shoved into his side. He looked down and saw the dullish metal of a gun barrel. It was in the hands of a man dressed as a security officer. Dominic glanced over to Johann. There was another security officer at his side.

"What are you doing?" demanded Johann.

"Gentlemen, please come with us," said the security officer next to Johann. "You are required for medical processing."

The bag over Dominic's head made it difficult to breathe. A strap secured it tightly around his neck, and the thick weave of the bag only allowed a restricted airflow. He lay on his side with his wrists and ankles tied together behind his back.

The security guards, if that was what they were, had escorted him and Johann from the airport arrivals hall to a long, white truck parked outside. There had been blue Cyrillic text on the side and an open metal door at the back with three steps up to it. The guards had forced them up the steps into the truck where the bag had been immediately thrown over Dominic's head and secured around his neck. He had been pushed to the floor, and his arms and legs hogtied behind him. The door had banged shut and there had been the clatter of feet on the metal steps outside.

He could hear Johann's breathing and feel him kicking out. He was on the floor beside him.

"Have they gone, Dominic?" Johann's voice was muffled.

Dominic paused to listen. Apart from Johann's breathing, the only other sound was a low-frequency hum. The truck was cold and seemed to be air-conditioned.

"Yes, they've gone," replied Dominic. "Are you okay?"

"Hah!" Johann's response summarised Dominic's feelings exactly.

"Well, you said you wanted to be part of a Dominic

Delingpole adventure," he replied. "And now you've got what you wanted."

"*Scheiße*." Dominic heard Johann struggle, slipping around on the floor.

"Hold still." Dominic moved until he made contact with Johann's body. "If you turn around, I'll see if I can undo the straps on your hands. Then you can get us both free."

Dominic fumbled with the straps around Johann's wrists and ankles. "I can't see what I'm doing," he said. "Can you undo the strap holding this bag on my head? It'll be a lot easier, and I'll finally be able to breathe again."

The two men shuffled around the floor until Johann found the buckle of the leather belt securing the bag over Dominic's head. Johann pulled on the belt tongue, and Dominic gagged as it tightened around his throat.

"Sorry," Johann said. The strap loosened again. "I can't see what I'm doing either."

"I thought you said you'd had a lot of experience in dark rooms." Dominic coughed and breathed as best he could through the fabric of the bag.

"I do," Johann replied. "But bondage isn't my thing."

The strap tightened around Dominic's throat again. But this time he heard the rattle of the buckle as it fell loose. Johann fumbled up the outside of the bag to the top and pulled it off Dominic's head.

Dominic squinted against the bright fluorescent light flooding the inside of the truck from the roof panels. The floor and walls of the truck were covered with some kind of smooth, white panelling. At the far end of the truck, away from the entrance door, was a long, cushioned table with straps hanging down on either side.

He turned to Johann. It was going to be a difficult task to untie him. Although he could now see, Dominic's hands were still tied behind him. It would be hard to crane his neck around to see what he was doing as he attempted to release the straps securing Johann.

There was the clatter of shoes on the steps outside the truck. A moment later the door opened, and a woman stood on the threshold. From Dominic's low vantage point she looked extremely tall. She wore a white lab coat, and her platinum blonde hair was tied in a tight bun on the top of her head. Behind her stood the two security guards. The woman stepped into the truck and the door closed behind her.

"Mr Delingpole. I see you've already started your escape. My sister warned me you were very resourceful. She was right."

The woman delicately kneeled down on the floor of the truck in front of Dominic.

"I am Professor Katerina Vniz Patrikova. My sister is Janet Downpatrick of the Natural Family Association. It's thanks to you she's now in jail."

Patrikova leaned forward. Her face was only a few inches away from Dominic's.

"It's my job to deal with you once and for all, Mr Delingpole."

28

PATRIKOVA'S EYES glowed with hatred. They sparkled, wide and manic. Her expression was that of a child that had been offered the run of Santa's grotto. As she crouched before Dominic on one knee, she tapped her long fingernails rhythmically on the white panelled floor.

"I'm so glad you took the bait," she said. "Or rather, your stupid son took the bait. Once he decided to come, we were certain you'd follow."

She stopped tapping her fingernails.

"You are puzzled, Mr Delingpole. It's very simple. When we found out Professor Alex Krovopuskov was using that disgusting homosexual app to communicate with your son – his boyfriend." She almost spat the words at Dominic. "We simply intercepted the message streams and decrypted the childish code. Then we replaced Krovopuskov's messages with ours. Our messages begged your son to come to St Petersburg, and we gave him simple instructions on how to make the journey. Meanwhile we replaced your son's messages to Krovopuskov with our own." There was a look of triumph on her face. "They thought they were talking to each other when in fact they were talking to us."

Patrikova stood up, smoothed down the creases in her lab coat and stared down at Dominic.

"But it wasn't your son we wanted. He was only the bait. To bring you here."

"Why do you want me so much?" asked Dominic.

"I told you." Patrikova sounded impatient. She walked to the side of the truck and propped herself against the wall. "You kept interfering in the work of the Natural Family Association. You and your queer friends. And because of you, my sister is in jail."

"How on earth is Janet Downpatrick your sister?" Dominic thought back to the soft Irish lilt of the woman that had almost succeeded in killing him two years previously. The two women did look similar, but how could Downpatrick be related to this Russian woman?

"Janet is my twin sister," Patrikova corrected him. "We were separated at birth. A tragedy. But Janet tracked me down, and we were reunited when we were nineteen years old."

Dominic could feel Johann fumble with the straps securing his hands. If he could keep Patrikova talking, Johann would have more time to loosen them and get him free.

"Why were you separated?" he asked.

"Because of you people." Patrikova almost shouted the words at him. "Our...father, was one of you types. Homosexual. He lived with a man in Ireland. They called it marriage. Of course it was illegal. But they still found some lesbian woman to have children for them." She sighed, and her voice became subdued. "That was me and my twin sister

Janet. Fortunately the church found out and rescued us. They took us away from the deviant men."

To Dominic's surprise she spat on the floor of the truck. "It was unnatural. Disgusting. The church found good homes for both of us. Sadly, not together. Janet stayed in Ireland. I was adopted by Christian missionaries living in Ireland, who travelled to the Soviet Union at the end of communism."

Dominic could feel the straps around his wrists loosen. Johann was making progress. If he could get them free, Dominic still needed to find a way to immobilise Patrikova. His ankles would still be bound together. Johann was unlikely to have time to release those as well. He had to keep Patrikova talking, to buy them both more time.

"That explains a great deal about Janet." Dominic decided to adopt a conciliatory tone with Patrikova. "I'm sorry you had such a disruptive childhood. I can understand why you're both angry."

Patrikova laughed. She walked across to him, and her high-heeled shoes clattered on the floor. Johann's fingers froze and slid away from the straps on Dominic's wrists.

"I'm not angry, Mr Delingpole." Patrikova's voice was uncomfortably quiet. She kneeled down to examine him more closely. "Not anymore. Because now that we have you, you'll be used in our next experiment."

The chill of the air conditioning inside the truck made Dominic shiver.

"What experiment?"

Patrikova stood up. She began to pace up and down the length of the truck. "Oh, but you know all about our triumph in Berlin at the weekend, don't you? The latest total is fifteen dead and eighty-four injured."

"You're responsible for that atrocity at the Prinzknecht?"

Dominic felt nauseous. Johann frantically restarted his work on the straps around Dominic's wrists. Dominic tried to pull his arms apart, but they were still secured.

"Yes." Patrikova stopped pacing and stood with her back to the door. She smiled at Dominic. "We successfully trained one of our implant soldiers to travel all the way from St Petersburg to Berlin. And he placed the gas bomb in that... homosexual bar." She wrinkled her nose at the phrase. "Sadly, he didn't succeed in making the return journey. But we're working on that problem."

"What do you mean, your 'implant solders?'" Dominic asked.

"Oh, it's very exciting." Patrikova walked up to Dominic and kneeled in front of him again. Her eyes were bright with excitement. "We implant a device in the subject's brain." She lightly tapped the top of Dominic's head, and he flinched. "Then we can control him. It's based on Professor Zimmermann's work."

"Zimmermann's involved?"

Patrikova shook her head. "Sadly not. We tried to recruit him. There was an opportunity when he came to St Petersburg for the academic exchange with Krovopuskov. But Zimmermann refused. A great loss. He could help us so much. And so could Krovopuskov."

"You're trying to recruit Alex?"

Patrikova laughed. "If only we could. Sadly he's far too weak a man to be involved in military projects. He has a conscience."

Dominic remembered Strelnikov telling him the identity of the man who had attacked the Prinzknecht Bar.

"Is that why you chose to use Alex's twin brother to plant the gas bomb? To threaten Alex?"

Patrikova tipped her head, lost in thought for a moment.

"What a good idea that would have been." She smiled at Dominic. "What a devious man you are, Mr Delingpole. No, it was simply a coincidence. We did not deliberately choose Karol Krovopuskov. He happened to be a patient in the psychiatric hospital where we selected our subjects. He was an exceptional candidate."

She stood and walked to the door at the rear of the truck. "And that's where we're taking you now, Mr Delingpole." She stared down at the hooded body of Johann. "You and your...friend. We didn't expect to have two of you, but I see no reason why we shouldn't include this one as a subject as well."

Patrikova banged on the door behind her. It opened, and the two security guards came back inside. They walked over to Dominic, tightened the straps on his wrists, replaced the hood over his head, and refastened the strap around his neck.

"After all." Patrikova's voice was muffled through the hood. "You're both queer. The world will be better off without you."

The truck shuddered as the engine started, and the floor began to vibrate. The low-frequency hum of the air conditioning was drowned out as the rumble of the truck's engine increased in volume. Dominic rolled from side to side several times and crashed into Johann as the truck picked up speed.

"*Scheiße*." Dominic felt Johann reach for the bag on his head once more. "There'll be nothing left of my fingers soon. I was making such good progress as well. Bastards."

"Do you want to give your fingers a rest?" Dominic asked. "I can try to untie instead."

"Oh, no," replied Johann. "I'm an expert now." He had already loosened the buckle around Dominic's neck. "After all, I'm doing it blindfolded."

Dominic laughed. "Perhaps you'll find a new liking for bondage the next time you're in a darkroom."

Johann pulled tight on the buckle around Dominic's neck, and he gagged. "Any more suggestions like that," Johann said. "And I'll leave you here with that nice lady."

The strap fell loose, and Johann pulled the bag from Dominic's head once again. Dominic looked around him. He could not understand why the security guards had not made it harder for them to escape. Were they watching them from the cab of the truck? He could see no visible cameras, but perhaps they were well hidden.

Johann was much quicker at releasing the straps around Dominic's wrists this time. As soon as Dominic got his hands free he unbuckled the strap around Johann's neck and pulled the hood from his head.

He blinked against the light and smiled at Dominic. "Hello again, my friend." He leaned forward and kissed Dominic on the lips. "That's better. Now please get these straps off me. They're cutting into my wrists."

He turned his back to Dominic and offered up his hands.

Within a few minutes they were both standing and stretching their aching limbs.

"Now what do we do?" asked Johann.

"You're asking me?" Dominic bent down and massaged his ankles.

"You've got more experience at this kind of thing than I have," Johann replied. "I'm guessing we need to get out of this truck before they get us to the psychiatric hospital. Once they've got us in there, I think it will be too late."

As the truck swayed from side to side he staggered over to the door and felt around its frame.

"There's no handle, and I can't see an easy way to lever it open," he said to Dominic. "Any ideas?"

Dominic made his way to the opposite end of the truck and inspected the adjustable couch he had seen when he was lying on the floor. It was a hospital operating table. He looked around for equipment, or some kind of tools, but he could find nothing. Haltingly, he walked back down the truck to join Johann by the door.

"It opens outwards," said Dominic. "So perhaps if we throw our weight against it, we'll be able to force it open."

"For God's sake, Dominic," said Johann. "We're probably travelling at about eighty kilometres an hour. Or even more. If that door bursts open, we'll fly out through it. Although I don't want to die at the hands of that bloody woman, I certainly don't want to die on a Russian autobahn." He nodded towards the front of the truck. "Did you find anything up there?"

"Nothing obvious," replied Dominic. "There's only the operating table. I couldn't find anything else. Perhaps I can break something off the table and use it as a lever to force open the door."

"Is there no way we can break into the cab?"

"It's sealed from the outside world." Dominic looked up at the roof. "I think that's where the air-conditioning unit is. Maybe there's a way out up there." He stretched up, but his fingers were several inches away from the panel above him. "Perhaps if I stood on your shoulders..."

"No way," Johann replied. "Not while we're swaying around like this. And I'm not going to stand on yours either.

This truck is swaying far too much for either of us to stand still for long enough." He pointed to the operating table. "Can't you stand on that?"

"I'll have a go." Dominic hurried up the truck and hauled himself onto the table. Johann followed and held onto Dominic's legs firmly. Dominic reached up and pushed his palms against the panel. It flexed and buckled. He pushed again. A crack formed along one edge and revealed a dark cavity behind it.

Dominic took a deep breath and pushed with all his strength against the panel. At that moment the truck braked suddenly. Johann let go of Dominic's legs, and Dominic fell forward from the operating table. He crashed into the front wall of the truck, bounced off it, and landed on the floor.

Johann kneeled down beside him. "Are you okay?"

Dominic looked up at the broken panel above them. There was a gap about six inches wide that revealed the metal skin of the truck above it. The truck was moving slowly now, and it no longer swayed from side to side. He got to his feet and clambered back onto the operating table. As he reached up to the panel, the truck lurched to a halt. He managed to keep his balance and pulled down hard on the edge of the fractured panel. It made a loud crack and came away in his hands.

"Wait," Johann whispered. "I can hear voices."

With his hands still above his head, Dominic strained to hear what was going on outside the truck. There was the sound of footsteps around the side of the truck. Johann pointed to the rear door.

"I think they're going to open up," he whispered. "Keep that piece of broken panel. It's our best chance of overpowering them."

Dominic climbed down from the operating table as

quietly as he could. He followed Johann back down the truck. Johann picked up the discarded cloth hoods on the way. He stood on one side of the rear door, with Dominic on the other. Then they waited.

Feet rattled on the metal steps that led up to the door. There was the creak of a latch turning, and the door swung open. A man appeared in the doorway and looked into the truck. Dominic swung the piece of broken panel down onto the man's head with as much force as he could muster. Johann followed through with a kick into the man's stomach.

The man fell backwards from the steps. Dominic and Johann pulled back and hid on either side of the doorway.

"Herr Delingpole," said a familiar voice. "And Herr Hart-mann. Move away from the doorway and lie face down on the floor. Put your hands behind your heads. If you try to attack one of my men again, we'll shoot you."

It was Kriminalkommissar Schutz.

29

DOMINIC'S HEART thumped in his chest. He pressed his hands against the back of his head to stop them from shaking. The floor covering was cold against his cheek, and he struggled to breathe. He desperately wanted to shift to a more comfortable position, but dared not move a muscle. A man in army boots stood inches away from his head.

Outside the truck, men shouted in Russian, and Dominic could hear Patrikova arguing fiercely with them. Boots thudded on the steps outside the truck, people entered, and the door slammed shut. The engine revved, and the truck lurched forward. The voices outside the truck grew fainter as it sped up.

"Please. Stay on the ground," ordered Schutz. "We have a short journey to make."

The truck slowed and swayed as its driver negotiated a series of turns. After ten or fifteen minutes it came to a halt and the engine cut. A man outside the truck shouted in German and banged on the rear door. The door opened, and Schutz called out to the man.

"*Mein Gott*," Johann whispered to Dominic. "I think we've been hijacked by the German police."

"You're right, Herr Hartmann," said Schutz. "You could say rescued by the German police. Or, to be precise, the anti-terrorist branch of the Bundespolizei. Please, gentlemen. You may sit up. Unless you would prefer to stand."

Dominic lifted his head from the floor. He rolled into a sitting position and got to his feet alongside Johann. Two men wearing bulletproof vests stood either side of them. Schutz was by the open rear door. Through it, Dominic could see they were parked on the side of a quiet street.

"You do realise," said Schutz. "That you, your son, and Professor Krovopuskov have caused a major diplomatic incident? Fortunately for you, we're about to enter the German consulate in St Petersburg." He gestured to the men flanking them. "My men will escort you inside. Herr Delingpole, technically you should be in the British consulate. But the German consul has graciously invited you to be her guest." He shook his head. "God alone knows why. If I had my way, you and your wayward son would be in a police cell by now."

Schutz walked out of the truck. The two police officers stood either side of the doorway.

"*Bitte*," said one of them and gestured to the open door.

Johann stepped forward, and Dominic followed him. Schutz was at the bottom of the steps. "Follow me, gentlemen," he said. "You're about to enter German territory."

Dominic and Johann sat on a plain wooden bench to the side of the entrance hall inside the German consulate. High above their heads, the German and European flags fluttered in the draft from the air conditioning. A large portrait of the German president hung on one of the off-white walls, lit by a pair of spotlights. It was a plain, austere space with minimal adornment. In the far corner of the hall, Schutz was in conversation with a consulate official.

Dominic examined the scuffmarks on his suit. There was a small tear in his jacket, which had probably happened when he had fallen off the operating table in the truck. He rubbed at several white marks on the fabric, but the stains stubbornly refused to go away. He leaned over to Johann.

"I feel like a naughty little schoolboy," he whispered. "Waiting to see the headmaster."

Johann laughed quietly. "Do they still beat you in English schools?" he asked. "No wonder you have so many clubs devoted to S & M in London."

"We do not," Dominic retorted. "Certainly not as many as I've seen in Berlin."

The consulate official shook hands with Schutz and left through a door at the side of the hall. Schutz walked back towards them. Dominic abandoned his attempts to erase the stains from his jacket.

"Get ready," he whispered to Johann. "I think it's going to be a bumpy ride."

The two men stood as Schutz approached down the hallway.

"We have a lot to talk about." Schutz cleared his throat. "I have an apology to make, Herr Delingpole." He coughed again and smiled. "But first, you have some people to meet. Please. Follow me."

Schutz led them through a door at the back of the hall and across a grand reception room to a set of French doors that opened onto a small garden. Schutz stopped and gestured to the open doors.

"Please," he said. "I'll give you some minutes for your reunion. Then I will join you."

Dominic walked out onto a paved veranda. On the other side of it sat Matty and Alex.

"Hi, Dad."

Matty ran across and the two men hugged. Dominic wiped his eyes.

"I'm so relieved to see you," Dominic said into Matty's ear. "Your mother's worried sick about you. And so was I."

"I'm sorry," Matty whispered back. "I've just spoken to Mama. She wanted me to tell you thank you."

"Thank you?" Dominic released his grip on his son. "I didn't do anything." He smiled apologetically at Johann by his side. "Except lead this man into an awful lot of danger."

Alex stepped forward. He held his arms out wide to Dominic and they hugged.

"That's not true." Alex took a step back and put an arm around Matty. "When you learned that your son was in danger, you took a great risk to come and help him. Matty is very grateful for that. And so am I."

Dominic shook his head. "Do you know what happened to Johann and me? We were kidnapped as soon as we arrived in Russia. I don't think we've been much use."

"On the contrary, Herr Delingpole." Schutz walked out into the garden and joined the group. "It may be true that you and Herr Hartmann have been a little impulsive. And it would also have been helpful if you'd told me more about what you knew."

Schutz coughed. Dominic noticed the Kriminalkommissar had a habit of coughing when he was about to demonstrate a rare moment of humility.

"But it's also true," Schutz continued. "That I was unwilling to move our investigation away from Professor

Krovopuskov and your son, when you had given us more than good reason to end that line of investigation. For example, when I questioned you in the police station, you told me that Professor Krovopuskov suffers from amblyopia."

Alex turned to Dominic. "You know about that?"

"I told him," Matty said. "I'm sorry, but I thought it might clear your name."

"Don't apologise." Alex smiled. "I'm not ashamed of it. And it sounds like it was useful information for the Kriminalkommissar."

Schutz nodded. "I got the team to review all the images of the suspect they could find, including some from earlier in the day when the man took a moped from the City Transport Department. There were several clear images of him that we were able to process against photographs of Professor Krovopuskov we had collected from his apartment."

"You took things from Alex's apartment?" Matty's tone was sharp.

"And I'm pleased they did." Alex patted Matty's arm reassuringly. "Otherwise I might still be a suspect."

"Exactly," agreed Schutz. "We took longer than we should to recover the extra images. When we did, we uncovered several discrepancies in the evidence we had pointing to you. It was the security camera video from the university and from the U-Bahn that cleared you. It showed you couldn't have been at the Prinzknecht Bar." He coughed again. "I'm sorry, Professor Krovopuskov. But once we had you as the main suspect, it took us too long to admit we were wrong."

Dominic thought back to his conversation with Schutz at the police station. He had failed to tell Schutz about the messages passed through the Papi app between Alex and

Matty. He recalled how he had suspected Schutz already knew that Alex was in St Petersburg.

"How did you know Johann and I were locked in that medical truck?" he asked. "Did the Russian secret service tip you off?"

Schutz laughed. "I'm afraid they were extremely unhelpful. What we did to recover you from that truck was not with the permission of the Russian authorities. The German consul has a lot of explaining to do." He smiled. "But at least you're safe."

"But how did you know?" Dominic asked again.

Schutz held up his hands as if in surrender. "I'm afraid it was luck," he answered. "As soon as I'd confirmed Professor Krovopuskov was here, I flew out with my officers yesterday evening. This morning I was alerted that you two were on a flight. So we decided to meet you at the airport."

He spread open his arms towards them. "A little German welcoming committee. Before we could get to you, we saw you being escorted into that truck, and we had to change our plans." He shrugged. "I did something very much against my nature. I improvised."

Johann stepped forward. "I must shake your hand, Kriminalkommissar," he said. "I know how difficult that must be for you."

Dominic watched as the two men solemnly shook hands. He wondered if Johann was being ironic.

"What's happened to Patrikova?" Dominic asked. "Did you arrest her?"

Schutz shook his head. "We have no jurisdiction here. Her fate is in the hands of the Russian authorities. Professor Zimmermann has told us what he knows about the Natural Family Association and their experiments at the Correctional Hospital. Our consul is making strong representations to the Russian authorities at this moment about how her experiments led to multiple murders on German soil."

"So she'll be tried and go to jail?"

"Maybe not," Alex replied before Schutz could speak. "It's possible the Russian authorities themselves are behind this."

Dominic thought back to Pavel Strelnikov's comment that Alex wanted to clear his brother's name.

"Are you still going to stay here until you expose the people who did this gruesome experiment on your brother? If it's the Russian authorities, and you accuse them, surely you'll be in danger?"

"You're right," replied Alex. "I'm not going to stay. I want to come back to Berlin with Matty. I have nothing left to hold me here, now that Karol is..." He turned away and Matty put a comforting arm around his shoulder.

"I'm sorry for your loss, Professor," said Schutz sympathetically. "But you can be assured that Germany will welcome you back with open arms. From what I understand, your research work is far too valuable for us to lose."

"Thank you." Alex straightened up and wiped his eyes. "And my brother's body is in Berlin. I need to organise his funeral."

"What about the Natural Family Association?" Matty asked. "I thought they'd been defeated once. How did they spring up again?"

"They had, replied Alex. "In the West at least. But Patrikova was clearly out to avenge her sister's imprisonment. And you know what Russia thinks about homosexuality. Patrikova and the Natural Family Association found a lot of sympathisers here."

Schutz nodded. "And I'm afraid their support extends to high levels in the Russian government."

"I don't understand, Alex." Matty shook his head. "You got out to avoid persecution here in Russia using the academic exchange program. But you exchanged with Professor Zimmermann. Isn't he gay as well?"

Alex nodded.

"Then why did he come here? Surely he now experiences the same hatred that you did?"

Alex sighed. "Because Mickey is a very wonderful man. He's much older than me. His husband died three years ago, and he wanted me to get a chance to live freely as myself. The same way he used to do when he lived in Berlin. That's why he suggested the exchange."

"That's not quite correct, Professor Krovopuskov."

Dominic turned to see a woman with perfectly coiffured hair wearing a tailored charcoal suit. Schutz held out his arm to welcome the new arrival.

"Gentlemen," he said. "This is Frau Leibnitz, the German consul based here in St Petersburg."

"Good afternoon, everyone," said Frau Leibnitz. "I'm sorry to interrupt your reunion. I'm so pleased to hear that you're all safe and well." She smiled. "Now all we have is the little matter of getting you back to Germany safely without upsetting the Russians."

Alex stepped forward and bowed his head. "I'm delighted and most grateful to meet you, Ma'am," he said. "But, please tell me. Did you say there's another reason why Mickey Zimmermann exchanged with me and came to Russia?"

"There is," replied Frau Leibnitz. "He's been working for us for several years. He suggested that you should work in the West. Your work is of enormous value. And Professor Zimmermann offered himself in exchange, in order to placate the Russians. Since he has been there, he has collected significant evidence about the activities of the Natural Family Association and their work at the Correctional Hospital. Once we have you all safely back in Germany, there'll be diplomatic efforts to bring them to justice."

30

Berlin, March 2020

Dominic rolled over and peered at the clock on the nightstand beside the bed. It was shortly before six in the morning. Another hour before the alarm was due to go off. He had been awake for nearly half an hour. It had become difficult to sleep in the past few weeks. World events were too distracting. Dominic looked beyond the nightstand to his suitcase, open on the floor. A reminder he was due to go home today.

Six months.

He slid up against the curve of Johann's spine and adjusted his position until they fitted together snugly. Johann stirred, intertwined his legs with Dominic's, and mumbled something incoherent. After a few moments, Johann's breathing dropped into a regular, slow pattern. Dominic tried to match his breathing with Johann's until a calmness settled on him once more.

Six months.

Six months of travelling back and forth between his home in rural Oxfordshire and Johann's apartment in

Berlin. One weekend in Oxford, one weekend in Berlin. With the occasional week or ten days together, usually in the Canary Islands or the Swiss Alps.

It was exhilarating. But also exhausting.

The regular trips to Berlin meant Dominic got to see Matty regularly. On two occasions he had had lunch with Amélie. His German was improving, and Johann had grudgingly admitted a love for British operetta. Well, Gilbert and Sullivan at least.

It was a start.

There was something significant about this week. He tried to remember what it was. His assistant had told him about it before he had come out to Berlin last Friday. Now it slipped his mind.

Johann shifted his position and nestled farther into the curve of Dominic's torso. Dominic felt his cock stiffen in response. He wondered whether they might have time to make love before they got up this morning. He tried to recall what Johann had said about his diary. Often, he kept it clear on the morning of Dominic's departures for England.

Had he kept it clear this morning?

Dominic slid his hand down Johann's chest and made contact with his cock. It was hard. He started to massage it and felt it twitch. Johann sighed contentedly.

"Good morning," Dominic whispered in his ear. "Do you still have any energy left after last night?"

The night before they had gone for a drink at the Prinzknecht Bar and met some of Johann's friends. The bar had been commemorating the six-month anniversary of the attack that had killed fifteen people. Matty had arrived with Alex, and they had partied until after midnight.

"Oh, shit," said Dominic.

"What's the matter?" Johann placed his hand on Dominic's arm and squeezed it.

Dominic disentangled himself from Johann and lay on his back.

"It's Matty's birthday tomorrow."

Johann rolled over and snuggled into Dominic's side. He stroked the hairs on Dominic's chest and rubbed his nose against his cheek.

"You know that already. He told you last night when we were leaving."

"Yes, I remember now. "Dominic sighed and turned his head to kiss Johann. "But I also remember that I'd already been told. Gillian told me last week. And I forgot about it as soon as I got here."

Johann chuckled and slipped his hand down Dominic's chest to his cock. "What happened? Something made you forget?"

"Yes. You did." Dominic laid his hand on top of Johann's to stop his distraction. "But it means I didn't give Matty a card or a present last night. I'm a terrible father."

Johann squeezed Dominic's cock, and he groaned with pleasure.

"We've got time." Johann kissed Dominic on the lips. "Your flight doesn't leave until this afternoon. We can go out and get something for him this morning, and you can drop it over to him before you leave for the airport."

He climbed on top of Dominic and sat with his legs straddling his chest. He placed his hands on Dominic's wrists and held them firmly against the mattress.

"Before then, there's something down here asking for a goodbye kiss." He looked down at Dominic's erect cock. "And it would be rude of me to refuse."

"Dad? Aren't you awake yet?"

The sound of Matty's voice shook the last remnants of sleep from Dominic's befuddled brain. He sat up with the phone pressed against his ear. The clock by the bed showed it was nearly half past nine.

"Shit."

"You're not, are you?" Matty sounded indignant. "I thought your flight was this morning?"

Johann stirred beside Dominic. He reached out an arm and nearly knocked the phone from Dominic's hand.

"This afternoon," Dominic replied, juggling the phone as it slipped in his fingers. "Look, Matty. I'm so sorry about last night. I completely forgot to bring your birthday present with me." It was a version of the truth.

"Don't worry about that. Gillian warned me you'd probably forget."

Dominic was affronted. He had had no idea his assistant would go behind his back.

"Anyway, it doesn't matter," Matty continued. "Have you seen the news this morning?"

Before Dominic could reply Matty answered his own question. "No, I suppose you haven't. You've been too busy sleeping. Patrikova's been arrested."

"What?" Dominic nearly dropped the phone.

"What's happened?" mouthed Johann. Dominic waved him away.

"Yes," Matty went on. "They've arrested her and a whole bunch of people from the Natural Family Association. The online news service says it's a triumph for German diplomacy. But Alex says the Russians are sacrificing her and her cronies in return for research cooperation from his labs. He's not very happy about it."

Dominic sighed. "Nothing's for free in this life, Matty."

"I guess so," Matty replied. "Did you see the other news?"

"There's more?" asked Dominic. Johann had propped himself up on his elbow. Dominic mouthed "*Sorry*," to him. Matty seemed unusually eager to chat that morning.

"It's about the virus. They're talking about locking down the UK. Like France is."

"That rumour's been floating around for a few days," Dominic replied. "What's new?"

"I'm only thinking about you and Johann." Matty sounded impatient. "The online news says a UK lockdown is much more likely now. What if you go back to England today and then get locked down there? You could be stuck for months."

The deadly virus had spread across Europe alarmingly. When the Italian government had ordered a lockdown ten days previously, most people had thought it would be enough to contain the outbreak. But when several more European countries had ordered lockdowns, Dominic and Johann had talked about the possibility of being trapped in different countries.

"Why are you going back?"

It was a good question. Because his flight was booked. Because he had a court hearing at the end of the week. Because his assistant was there. None of them were compelling reasons to leave Germany. He could delegate the court hearing to an intern he had taken on at the start of the year.

"I don't know," Dominic replied. "Maybe I'll delay for a few days and see what happens." He rested his head on

Johann's chest. "Listen. What are you doing tomorrow lunchtime? Do you want to meet up for your birthday?"

"Sure, Dad," Matty replied. "As long as you don't take me to the Alt Schwäbisch again."

Dominic laughed. "Anywhere you like. Text me later."

They ended the call, and Dominic sighed.

"What's happening?"

"Do you want to come shopping with me this morning?" Dominic asked. "I need to get Matty a present. And I'm going to have to buy some more clothes." Dominic reached over and kissed Johann. "I've decided to stay for a while."

ABOUT THE AUTHOR

David C. Dawson is an award winning author, journalist and documentary maker, and lives in London and Oxford.

His debut novel *The Necessary Deaths* won Bronze for Best Mystery & Suspense in the FAPA awards.

As a journalist he travelled extensively, filming in nearly every continent of the world. He's lived in London, Geneva and San Francisco, but he now prefers the tranquillity of the Oxfordshire countryside.

In his spare time, David tours Europe with his boyfriend, and sings with the London Gay Men's Chorus.

ALSO BY DAVID C. DAWSON

The Necessary Deaths

The Deadly Lies

For the Love of Luke

Heroes in Love

THE NECESSARY DEATHS

Book 1 in The Delingpole Mysteries series

Award winner in the 2017 FAPA President's Awards for Adult Suspense and Thrillers.

A young man. Unconscious in a hospital bed. His life is in the balance from a drugs overdose.

Attempted suicide or attempted murder?

British lawyer Dominic Delingpole investigates, with the help of his larger than life partner Jonathan McFadden.

Compromising photographs of senior politicians and business chiefs are discovered.

Is the young man a blackmailer?

Dominic and Jonathan uncover a conspiracy reaches into the highest levels of government and powerful corporations.

Three people are murdered, and Dominic and Jonathan struggle for their very survival in this gripping thriller.

THE DEADLY LIES

Book 2 in The Delingpole Mysteries series

A man is murdered, and takes a deadly secret to his grave.

Is it true the murdered man is Dominic Delingpole's former lover? And were they still seeing each other just before his recent wedding to husband Jonathan?

Or are these simply lies?

This is more than a story of deceit between husbands. A man's death plunges Dominic and Jonathan into a world of international espionage, which puts their lives at risk.

What is the ruthless Charter Ninety-Nine group, and why is it pursuing them across Europe and the United States?

Dominic and Jonathan are forced to test their relationship to its limit. What deadly lies must they both confront? And if they stay alive, will their relationship remain intact?

FOR THE LOVE OF LUKE

A handsome naked man. Unconscious on a bathroom floor.

He's lost his memory, and someone's out to kill him. Who is the mysterious Luke?

British TV anchor and journalist Rupert Pendley -Evans doesn't do long-term relationships. Nor does he do waifs and strays. But Luke is different. Luke is a talented American artist with a dark secret in his life.

When Rupert discovers Luke, he's intrigued, and before he can stop himself, he's in love. The aristocratic Rupert is an ambitious TV reporter with a nose for a story and a talent for uncovering the truth. As he falls deeper in love with Luke, he discovers the reason for Luke's amnesia. And the explanation puts them both in mortal danger.

HEROES IN LOVE

NOT EVERY HERO WEARS A UNIFORM

Can love last a lifetime?

Billy and Daniel never intended to be matchmakers. After all, they're only at the start of their own love story.

But Billy uncovers a failed love affair that lasted over fifty years until it fell apart.

He and Daniel see their own fledgling relationship through the lens of the now estranged couple.

They vow to reunite the elderly lovers. But as they set about their task, the pressures of modern life threaten to tear them apart.

Made in the USA
Middletown, DE
03 June 2021